Introduction

The story of a beautiful yet shy and bashful girl that had an unusual and sometimes turbulent childhood into a woman that changed each year as she grew from humble and troubled beginnings, to become a woman that a city would never forget. A story of how a person's past could sometimes shape their future, how a person's life experiences can change them into someone they never knew they could be.

A West Baltimore female who wanted the best out of life and everything it had to offer her. But life is a constant change. Some of us while seeking the better things in life change for the worst. The story of two sisters growing up in West Baltimore who shared an incredible bond but were two different people, or so most thought. Their lives would change throughout each trial and tribulation, their lives would somehow be in contrast with one another. No matter how different they were, at the end of the day they shared a sisterly bond through it all. And it was unmatched by no other. Like most young girls, early in their lives they had a lot of ambition, dreams, and desires that were at times the same but for the most part different as they got older. The price they pay for success would eventually affect both their lives, would either of them become successful ? And if any of them did, how would it affect their lives ? A wild ride into the life of two sisters, and everything that consisted of their lives, goals, and actions. Living in Baltimore, Maryland had its dangers and temptations.

Both girls would take different paths through life to obtain what many that grew up around them thought was the American Dream. But at what price would these two girls pay to get what they wanted out of life ? Only time would tell for either of them. Even though they had a strong sisterly bond, they both at times had to put their trust in other people's hands with certain things involving their life. As they both experience life even at young ages, they learned quickly that you had to watch who you trust. Experience the life and legend of a woman that some people grew to know as "Raspberry".

Chapter One "Shy Girl"

In the mid to late 80's a West Baltimore, Maryland family struggled to make ends meet like most families they knew that also lived in the area. Those families suffered through the crack era. Robert and Denise Knight had two daughters, Desiree the oldest and Deanna their youngest. They raised their daughters in their West Baltimore home amid the normal dangers associated with big cities. Drugs, murder, robberies and other dangerous crimes. They did their best to keep them safe from the realities they faced everyday.

Desiree was two years older than her younger sister Deanna, they both went to Baltimore City public schools. And their parents were both city workers, their father Robert Knight was a city bus driver and their mother was a cafeteria aide at a city school. Their mother was also in and out of their home at various points of their young lives due to her drug addiction. Their mother had fell victim to the crack era. She often times couldn't hold down many jobs because of her addiction, and as hard as their father tried to fill that void. It affected both girls lives. Battling drug addiction, she had a few stints in rehab before finally remaining clean for the last six months. Her current job didn't pay much, but it was a start and it was huge for her because she had promised her girls she would stay clean for good. Desiree and Deanna were both smart and ambitious growing up, wanting to be anything from doctors to fashion designers.

Desiree being the oldest was shy and bashful, her sister Deanna on the other hand was very outspoken no matter who wanted to hear it. Deanna was the little sister but had the personality of the big sister, Desiree was definitely a girly girl when they were growing up. Deanna was more of a tomboy, she was tough and often times got in numerous fights with kids throughout the neighborhood and surrounding neighborhoods. She developed a reputation for herself around the neighborhood as someone you didn't want to cross. Even though the sisters were like night and day, they had a very close bond. Both their parents were street smart after living in Baltimore for many years. Their father Robert was born in Baltimore, and their mother had moved to Baltimore when she was six years old from Columbia, South Carolina. Their father Robert was a very strict disciplinarian. And that was a fine line, because sometimes he was mentally and physically abusive.

Especially when he drank, which was basically every weekend. Their father Robert also had a part time job unloading trucks for a company. So during the week his time was occupied with his two jobs. Which was the main reason he didn't drink as much as he really wanted to. One thing that their father maintained throughout their childhood was being a good provider. He had his nasty ways about him, but he always made sure his family was taken care of. It was very important that he did, being that his wife was in and out of rehab. He had held things together while his wife got her life back together, more importantly he stood by her through it all. When their mother had finally came back home, things seemed good for the first three months. But as time passed, Denise and Robert's marriage began to be really rocky.

Many of nights the girls were awakened by their parents fighting and arguing, and at times seeing their mother being abused by their father. It was a hostile home at times for them growing up. And their father had the king in his own castle mentality. Whatever he says goes. With help from some local family members, their father was able to work and still take care of his daughters. By having them checked on by family members when he worked when his wife was in rehab. Often times he blamed her for the kids unstable childhood, which in turn started agruments. Robert Knight was a hard working man. But after dealing with the pressures of providing for two children on his own, for a period of time. And his wife being a recovering addict, it began to take a toll on him. Robert as a child dealt with mental and physical abuse from his own father. But instead of breaking the cycle, he continued it with his own children. The girls loved their father, but they also resented him because of the way he treated their mother. They believed that their mother really wanted to get clean and stay clean, but often times he stressed her and made her want to relapse. He didn't know how to deal with a recovering addict, all this was new to him.

Recently their mother had been able to overcome her rocky marriage and stay clean for six months, something both girls were extremely happy about. As the girls grew one thing was obvious, Desiree was growing into a stunningly bright and beautiful young lady. And she was envied by many of her peers in school and around her neighborhood. Desiree found herself being picked on and sometime bullied. Because she wasn't a fighter, and a lot of girls were jealous of her. Because of her looks and personality. Her younger sister Deanna would stick up for her as much as she could. And after some kids who didn't know that Deanna was Desiree's sister got dealt with physically, all the fighting for Desiree stopped. Deanna spent a lot of time around boys, while Desiree was playing with Barbies and being a girl. Deanna developed a tough mentality being around boys. One day after school and after they were in their rooms, Deanna had a talk with her older sister.

"Sis you can't let these people run all over you, or they will do it forever" Deanna said to Desiree.

"You like to fight Deanna, I try to avoid confrontation as much as I can unless I absolutely have to. You on the other hand, no one can say nothing to you. You automatically snap, and be out for blood in an instant. You always like to fight" Desiree said.

"I dont start fights sis, I finish them. Always remember that. And im getting in fights saving your butt, big sister" Deanna responded as they both laughed.

The two girls had fun even though they lived through some turbulent times within their own home and city. Just joking around and being the girls they were was fun to them, they both learned early to be street smart. Their parents knew they both would come across things and situations in the street. Each day coming home from school was an adventure. Anything from kids fighting, Deanna fighting, or them getting chased by some boys. Once they got home, it was a whole other situation. Their father Robert had strict rules and a very strong character, that didn't mesh well with his younger daughter Deanna's strong and outspoken character.

They were too much alike in a sense. Deanna was just like her father, and they always bumped heads. As Deanna's reputation grew on the streets and around the neighborhood, she no longer feared her father like she once did. And it reflected on how she began not listening to him and bending some of his rules, much to the dismay of her father. The walks to school were the one on one conversations between the sisters about the situations going on in their home. When they would walk with their friends they didn't mention it out of fear and embarrassment. But when it was just them, it was like their therapy sessions for themselves. You can say they got each other through those rough times, those were the conversations they didn't want their father to hear.

"I don't know why she takes that from him" Deanna said as her and her sister walked to school.

"I don't like it either Deanna, but he is our father and it's his house. And we don't have no other place to go. I think sometimes mom feels trapped because she has us. And after being gone for periods of time she feels guilty about taking us out of our home. Maybe if she didn't have us she would leave" Desiree replied.

"I think we can leave if we really wanted to. I just know if he puts his hands on me again, I'm going to do something about it." Deanna said.

"Deanna what are you going to do ? He's our father and we live in his house, and he also has the right to discipline us. I don't want him to hurt you or any of us anymore than he has to" Desiree replied.

Page 3

Desiree pleaded with her sister not to do anything or say anything disrespectful to their father and make him even more angry. But Deanna had a mind of her own and once it was made up, there was nothing that no one could do to change it. Once her fear for him was gone, she was ready to put her defiance to the test and conquer anything in her way. Seeing what their father did to their mother made her look at men differently than most females did. She vowed that she would never be a victim to anyone's abuse again. She had a conversation with her mother before she decided to act on what she said she was going to do.

They were setting the table for dinner before her father came home. At the time Deanna was fourteen and had seen enough for a person much older.

"Mom can I ask you a question" ? Deanna asked.

"Yes Deanna, what is it" ? Denise replied.

"Why do you let him do the things he does to you"? Deanna said.

"Deanna your father is a good man and he loves us all, marriages and relationships have arguments and sometimes things get physical. I'm not condoning the physical, but sometimes it happens in the heat of the moment." Denise replied.

"You know mom, one of my friend's from school. Her mom used to say the same things, until her husband killed her" Deanna said.

A friend of her's mother was murdered by her husband after years of abuse, Deanna didn't want to see that happen to her mother. She was concerned, and more than anything she didn't want her mother going back to using because of the stress inflicted on her by her husband.

"Don't worry Deanna, I'm fine and your father is not going to kill me. Or anyone else for that matter." Denise replied.

Her mother responded reassuring Deanna that she was fine and it wasn't as bad as she thought it was. Regardless of what her mother said, Deanna's mind was made up. And she was no longer taking any abuse from her father. And she still planned on challenging his authority. At age sixteen, Desiree had matured and her body did as well. She often times looked older than sixteen, and would get hit on by older guys. Almost every guy at school yearned for her attention. Despite what was going on at home, the girls still did well in school.....at least for now.

Desiree herself maintained a 3.9 grade average and was primed to get a scholarship to basically any school she wanted. She was that smart. Deanna also did well but began to let the streets consume more of her time than it should have. And really didn't have any plans of furthering her education. As Deanna got older, she wasn't ambitious as she once was. The family noticed a change in her and knew it was only a matter of time before Deanna experienced sexuality. Deanna had told her sister that she was interested in sexuality with someone of the same sex, she was always a tomboy growing up so it didn't surprise Desiree. Desiree had liked some guys and talked to some here and there but nothing serious.

All of this information was of course kept a secret from their parents, especially their father. One day

Deanna had gotten caught by their father walking down the street hand and hand with another girl. This was a surprise to their father. Because although he knew she was a tomboy, he figured she would grow out of it. And even just seeing her with his own eyes dating already had him angry. His anger exploded on a city street, as he got out of his car and yelled for his daughter to get in his car. Deanna refused and her and her friend fled on foot running away from her father as he couldn't catch them. Deanna didn't care anymore about what her father thought. A few hours later Robert Knight was at home still waiting for his youngest daughter, and angry as hell.

"Where is she, where the hell is she" !!? Robert Knight said pacing back and forth in the living room.

"Calm down Rob, I'm sure she will be home soon. Just relax and sit down" Denise replied.

"Hell no I'm not sitting down, a child of mines disobeying me living in my house. Her ass is mines once she gets here." Robert said angrily.

There was no calming him down, he was enraged that his daughter didn't obey him. Desiree listened quietly in the room they both shared. Feeling concerned what their father would do to her sister. That night went on with their father falling asleep on the couch after having a few beers with his leather belt still in his hand. But suddenly the door opens and it's Deanna. Robert Knight got up right as Deanna came through the door.

"Where in the hell have you been ? And why didn't you come when I told you to get in the damn car" Robert yelled walking towards Deanna.

At that moment Denise got in between Robert and Deanna.

"I didn't want to come home, because I'm tired of the way you been treating my mother and the way you been treating us." !! Deanna said.

"Who the hell are you to tell me how to treat anybody, you live in my house under my roof. And as long as you do, you will do as I say or get your ass outta here" !! Robert replied.

"Maybe that's exactly what I should do" Deanna said walking towards the room the girls both shared.

But before she could make it to her room, her father walked in front of her mother and spun Deanna around and smacked her across the face, hard enough to knock Deanna to the floor. Deanna immediately jumped up grabbed the empty beer bottle her father had just finished drinking and attempted to strike him in the head with it.

Deanna's mom Denise quickly grabbed the bottle from her daughter as her father Robert just stared at her.

"Now get your shit and get out of here since you can't respect me in my own house" Robert shouted.

"Rob calm down, all this yelling isn't going to solve anything. Let me talk to her so we can get this straightened out. In the room Deanna, let's go" Denise said leading her daughter into the girls bedroom where Desiree was sitting on her bed listening quietly.

"Mom I have made up my mind, I'm leaving. I no longer want to be here dealing with his bullshit, and you both should leave with me too" Deanna said packing clothes.

"And go where Deanna? Think about what you're doing Deanna, where are you going to stay" ? Denise asked.

"I have a friend I can stay with mom, and that's where I will be until I get my own place." Deanna replied.

"With what Deanna ? You don't have a job to afford a place to live." Denise said.

"Mother I have my ways, I will keep in touch. I love you both" Deanna said giving her mother and sister a hug.

But before she walked out, Desiree got up and stopped Deanna.

"Deanna, you really want to do this ? Can't you wait until you get enough money to move out? Think about what you're doing Deanna" Desiree said pleading with her sister.

"I have to go Desiree....I have to go" Deanna said as she walked out.

Even though Robert had hit his girls before, it never got this bad and he never hit any of the girls as hard as he hit Deanna that night. Regardless Denise couldn't sleep knowing her daughter was out there in the dangerous Baltimore streets. Those same streets that Deanna had earned a rep for being a tough female that didn't take anything from anyone. Deanna had end up staying with her best friend Anita Washington, who was also a female that came up hard in Baltimore streets. Anita's mother who was hardly home from working two jobs trying to support her and Anita as a single parent. Anita's house was usually the hangout spot. The girls mostly hung out with some friends that came over, no more than a few. Anita and Deanna was very close friends.

Anita lived a few blocks away from the girl's home. So now Anita and Deanna would meet her sister Desiree and walk to school together everyday. After being a sought after and very beautiful young lady who was strictly into school and few boys. Desiree had finally met a guy that changed her mind about boys. By this time Desiree was a senior in high school. The school's star wide receiver Ricky Stanton, who was also very sought after by all the girls in school. Except Desiree. I guess for some reason that intrigued him, besides the fact that she was very beautiful. And the fact that she was smart was the icing on the cake. They began dating and were pretty much together everyday. After a few months things continued going strong and they both were happy. Desiree had plenty of guys after her and probably could have had any guy she wanted. But there was something about Ricky that made Desiree open herself to him. At the beginning

Desiree made it challenging for Ricky, despite him being the most popular guy in school. And also a football star. He was a very attractive young man, she would wear his football jersey and go to his games when she could. Life was going so well. But after hearing about her dating a guy, her father Robert wasn't too thrilled. So at times seeing Ricky was difficult. A few of Desiree's friends used to get fake ID'S to get in local adult clubs around the city. Desiree was too scared to even try, in fear of someone seeing her and telling her father.

Page 7

The fact that she dated a star football player only added to her shine, it also came with a lot of jealousy. Even more jealousy than she faced before. She took it all in stride and handled it with class. Even though she was once the shy girl who was very bashful, she began to develop tough skin from all the jealousy and envy. Deanna had settled in to Anita's house and they began selling clothes they had got cheap from a friend of Anita's mom. She would give Anita clothes to wear that were too small for her daughter who was a few years older than Anita. The clothes Anita didn't want, they would sell to some of their classmates. They made a pretty good amount of money, and with that money they would sometimes buy better more high end clothes and sell them.

As Deanna grew older she discovered she was bisexual, and as time went on further it was obvious she was gay. Her attraction for girls was obvious, even her and Anita had some sexual experiences together. Regardless of it all, they remained the best of friends. Deanna had been with only a few boys in her life. Her older sister Desiree was still going strong with her first love Ricky Stanton. Desiree was a virgin. But as the prom was approaching, her and Ricky would have conversations about sex. Desiree was always nervous of the thought of sex. But she knew no matter how much she was scared and tried to avoid it, that it would come up sooner rather than later. Especially from Ricky, who was very manly and was definitely ready to go all the way with her. They had been dating for almost the whole school year, and the year was winding down to the prom. Desiree had started to feel the pressure. Deep down she liked Ricky a lot, and she wanted to go all the way also. But was still a little nervous. So her and Ricky was sitting in the library one day talking.

"The prom is coming, so excited. And I booked us a room, I'm ready to spend the night with you" Ricky said smiling.

"Oh yeah ? A room" ? Desiree said surprised.

She was a little thrown off because Ricky knew how strict her father was, how was she supposed to spend the night with him ? Ricky had it all planned out, Desiree was to say she was spending the night with her friend after the prom. And everything was set. It was also right around the time Desiree found out she had been offered a full scholarship to the University of Maryland. Which also happened to be where Ricky had already signed a letter of intent to play football on a full scholarship himself. So everything fell into place perfectly.

Page 8

Anita and Deanna selling clothes would take a turn as they would meet a local drug lord who would try to change their mind about what they were selling. One day walking home from school they would have an encounter with that very drug lord. They didn't know it yet, but Francisco was watching them from a far selling their clothes. He loved their drive and commitment and he wanted them to work for him. As the girls were walking, a late model Cadillac drove up beside them and the window came down, the girls were shook at first and then a voice.

"Hello ladies, I see you two have done well selling clothes, I admire your spirit and I can make you two even more money working for me." Francisco said.

Without hesitation Deanna replies, "We don't even know you, how do you know us and what we sell" ?

"Let's just say I have ways of finding things out. And I know more than you think I know. But right now that's not the point. I would love for you and your friend to come work for me, trust me you won't regret it. And you will make a lot more money than you been making" Francisco replied.

Anita and Deanna looked at each other, Deanna nodded in approval.

"What you talking about us selling" ? Deanna asked.

"Well I will start you ladies off small, let yall sell a little weed. See how you handle that. If yall do yall thing and move it in a swift amount of time, I will increase yall handle." Francisco said.

"Sounds fair enough to us, when we get the product" ? Deanna asked.

"I will have one of my soldiers drop it off to yall right here where we're standing. Don't fuck this up, you hear me ? It can only benefit you more if you both handle shit" Francisco added before driving off.

The girls didn't know what to expect or if he was being real because they didn't really know Francisco. They only knew of him. One thing they did know, he was that dude when it came to making money. So they trusted that he would come through on his word alone. A few days later as promised, a stocky man with braids met the girls in the same spot they had met Francisco just a few days prior with a half pound of weed.

It was the most product the two girls had ever seen in their lives and it was also the last day the girls would sell clothes ever again. As they sought out on a new journey to become major players in Francisco's organization. Meanwhile the prom was quickly approaching and Desiree was trying on her dress with the help of her mother. Something her mother had always dreamed of doing. Helping her get ready. And after all her mother had been through up until this point, she was happy and blessed to be involved.

"You know I always dreamed about doing this ever since I thought about having kids, you are my first child that I have experienced this with. And will probably be the last. I don't think your sister will be into going to the prom." Denise said helping Desiree get ready.

"You never know mom, Deanna may surprise you. She may just show up to her prom and be the most beautiful girl there. You know she's capable." Desiree replied.

"I really hope you're right Desiree. Now let me see just how beautiful my first born looks" Denise said smiling looking at Desiree in the mirror.

Like most mothers Denise had envisioned herself doing these things with both her daughters, it was an exciting time for the Knight family. Seeing Desiree going to her high school prom. Desiree looked absolutely beautiful as always from head to toe dressed in a stunning purple dress. That came down right below her knees and showcased her beautiful legs, down to her very nice heels that her mother bought for her. Desiree's boyfriend Ricky had got a limousine for them to ride to the prom in. Along with a few of his friends and their dates.

They were indeed going to be the main attraction, the star football player and his beautiful girlfriend. Ricky came to pick her up looking handsome dressed in his black tuxedo with the purple bow tie to match Desiree's dress. They looked great together. As they walked out the house and headed towards the limosine, Desiree's sister Deanna walks up.

"Hey sis, you look amazing." Deanna said.

That voice that Desiree knew all too well, she knew it was her sister as she turned and walked towards her as they both embraced each other with a hug.

"Thank you sis, how are you at Anita's" ? Desiree asked.

"I'm good, and we're doing well" Deanna replied.

It was the first time the sisters had seen each other since Deanna had left home. It made Desiree feel good that her sister had seen her before she left for the prom. She was wondering if her sister would show up and she did. As Desiree got in the limosine after Ricky opened the door for her. Deanna, her mother Denise, and a few people from the neighborhood waved as she rode off. This was Denise chance to try and convince Deanna to move back home. "How are you Deanna ? I'm really worried about you out there in them streets." Denise said.

"I'm fine mom, don't worry. I'm at Anita's and you can call me if you need me" Deanna replied.

Deanna had her mind made up, and she was about to embark on a new journey that she felt would help her live comfortable. Working for Francisco and his organization. She and Anita both wanted all that was offered to them and they was hungry to get it. And it showed from the very start, as soon as they got the product they hit the streets with a purpose and spirit like no other.

The prom was everything Desiree imagined, as her and Ricky enjoyed themselves dancing and mingling with classmates. It all came full circle for Desiree, once being such a shy girl. And now being the girlfriend of the most popular athlete in not only her high school, but the state of Maryland. After having a great time at the prom, the two were headed to their hotel suite that Ricky had reserved for them. Upon entering Desiree had to pause before going into the room.

"Whats wrong baby, you ok" Ricky asked as she paused.

"Oh nothing I'm fine, just amazed at how perfect the night has been" Desiree replied.

"Well its about to get even better beautiful" Ricky said taking Desiree's hand leading her into the room.

The night was finally here, the night Desiree and Ricky had talked about so long, the night Desiree would lose her virginity to her first love. After kissing since being in the elevator, Ricky and Desiree finally entered their suite. It was an absolutely beautiful night as their suite overlooked the Downtown Baltimore skyline and Harbor.

Looking out on the skyline, Ricky went behind Desiree softly kissing the back of her neck and slowly unzipping her dress, taking it off while passionately kissing her shoulders. The mood was right and the passion was thick. Desiree followed Ricky's lead as their clothes came off and Ricky reached in his pocket for a condom.

"Are you ready for me sexy" ? Ricky whispered into Desiree's ear.

"Yes I been ready" Desiree replied as they lay on the bed.

So as Ricky slid the condom onto his penis and slowly inserted it into Desiree's vagina. A quiet whisper of a moan came out of Desiree's mouth as he began to penetrate her with each stroke of his hips. They were completely naked as he continued penetrating her with rhythmic strokes as she moaned softly and as they kissed passionately. It was indeed somewhat painful at first for her first time as expected. But as it went on she enjoyed it more. And at the time she couldn't think of a better guy to lose her virginity to.

"Are you ok" ? Ricky asked.

"Yes I'm fine, keep going" Desiree replied as she let out a medium pitched yell.

It became even more intense as the minutes turned to an hour and the passion remained thick throughout. As they both climaxed they looked up at the clock to find the time at 1:11 am. Ricky jumped up.

"Wow I didn't realize what time it was, I have to get you home" !! Ricky said sounding nervous.

"Relax, I'm staying over a friend's house remember" ? Desiree replied smiling.

"Oh yeah, right" Ricky said calming down.

"Don't tell me you're scared, Ricky Stanton the star wide receiver the beast" ? Desiree said jokingly giving Ricky a kiss.

"You got jokes. No I just want to see your ass again, I know how your father can be" Ricky replied.

After spending the night together and having her first sexual experience, she came home the next morning to see her father sleeping on the couch. At first it intially scared her because she didnt see him at first.

"Oh my God dad, you scared me. Didn't see you at first" Desiree said coming into the house.

"I was up waiting for you, dont you know your curfew young lady" ? Robert Knight said.

Before she could say anything in response, her father smacked her across the face.

"Daddy" !! Desiree said hoping her face.

"Daddy what ? Don't ever come into this house again after your curfew, or the door will be locked" Robert Knight said angrily.

Desiree just ran into her room crying. It was another moment in Desiree's life that she wanted to forget. After a night that was so special to her. She had asked her mother was it ok if she could stay at her friend's house and her mother said yes. But her father had came in very late the previous night and was still in a drunken rage.

The commotion did wake Desiree's mother Denise up, but Desiree had already went into her room and closed the door. She thought her father would be a little more lenient with it being prom and all, but she realized then her father would never change his ways. And she was glad to be leaving and going off to college soon. Desiree's father didn't approve of her relationship with Ricky and tried his best to make it hard for her to see him. Desiree and Ricky both knew this, so they adjusted to make time for each other whenever they could. Resentment set in even more as Desiree had so much animosity towards her father. Not only for his non approval for her and Ricky's relationship, but also for the way he treated her and her mother. Not to mention the fact that he drove Deanna to move out, it was tense times in her household as usual. Desiree tried to remain positive knowing she was going away to college in nearby College Park soon. And she was excited about it. Adding on the fact she would have the love of her life Ricky going to the same college with her.

Ricky was just as smart as Desiree, they both carried between 3.5 to 3.7 GPA'S throughout their high school years. And both were offered full scholarships to the University of Maryland. His was for football as well as his academics. Her's was for academics. It was a bright future ahead of them, and they were excited about sharing their lives together.

Page 12

Deanna and Anita did well with the product Francisco had initially gave them, a half pound of weed in which they moved rather quickly without having much clientele. The kids that were their customers knew them for selling clothes not weed, so their customers changed. It began to be older men and women from in and around their neighborhoods. Some of them were their classmates parents, some older people they knew from the area. Francisco was happy but not surprised the girls sold the weed so quickly, he knew they had the drive in them to be great. So he decided to meet with them in a location just outside the Baltimore City limits, they were to be picked up near Anita's home and driven to where Francisco was in a warehouse outside the city.

"I see yall took care of business just like I thought you would, good work. You now have the freedom of getting as much product as you want as long as you move it in the allotted time. Whatever product you get, you must move it. We don't take back product, we take money back in return for that product. No excuses. So be very careful how much you ask for, and be sure to sale all that you have. Any questions ladies" ? Francisco said.

"No not at all, we understand and we know what we're getting into" Deanna replied as Anita nodded in approval.

"Ok well yall set then, let my man's right here know what you need and yall do what you do. Grind and get that paper, I will be in touch" Francisco said as he got back in his car with his driver and drove off.

The girls decided to talk in private between each other to decide how much they would ask for and eventually move. Because they knew now that they had to be sure they could sell it all in the time period that was given. They didn't want to be on Francisco's bad side at all, their mission was to climb the food chain as quickly as they could. About this time word had traveled on the streets as well as school, that Deanna and Anita were drug dealers. It had spread through the students but none of the school officials, somehow they never found out. Deanna was beginning to realize her name was in the streets. So she decided with the money they both made off moving the first half pound that they needed a gun. Being in the streets and the fact they were both young girls. It was pretty much a necessity for their survival and to keep them from getting robbed of their product and money.

So the girls got in touch with someone who knew someone else who sold guns on the street. It was risky because of the possibility of the gun having bodies already on it, but Deanna and Anita was desperate. So they decided to purchase a 38 revolver. And would eventually learn how to shoot it using a make shift range, because at the time they were both too young to legally own a gun.

Page 13

Although Deanna was known on the streets for handling her own when it came to fighting, she had never been one to handle a gun. But she would quickly get herself comfortable with the 38 Revolver she had just purchased. Anita had handled guns before, being raised by a single parent who worked two jobs and was hardly home. Her mother kept a gun in their home. Anita had to learn quickly herself. The girls had a spot behind some abandoned houses a few blocks away from Anita's house where they could have target practice. They would go there everyday and practice until they felt they were comfortable enough to handle it. They were a few stashes around Anita's house for their product and the gun, they hardly ever carried product on them. They knew that people around their area knew that they sold drugs, and certain cops began watching them. They could feel it. The more Deanna hustled, the more school became less important to her and her time was dedicated primarily to hustling. Her and Anita was making money hand over fist, and slowly making their way up the food chain in Francisco's organization. So much so that a few of Francisco's other workers became jealous and envious, one in particular. One of the lower level dealers by the street name "Snake" had gotten into a heated argument with Deanna over territory which led to "Snake" threatening to take everything Deanna had and Deanna threatening to slit "Snake's" throat.

It was competitive like that within Francisco's organization, that's the way he liked it. He felt it kept all of them hungry to do better. But the rule was to never get in the way of one another making the almighty dollar. Never lose money to the organization for inner personal conflicts. It would ultimately lead to losing your life. So even though some within the organization had issues with one another, they were very mindful of their personal beefs. And the business side of it was a totally different situation. Deanna had her gun for a little while now, and she was very hesitant about letting her sister know about it in fear of telling their mother. They had such a close relationship and told each other everything that it was only natural for her to tell her sister Desiree. She also hadn't told her that she had went from selling clothes to drugs. Word had got back to Desiree, but she didn't want to believe it knowing how they both hated drugs because of what it had done to their mother. So Desiree was hesitant to even ask Deanna about it. But one day seeing Deanna on the street, Desiree finally asked her sister about it.

"I been hearing that you and Anita been selling weed. Tell me this isn't true Deanna." Desiree said.

"I'm sorry sis I can't tell you that, because it is true." Deanna replied.

Somewhat stunned at the answer Desiree just shook her head.

"So this is what it's come to Deanna? Clothes wasn't enough for yall" ? Desiree asked.

"To be honest with you no it wasn't, look I know we personally hate the shit because mom was on drugs. But she wasn't smoking weed. She was snorting coke and smoking crack." Deanna replied.

Deanna even told Desiree about how much money she was making, and then offered her fifty dollars to take home to help out around the house. At first Desiree refused, but after a little more convincing Desiree took the money and went home. Deanna also told her not to tell their parents where she had got the money from, but lie and tell them her boyfriend Ricky gave it to her. That didn't matter too much because the girl's father didn't like Ricky anyway. Deanna just wanted to help her family out with what she could at the moment. And she vowed that there was more to come. As soon as she got on her feet and made more money. Amid their conversation, Deanna didn't even mention anything to Desiree about the gun she had bought. And after thinking about it after she left Desiree, she felt it was better that her sister didn't know. Desiree was about to go away to college and Deanna didn't want her sister worrying about her and what she was doing. So she just kept it to herself.

In the coming months, Desiree would graduate and go off to college at nearby University of Maryland, which was in College Park, Maryland. About an hour and ten minutes away from Baltimore. Desiree was nervous and anxious at the same time, starting basically a new life and her first time away from home. She was also worried about her sister, who she knew now was selling drugs and was heavy in the streets. The one thing she did have on her side and was accompanying her to college was the love of her life Ricky Stanton. Who was just as excited to be going to college and playing football in the Fall. Everything was set and things were going really well. But Desiree couldn't hide her concern for her mother. Desiree felt like she was the last piece holding the family together. Being there with her mother and bringing some sort of peace between her parents. Her father would never change his ways, he also began drinking even more often right before she left. There were a lot of things weighing heavily on Desiree's mind heading to her first semester in college. But she tried her best to block out the distractions and focus on having a good year. Upon entering College Park and the campus, Desiree checked in and was shown to her dorm. She had a roommate by the name of Candice who she met upon entering her dorm room.

"Hey girl, you must be Desiree. Hi I'm Candice, nice to meet you." Candice said extending her hand.

"Hello Candice it's nice to meet you too" Desiree replied.

Candice was from Washington, D.C. and she too was a Business Major. She was also a very beautiful woman and a plus size female who carried it well and wasn't ashamed that she had weight on her. She was a very proud plus size woman and would let you know it in a minute if you said anything otherwise.

She was friendly and was willing to help get Desiree comfortable. Candice came a day earlier and visited the school prior to coming to the University of Maryland. So she knew her way around so to speak.

"As I told you before, I'm from D.C. Southeast to be exact. Where are you from" ? Candice said.

"I'm from Baltimore, the West Side. And I'm a Business Major, and I hear you are too" Desiree replied.

"Yep, you heard right. I was going to go with Communications but I decided Business was better for me" Candice said putting some of her clothes away.

After the girls talked a little longer, they went to get something to eat. Desiree was also planning on working a part time job, she didn't have much money. Only the fifty dollars her sister Deanna gave her, she never did give it to her parents. She kept it. She figured her mother would only question her as to where she had gotten it, and that would've led to more questions. Plus she knew she was going away to school soon so she kept it for herself.

It was a smart decision because it was very useful for her just starting out. Desiree did look for work and it didn't take long for someone to call. As she began working at an eatery a little off campus in the evenings. She knew doing that, she wasn't going to be able to spend much time with Ricky. Adding on the fact he was practicing and getting ready for the season. So whatever time they could spend together, they made the most of. In between studying and going to her classes. This was her new life. And even though she was away from the big city life of Baltimore, her life seemed at its fastest in the present time. Her and Ricky would often times walk through campus talking to each other about their classes and experiences so far on campus.

"How are you enjoying being away from your parents ? I know this has to be a shock to your system, coming from how strict your father was" Ricky said laughing.

"Oh indeed it is, smart ass. So how is life on campus for the big time Freshmen football star" ? Desiree asked.

"I ain't shit yet, I was a high school star and these people believe in me. That's why they offered me a full ride. Now I got something to prove, there's a lot of pressure on me, and these upper classmen really don't want a Freshmen to take their spot. No matter how much of a star I was in high school, I haven't done nothing here yet. My father has been schooling me on this, you know he used to play football in college too. He played at the University of Illinois." Ricky replied.

"No I didn't know, that's interesting. And I'm glad he prepared you for this moment, just know you have my support always" Desiree replied kissing Ricky on his cheek.

"And that's why I love you girl, cause you hold a brotha down. Now let's get you back to your dorm before it gets dark" Ricky said as they walked hand and hand.

Back in Baltimore Deanna and Anita was steady grinding, moving product and making money like they had imagined. They were making enough money to stash to save for an apartment of their own. Anita's mother had eventually caught on to what her daughter was doing, and she wasn't too happy about it. She told her she had a few weeks before she had to go. And Anita herself wanted to leave, her and Deanna felt it was time to have their own space. Plus they didn't want to bring any heat to Anita's mother's home. Like Denise, Anita's mother pleaded with her daughter to give up selling drugs and go to school. In which it fell on deaf ears as Anita was in and out of trouble since she was young, spent some time in a detention center as a juvenile. Her father was murdered when she was eight years old, and it's been her and her mother ever since then. Anita never really got close to anyone as a child until she met Deanna when she was thirteen, they had been close friends ever since. Now at seventeen they were full fledged hustlers deep into the street life, and about to get deeper.

Deanna had got Desiree's number up at school and called her one day, surprising her.

"Hello is Desiree there" ? Deanna asked.

"Yes this is her, who is this" ? Desiree replied.

"This is your sister knucklehead, Deanna." Deanna said.

"Oh Deanna, how did you get the number" ? Desiree asked.

"Can I get some love, damn. You asking all these questions, where's the love" Deanna said jokingly.

"I'm sorry sis, it's good to hear from you and I'm glad you called. How are you, how's mom" ? Desiree asked.

"I'm good, and as far as I know she is good. Just doing my thing, and oh yeah, you're going to receive a package. Remember the time we went to the carnival and you wanted that big ass teddy bear and dad wouldn't get it for you" ? Deanna said.

"Yes I remember, you teased me the whole way home. I wanted to rip your head off" Desiree replied.

"Yeah well I got it for you" Deanna said.

"You what " ? Desiree asked confused.

"I got it for you, and I put something inside it, just follow the cut I made to get it open and I put a little surprise in it. I'm not going to tell you what it is, so don't ask. Matter of fact, I have to go sis". Deanna said hanging up the phone.

"Deanna wait......Deanna" !!!! Desiree said. As usual Deanna escaped again, Desiree just smiled at the phone and shook her head.

A few days later her package had arrived and she was quick to grab it and run to her dorm room to open it. Upon entering the room, her roommate Candice just watched as Desiree took the teddy bear and opened it up where her sister Deanna said she made the cut. Candice at first was a little confused. But after opening the teddy bear and pulling out two one hundred dollar bills, she knew why Desiree was eager to open the bear.

"Very creative, whoever thought of stuffing money in a teddy bear" Candice said as she looked at Desiree.

Desiree just smiled and put the teddy bear back together.

"It was my sister Deanna, she sent me some money to help me out" Desiree replied.

"Oh so you have an older sister ? How old is she" ? Candice asked.

"No, actually she's younger. She has a job and she knows I'm only working part time so she sent me something to help out with my expenses here" Desiree replied.

She didn't know Candice well enough to talk to her about her personal business, or family for that matter. She seemed like a very nice person, but Desiree had to really get to know someone before she could confirm that. And besides that, just because she was a very nice person didn't necessarily mean she was a trustworthy person.

Only time would tell. In the meantime Desiree kept everything close and stayed to herself. Ricky had been very busy of late with classes and of course football that he and Desiree hardly seen each other. It was starting to put wear and tear on their relationship. They both loved each other but had conflicting schedules. With them now going through the ups and downs of a relationship on the college level. You would think because of the freedom they now had, it would be easier to work things out. But yet there were still distractions. Would their relationship survive and stand the test of time ? It would remain to be seen. There was a moment that made Desiree think. One day she was walking in between classes when she saw Ricky from a distance doing the same. And also talking to a female student as he was walking. They seemed to be having a good time laughing and smiling, she didn't think much of it. She just watched from a far then proceeded to go to her class. She tried her best not to make the situation bigger than what it seemed, but she couldn't help but think about it. She was wrestling with the fact on whether she should say something about it to Ricky or not. If it was nothing he would think she was overreacting and being insecure. Which could be a turnoff. If it really was something she would be protecting herself from being hurt in the end. Since she had no other reason to believe it was, she decided to play it safe and let it go.

There was a party coming up, the first major party of the school year. Everyone was talking about it around campus. Desiree had a lot on her plate, as she had to study for a few tests she had coming up. So she was torn between whether she was going or not. She was still undecided, but leaning towards not going.

"I saw you and wanted to catch up with you before you went to class, so I know you heard about the party, you going" ? Desiree asked after seeing Ricky in between classes.

"Not really sure if I'm going, got a lot of shit to do, couple papers due next week. Why are you going" Ricky replied asking.

"I was thinking the same thing, lot of things I have to do. So I will probably be home studying" Desiree replied.

"Well I gotta get going, see you later" Ricky said walking away.

Desiree was surprised that Ricky wasn't going to the party, he was the type to always be at every party. Especially one as big as this one. After going to her classes, Desiree returned to her dorm and laid on her bed. She was there for about fifteen minutes when her roommate Candice came in.

"Whats going on girl ? Why you laying there like you lost your best friend" ? Candice asked.

"Nothing just thinking" Desiree replied.

"Thinking about what ? You can tell me, it will stay between us I promise you that" Candice said looking concerned.

"Just thinking about me and Ricky, and what's going on with us. Things are changing and I seen him the other day walking with some chick smiling and laughing. I damn near ran to catch him this afternoon and he was acting like he didn't care if he seen me or not. It was weird, I asked him if he was going to the party and he said no. I have never known him to miss a party." Desiree said.

"Well just wait it out and see if he goes, I know I'm going. You not going" ? Candice asked.

"I don't think I'm going, I have some studying to do for some tests next week. But you can do me a favor. If you do see him there, don't say anything just let me know if he is there with anyone." Desiree said.

"Girl you know I got you. If I see him there with any female, I'm definitely going to let you know" Candice replied.

Back in Baltimore, Anita and Deanna continued to do really well moving the product they got from Francisco. And he continued feeding them whatever they wanted and needed, but he also had some other plans for them. Something new and something that would be a challenge like they had never seen before. He had asked to see them and discuss the plans he had for them. The girls got the news and quickly met up with Francisco and a few of his soldiers. The same spot as always, an abandoned warehouse just outside the city.

Page 19

"Y'all ladies ready to make some real money" ? Francisco asked.

"Of course we are, that's why we're here" Deanna replied.

"Yeah but this is going to be some different shit, this isn't about selling no weed. I need you to link up with my homie Chaos and do a job for me. Some muthafuckas robbed a few of my workers, and we need to get our shit back ASAP. Which means I need you two to ride wjth Chaos to get our shit back. Of course you two will be strapped up. I need yall on this one, so yall down" ? Francisco asked.

Chaos was Francisco's best friend from Jersey City, they both grew up together and were partners in this organization. Chaos was about 6'3 255lbs. and built solid after doing a few prison stints when he was younger. Even after doing a few prison stints that spanned the course of eleven years he was still very hot tempered. He linked up with Francisco after coming home from his last stint and has remained out of prison ever since. Chaos was accused of killing three people in two separate incidents, only to beat the case because of Francisco's very expensive and powerful lawyers. He looked out for Chaos, because Chaos more than looked out for him as his main enforcer. Catching cases behind some of Francisco's brutal and ruthless orders of vengeance against those who crossed him. For a good moment no one would dare to cross Francisco, so the two were free of any legal problems and mostly stayed low and out of the mix. But a week prior one of Francisco's workers was robbed by a rival East Side crew. Francisco always vowed if anyone robbed his people, there would be hell to pay. So he decided instead of sending Chaos in, or another one of his other soldiers. He would surprise the East Side crew with a few girls to distract them, and who better than the hungry duo of Deanna and Anita.

Francisco felt it was time for the two girls to step up into a new level of putting in work, and if they succeeded they would be paid generously.

"Yeah we down and we ready, as long as the money is right. We been ready" Deanna replied.

"Well here it is, you and Anita will go to this location, Chaos will drive. Once you get there, Anita knock on the door, Deanna stand on the side of the house with your gun drawn and your eyes open. Once the door opens you rush the spot and demand them clowns to lead you to the product and the money. Anita by that time you should have your gun on anybody else in the room right beside her. If anybody act stupid in there....... and I mean anybody. Don't hesitate to blast they ass on site. If that does happen, my man Chaos will be right behind yall with the big gun. So don't worry you got back up in case shit gets funny in there. After yall get what yall went there for, get the fuck out of there fast !! Chaos will be waiting in the ride. Any questions"? Francisco said as the girls listened carefully.

"No we understand, when do we get the guns" ? Deanna asked.

Francisco laughed a little and said, "You really anxious aren't you little mama? You will need some target practice, you both will".

Deanna and Anita had got their apartment, a decent place not too far away from Anita's mother's house. They had things only their friends and kids their age envied. A nice couch, a big screen TV and several video game systems. They were having the time of their lives so to speak. They had money and often times when they weren't hustling, they would be at the mall shopping. But they now were faced with and agreed to a very dangerous job to make even more money. They were headed in unfamiliar territory of a rival crew on the East Side. Regardless of what could happen, the girls had their minds made up and was totally focused on the job at hand. They went to the gun range everyday for a week to prepare them for the upcoming job. Surprisingly enough the girls weren't nervous, at least not yet they werent. The job was a few days away, but Deanna was amped up about it already.

"This is our shot Anita. We do this shit right, the sky is the limit. And he is going to come to us when he needs shit done instead of "Snake" and those other clowns that were hating on us. Man I can't wait" !! Deanna said sounding excited.

"I'm doing this for you. I want to make more money but I didn't want to be in the mix like that doing stick ups and shit. You know we going to ride for each other regardless, and I'm always down when you are. But I really don't want to be doing this after this job Deanna" Anita replied.

For the first time in their friendship Anita was partially against what Deanna wanted to do, it surprised Deanna but she also understood Anita's point of view. And they both shared that mutual respect for one another. That's why they went hard for one another and stuck together since they first met. This was their moment to shine, but more importantly to get out of it safe and unharmed.

"You know you do have a point, let's just do this and get out the stick up game. After this we can get back to what we do best, I will tell Francisco next time we meet" Deanna said as she sat in the rocking chair at their apartment.

Anita nodded in approval and the night went on as planned, the girls played dominoes and ordered some take out. Back in College Park the dance was tonight and Desiree was watching Candice get ready.

"Girl I can't believe you're not going, the first party of the year. Tomorrow is Sunday you don't have the test until Monday. Just study tomorrow" Candice said fixing her hair.

"Well actually I cant, I'm already behind and I have another test Monday also. Besides you're going and you can keep your eyes open for Ricky, in case he's doing some shady shit" Desiree replied.

"I told you girl, I got you. If I see him I will call you right away. I just know they going to be some fine looking brothers at this party, shit girl I might get lucky" Candice said dancing in the mirror.

Desiree just laughed and shook her head.

Chapter Two "College Life"

Candice finally made her way to the party and at first she was just mingling through the crowd, and didnt see any trace of Ricky. She talked to a few people she knew and danced a little before she seen a dude that looked like Ricky. She went a little closer and looked around the corner to see a familiar face, it WAS Ricky. He was talking to some female. She continued to watch from a far, out of plain sight. As they continued talking and then all the proof Candice needed happened. They both embraced each other and kissed. Candice just put her hand over her own mouth and quickly went back inside to walk out the front. Once she got out front she took out her cell phone and began to walk down the street calling Desiree. Candice was walking fast and was nervous, and felt bad about telling Desiree the painful truth.

"Desiree, girl I saw him with some chick out back. They were talking for a little and then I seen them hugging and kissing. I'm so sorry girl, you want me to come get you" ? Candice asked.

"No, just go back to the party, thanks" Desiree replied.

"What ? You're not going to check your man and handle this chick ? I got your back I'm here" Candice said confused.

"No I will handle it later" Desiree replied.

"But Desiree....." Candice pleaded.

"Candice, just go back to the party and have a good time, I'm good" Desiree said interrupting. "

"Ok girl, call me if you need me" Candice said before hanging up.

Desiree's worst fears and the painful truth had came to reality, her first love was seeing someone else. It was also something she had suspected, so in a way she wasn't surprised. Regardless of it all, it still hurt and instead of her flying off the handle and causing a scene at the party. She decided to stay at home and think about how she was going to handle this situation. That was just the type of person she was, a deep thinker who always was careful when making decisions in her life. The next morning Desiree had woke up and sat in her bed and cried softly as tears ran down her face. Not too long after, Candice woke up and tried to console Desiree.

"Aww girl, you gonna be ok. Forget his ass. He wasn't worth it anyway" Candice said wiping tears from Desiree's eyes.

"I'm going to need the room tomorrow" Desiree said drying her face with a napkin.

"You going to invite him over" ? Candice asked.

"Yeah I'm going to need some privacy" Desiree replied.

"Ok I will go to the pizza shop" Candice said. Page 22

The next night Desiree called Ricky to come to her dorm, and made it seemed as if they were going to have sex. She knew that would lure Ricky over to her dorm rather quickly. Once he arrived he was all over her and she played along with it until she stopped him as things were getting hotter.

"Well why did you invite me over for like you was trying to get it in? I got a lot of shit i could be doing right now" Ricky said sounding confused.

"Because I wanted you to THINK you were getting a taste of this again. You will never touch me again, now get out of my room before I call the campus security." Desiree said sounding angry.

"You can't be serious, you crazy bitch" Ricky said shaking his head walking out the door.

"That's right, a crazy bitch you will never have again. Go be with that bitch you were kissing on at the party" Desiree replied loud enough for some of the other girls in the same building to hear.

She was beyond angry, and had tears in her eyes. But she knew she made the right decision. Ricky is all she knew when it came to love. She didn't know if they were going to be together forever or not. But she believed they would be together longer than just a few months into their college years. Those first few weeks after the breakup were rough, she couldn't concentrate fully on her education. As much as she wanted to get over Ricky fast, it was going to take some time. Desiree did her best to avoid Ricky and move on with her life, so she got focused and kept her head in the books.

Back in Baltimore Deanna and Anita was a night away from their moment of truth and the time was ticking on their chance to show and prove. As Deanna was sitting on the couch just thinking, she thought about her sister and decided to call her. Desiree sitting in her dorm room studying and the phone rings.

"Hello" Desiree answered.

"Hey sis, how are you" Deanna asked.

"A little depressed, but I'm getting through it." Desiree replied.

"Why what's going on" ? Deanna asked.

"Me and Ricky broke up, he was seeing another chick. My roommate seen him at a party with her, kissing and all up on her." Desiree replied sounding upset.

"Something told me Ricky wasn't shit, I never really liked him. Anyway sis, you know there will be plenty of guys coming at you in the near future, you're beautiful. And I'm not just telling you this because you're my sister. Because if you was ugly I would tell your ass that too" Deanna replied as they both laughed.

That was their sisterly bond on full display, Deanna calling and talking to her sister when she needed it most. And also providing a smile and laugh when she needed it. After getting off the phone, Deanna just sat in her chair holding her 38 Revolver and thinking about the job that was ahead of her and Anita. As they were sitting there the phone rang, it was Francisco letting the girls know Chaos would supply the girls with brand new guns that had scratched off serial numbers. The street bought guns they owned could've been used in other crimes, Francisco of course wasnt taking that chance. The girls were a little worried about using different guns because they were so used to their own that they didn't know if they could handle them well, as always Francisco had an answer for that. He had reserved a spot for the girls at the range just hours before they were to do the job. After leaving the range they went home and changed before meeting up with Chaos to head to the location. Chaos would meet them at a separate location about three blocks from the girls apartment.

Chaos told them to be ready and at the spot for him to pick them up by 9:30 pm. The girls were both dressed in all black with black gloves and would also have black masks to hide their identity. They would also both be equipped with 9mm hand guns. Chaos of course had his 45 caliber handgun, most times his weapon of choice. It was time, and as promised Chaos came to pick the girls up in a van. Once they got in the van, Chaos wasted no time making sure the girls were on point.

"Yall ready ? It's time to show and prove. Like Francisco told yall, when you get in there have your guns drawn. Empty the spot out, take everything they got and get the fuck out of there. If you have to let off, let off. I will be in the van, if I hear some gunplay I got yall back and will be in immediately. Any questions" ? Chaos said.

"No questions, and we been ready. Just get us there and make sure you have our back" Deanna replied staring at Chaos.

Chaos just stared back as he continued driving the van through Baltimore streets to the East Side. Once they got to the location, Chaos parked a few blocks away. The girls then put their black masks over their faces and exited the van in route to the location. They walked a few blocks and across an intersection, and then preceded to the house.

Very slowly and quietly, Anita walked up to the house and knocked on the door. Deanna was along side of the house gun drawn waiting. After a short time the door opens and a man answers.

"Hello I'm sorry to bother you but, I have a flat tire and I could use some help" Anita said to the man sounding concerned.

The man then preceded to walk outside the house, that's when Deanna came behind him and said, "Shhh....get in the fucking house right now" with her gun pointed at his head. The man listened to what she said as he led them inside the house.

Once they got in the house there was another man who was sitting on a chair and was about to reach for his gun until Anita yelled, "Don't fucking try it, don't even think about it" pointing her gun right at him.

Deanna then instructed the man who led them inside the house to open a safe that was located in the living room. He just stood there. "Open the fucking safe before I blast your ass, hurry up" Deanna yelled.

He then walked over to the safe and started to open it, just then the other man went for his weapon again....boom !!! Anita fired a single shot into the man's knee dropping him to the floor in great pain.

"Now the next one going in your head if you move again" Anita said.

"I'm going to tell your ass one more time, open the fucking safe" !!! Deanna shouted.

The man then continued to open the safe while the other man Anita shot lay on the floor agonizing in pain from the shot to his knee. The safe was finally open and Deanna was just about to go over and empty it when another man started to open the front door. Deanna and Anita both looked at each other. Meanwhile Chaos seen the other man approach the front door from his sideview mirror.

Chaos then proceeded to grab his 45 caliber handgun and exited the van. As the door opened both Desiree and Anita drew their guns on the third man as he came through the door.

"What the fuck is this" ? The man said coming through the door as two guns were pointed at him.

"Get in here and sit down, and shut up before you get shot. Where's the rest of the product" Deanna asked yelling.

At that time, the other man that opened the safe decided to run out the back as Deanna fired a shot at his head, barely missing him. At the same time Chaos had entered the home and drew his 45 on the men in the house. Chaos then motioned Deanna to go out back after the man that fled. Anita had her gun on the guy she shot and Chaos had his gun on the guy that just came in the house. Chaos then went over to the safe and began emptying it out. There was about thirty thousand dollars in cash and about four bricks of raw cocaine in the safe. Chaos took it all and stuffed it into a bag that they had brought to collect the product in. Chaos knew there was more product and possibly more money in the house.

"Where is the rest of the shit at...huh ? Tell me where the fuck it is" ? !! Chaos yelled.

The man said he didn't know, Chaos then pointed and aimed his gun at the man's head and fired. Killing him instantly. At that point Chaos and Anita heard some shots fired out back.

Page 25

"Stay here with him, I'll be right back" Chaos said to Anita as he ran out back.

Chaos went out back and he could hardly see anything, but he kept hearing shots being fired back and forth. So he started firing in different directions of where he thought the enemy was. He didnt want to call Deanna's name to draw attention to himself. After some more shots were fired, they suddenly stopped and he heard a body drop. And someone running away. He fired in the direction of the person running, but they got away. He ran over to where he seen a body laying motionless, he looked closer and it was a female. Thats when he knew it was Deanna. He then ran back towards the house and inside the back door.

"We gotta get the fuck outta here" Chaos said as he continued filling the bag with money and the rest of the bricks of cocaine.

"Where's Deanna" ? Anita asked Chaos looking concerned.

Chaos completely ignored her and continued filling the bag. After filling the bag, Chaos walked over to the wounded man on the floor and shot him at point blank range in the head. Killing him, as Anita watched.

"Let's go" !!! Chaos yelled as him and Anita fled the house and got back in the van and sped off.

Inside the van Anita began yelling. "Where is Deanna Chaos, where is she" ?

"Listen, shut the fuck up !! She is gone, she is dead. We have to get out of here, and you must go home and get your ass out this city. If the cops catch up to you, you better keep your mouth shut or you're going to end up like them two dudes I just shot. Keep your mouth close, and get rid of that gun. If you get locked up for this shit, don't think you're safe because you behind them walls. I got people in the inside that will touch you if you put my name or Francisco's name in this shit." Chaos said.

He wanted to let Anita know, no matter what she better not say anything about him or Francisco. Or she would be killed inside or outside of prison walls. Anita terrified and still in shock was dropped off at the same location where he had picked her and Deanna earlier. After getting out of the van, Anita ran home at full speed. Once she got back to their apartment, she went in the bathroom and threw up. She was in the bathroom for about twenty minutes, throwing up and crying her eyes out. This had to be a bad dream, her best friend since they were young couldn't be dead. After really not wanting to do the job. Only doing it because Deanna wanted to, it seemed so much of a regret now. Anita wanted the night back, even the time back when Francisco first asked them to do the job. She wanted her friend back. But this was no bad dream, this was real life and this was reality. She just sat in the empty apartment and cried for most of the night. She could barely sleep thinking about what happened to her best friend, and how Chaos just left her there. By this time the news was out that two men were found shot to death in an East Baltimore home. With another body found in the back of the house.

Page 26

Deanna's body had been identified an hour later, as her mother was notified. The police ended up interviewing a witness that identified Anita as the female that fled the scene with an unidentied suspect. After she had removed her mask fleeing the scene. They showed up at their apartment. She was somewhat shocked, after the police asked her if she was Anita Washington. They arrested her at the girl's apartment. She felt very distraught thinking about if Deanna's family had thought that she had something to do with Deanna's murder. She was also stuck because she couldn't tell them the truth because in part she didn't really know what happened in that backyard that night. She feared Chaos and Francisco, she feared for her life on the outside and behind prison walls. They had ways of touching her even in the prison system. She had a decision to make, and it was weighing heavy on her mind as each minute passed. She went into police custody with no resistence. Meanwhile at the Knight household the mood was total sadness, as Denise and Robert Knight's youngest daughter had been killed in an attempted robbery. Friends of both the girls from school were seen in and around the Knight home in West Baltimore, paying their respect to the family.

Denise had to do the worst thing she had to ever do in her life. Call her oldest daughter to tell her that her younger sister had been killed. Even harder than fighting her drug addiction. Every time she picked up the phone and dialed the number she stopped and hung the phone up. She did that maybe three times before she had enough courage to actually complete the call. Desiree was putting some of her clothes away when the phone rang.

"Hello" Desiree answered.

It was quiet and seemed like no voice was on the other end, Desiree said hello again only for a familiar voice to speak on the phone.

"Desiree it's your mother, I have some terrible news....Deanna was killed tonight"

"Oh my God no....no...no" !! Desiree dropped the phone and dropped to her knees crying and screaming.

Her mother Denise could hear her on the other end, which made her breakdown. It was a very emotional time for them both, after that Desiree could hardly talk. But she did want to know what happened.

"What happened mom, how did this happen" ? Desiree asked.

"We don't know a lot right now, she was found in a backyard on the East Side." Denise said.

"East Side ? Deanna doesn't be over that way too much" Desiree replied.

"I don't know, that's what we were told. Just come home." Denise said.

"I will mom, I'm on my way." Desiree replied. And just like that, Desiree was on her way home to bury her sister.

Page 27

Desiree finally got home after her hour and fifteen minute drive from College Park, there were a few family friends at the house coming by to pay their respects. As Desiree's parents Robert and Denise Knight greeted each person. She got in the house and immediately embraced her mother with a hug as they both shed tears. Once Desiree got home the guests were asked to leave so the family could be in peace. Robert Knight decided to break the ice so to speak by saying something first.

"I know me and Deanna didn't have the greatest relationship, but I loved her like I love all of you. I would do anything for my family, I worked hard supporting you girls. I'm sorry for all the things from the past, I truly am." Robert Knight said.

Desiree just looked at her mother and then looked at her father, and nodded in approval. She could hardly speak, the moment added with the circumstances was too much emotionally for her at the time. Tears just rolled down her eyes, as her father embraced her with a hug.

Robert Knight felt like he of all people had to be strong for his wife and daughter, he felt guilty about the way Deanna's life ended up. If she wouldn't have never left home, would she still be alive now ? Desiree was never really over what her father had done in the past, but she knew she had to forgive him to move on with her life. She also felt at this moment in time it was better to have peace, so you can say she decided to coexist with him mostly for her mother's sake. And out of respect for her sister's death she wanted her family to be on good terms. Later on that day, some more people came by the house to pay their respects including Deanna's best friend's mother Shirley Washington. Whose daughter was in police custody in connection with Deanna's murder. Anita wasn't believed to be a suspect in her murder, but it was confirmed she was there. Denise and Desiree both were happy to see Anita's mother, and knew she herself was dealing with a tragic situation. Her daughter was locked up. They sat and talked, laughed about the times Anita and Deanna had together that they remembered. And even cried together. Two families and one case that changed a lot of lives.

A few days passed and a day before the funeral the official autopsy was released. Deanna was shot twice. Once in the back which went through her chest, and once in her stomach. The shot that went through her chest was the fatal shot. After arresting Anita, the police recovered her 9mm. It was the only other gun recovered in the case besides Deanna's and one of the deceased men found in the house. But the two bullets that were recovered from Deanna's body were a 45 and a Clock 40. After learning that, Anita knew that Chaos had the 45 caliber and was partly responsible for Deanna's death. All she could do was shake her head in disgust. She began to think her and Deanna had been set up, maybe even set up from the very beginning.

Page 28

It was something that Anita had no answer to, but would think about for a long time. But for now, Anita had to stick to her story. Her story was her and Deanna went to rob the men on their own and the robbery went bad resulting in Deanna's death. Anita's gun was traced to the one man who was killed. The shot to the deceased man's knee was fired from Anita's gun. The fatal shot to the head that killed him was fired from a different gun. That same 45 that was used to kill Deanna and the other man was the same gun that killed him. So the one thing that was in common in this case was that the 45 caliber was used in all three murders. So the question was, who had the 45 caliber ? And who was the shooter ? It was something law enforcement was trying to find out and had to find out to solve this case. The detectives tried to get Anita to give up any information that she knew about a possible shooter. But she stuck to her story that she and Deanna went to rob the men and she had no idea who had the 45. There was no way she was giving up Chaos or Franciso.

She did know she was going to do some kind of time being that she was involved in the robbery. And she did shoot someone. She was going to let the police do their job. Meanwhile back at the Knight household they were getting ready to go to the funeral. A packed church came to pay their respects to Deanna. Everyone from classmates to people from the neighborhood, to people who hardly knew Deanna that just heard about the story. And also whose lives she touched in some form or fashion also came out. It was a beautiful uplifting service for Deanna, although very sad at moments. The Knight family appreciated the outpouring of love and respect shown to them throughout the city. Desiree was dealing with the hardest thing she ever had to deal with in her life. And she had also just got her heart broken by her first love. It was a lot to take all at once, but she did her best to hold it together. She still couldn't believe that her sister was gone until she actually seen her laying in the casket. Desiree was froze, just standing over the casket staring at her sister until a friend of the family came and helped her to her seat. As much kids as Deanna fought growing up, it was just as much love and respect showed at her funeral.

As much as Desiree and her family was going through it, so was Anita. Who was in police custody and couldn't attend the funeral. She sat in her cell the day of the funeral and cried her eyes out. Not only did Anita lose her best friend and was in the city jail, she was more than likely going to be in prison for a long time. She couldn't say goodbye to her best friend, which hurt more than any prison sentence they could give her. That was the only thing on her mind at the time.

Page 29

But she had to stay strong and stick to her story, it was very important and would play a major role in determining her fate. After grieving the day of the funeral, Anita had to get her mind right because she had a Detective coming to ask more questions about that night. So as she sat in a waiting room accompanied by her lawyer, the Detective then comes in.

"Hello I'm Detective Burns and I got you here with your lawyer to ask some questions about the night your friend Deanna was killed. So let's start from the beginning again. Now before you were questioned by my partner, that's why I'm asking you to start from the beginning. So where do we begin" ? Detective Burns asked.

"Like I said before, me and Deanna went to the house to rob these guys. And in the midst of robbing them, things got out of hand." Anita said.

"Ok well how do you explain the 45 caliber bullet being the fatal shot that killed all three of the deceased" ? The Detective asked.

"I don't know I didn't have a 45, and Deanna didn't either. So maybe it was the guy that got away because one of the guys fled on foot, the guy that was shooting at Deanna in the backyard." Anita replied.

"No see I believe you know who had that 45, and you holding out protecting them. But why Anita ? You give them up and you probably only do maybe five years tops....maybe even less. But if you dont, you going to do a lot more time than what you deserve." The Detective said.

"You can't stick me with this, my gun didn't fire the fatal shot in any of those who were murdered and you know it. Im telling yall, you should look for the guy that fled on foot" Anita replied.

At that moment Anita's lawyer interrupted by asking if there were any more questions, the detective shook his head no while staring at Anita. Anita staring right back. It was a tense moment, but Anita wouldn't break. She stood tall like always and called the Detective's bluff. She would never give up Francisco and Chaos, she knew what was at stake for her personally. She had a plan, and that plan she kept to herself until the time was present to execute it.

Desiree was on her way back to College Park, still grieving the loss of her younger sister. The drive back seemed so long to her, she had some time to think and a short time to cry again. Desiree had thought about taking a leave of absence from school, but later changed her mind because she didnt want to just sit around and continue thinking about it. She knew Deanna would've wanted her to go back to school and follow her dreams. What was she going to do without not only her sister but her best friend ? The only person she has shared so many of her life experiences with, good and bad. She thought about her father, and how he was during the time she was home for the funeral. Was her father going to change for the better ? Was her family going to become closer after Deanna's death ? A lot of things crossed her mind during that hour and fifteen minute drive.

After finally getting back to school and in her dorm room. She seen her roommate Candice for the first time in a while.

"Hey girl, I'm so sorry to hear about your sister. You left so fast I wasn't able to give you my condolence. Im here if you need to talk" Candice said.

"Thanks Candice, and I just need to get some rest right now" Desiree replied.

Desiree had still been working part time at a local eatery, but was growing tired of the hours and the pay. And she also realized that Deanna was no longer around to send her money when she needed it. It was the harsh reality that she faced. Until one day she had a conversation with her roommate Candice that would change her life forever. One day returning to her dorm room after a long day of classes and work, Desiree was exhausted.

"Damn girl you look tired, they working you hard at that spot huh" Candice asked.

"Yeah and I'm sick of that place, I need another job" Desiree replied.

"Well my cousin Simone works at this club called "Melvins" on the other side of town" Candice said sitting on her bed.

"And what do they do at this club" ? Desiree asked.

"Come on girl, you know what they do, dance and strip.....get your money" Candice replied dancing.

"I'm not dancing. In front of some creeps ? No I'll pass." Desiree said

"Them creeps got money girl, my cousin makes good money there and she doesn't dance that much. She's actually the emcee, but she can put you on" Candice said.

"You really think I could dance there ? I never done anything like that before in my life" Desiree said.

"Girl look at you, look at your body. Look at that ass and them titties. Of course you can, as long as you can move to the beats you good" Candice replied.

Desiree thought about it, even though she wasn't too thrilled at the idea. She needed to make more money than she was. So after thinking about it for a day, Desiree decided to get Candice cousin Simone to hook her up. Candice had arranged for Desiree and Simone to meet at Melvins, so Desiree and Candice could check the club out.

"Hey cousin, how are you ? And I see you brought your friend.....damn she is fine as hell too. Nice ass and nice titties, this could definitely work. You're a fresh face, they going to love your ass. Let me know, I will put you on" Simone said looking Desiree up and down. Admiring her beauty.
Page 31

Her body was made for the stage, her beauty was undeniable and she just needed a shot. And she had it at "Melvins". Desiree agreed to take the job, besides she had nothing else going on at the moment. Her first night she was very nervous, as it was to be expected. But she was driven by the potential of how much money she could make each night. Regardless, after some coaching from Candice and Simone, she was ready. Upon arriving at "Melvins," Desiree was instructed to go downstairs to the dressing room. As she entered the dressing room, there were women everywhere talking and getting dressed. About nine women were there at the time when Desiree came in, at that moment one of the women said.

"Hey....you must be the new chick. Welcome.....better get your game tight or you going home light sweetheart."

Desiree said hello and just stared for a second at the women. You could hear the music banging upstairs as the DJ was preparing the crowd for the first set.

After Desiree got dressed in her sexy outfit, she was sitting in one of the chairs when Simone came downstairs.

"Hey girl, I hope you ready. There's a lot of money up there to be made, and you better get it. You new, you have to set the tone for these niggas. Go out there and make them never forget you and make them want more. That's the only way you gonna get paid. And oh yeah, we need a name for you" Simone said.

Simone noticed Desiree was chewing gum, and she told her to remove it. But before she did she asked Desiree a question.

"What flavor gum are you chewing" Simone asked.

"It's Raspberry flavor" Desiree replied.

"That's it, that's kinda slick. Yeah you going to be Raspberry" Simone said sounding confident.

Desiree just stared looking a little confused, but decided she guessed it would work and went with it.

"Now I gotta go back upstairs, you on next so be ready. And don't worry girl, you gonna kill it tonight, I just got a feeling" Simone said going up the steps.

"Thanks Simone for believing in me, I won't disappoint you" Desiree replied.

After Simone went upstairs, Desiree was all alone in the dressing room staring at herself in the mirror. A lot of things went through her mind, her doubts turned to confidence and before you knew it, Simone was on the mic about to introduce for the first time, "Raspberry."

"Ladies and gentlemen live from Melvins for the first time making her debut tonight, the sexy and gorgeous "Raspberry" !!! Simone said.

She was of course nervous at first when she hit the stage, but as she continued on she felt more comfortable. And just like Simone said, the crowd loved her. It was a great start to Raspberry's new career in the exotic dancer field. Simone and Candice was right about Raspberry's ability to control a crowd's attention. Desiree was happy and excited for what was next to come, it was also the night Desiree transformed into Raspberry. The next morning Raspberry woke up and grabbed the bag next to her that was filled with all the money she made the previous night at the club. Much to her surprise, she made about three hundred dollars. Which was a nice take for her very first time on stage. Such a great start prompted the owner Melvin Charles to want to meet Raspberry. So Simone arranged for Raspberry and Melvin to meet in his office. Making their way to Melvin's office one day, the two women entered and Melvin was sitting at his desk. Melvin was a medium build man that had a bald head and goatee. He was in his 40's and always dressed business like. When the women entered Melvin got out of his chair at his desk and extended his hand as he was introduced to Raspberry.

"You did great last night, actually better than anyone I could remember" Melvin said puffing on a cigar.

"Thank you Melvin, I appreciate it. And thank you for giving me an opportunity" Raspberry replied.

"You're a very beautiful woman with a bright future ahead of you, I want to personally welcome you to Melvin's. And I appreciate you being apart of the team." Melvin said.

"I'm happy to be apart of the team" Raspberry replied.

She knew in her mind meeting with the owner after just her first appearance on stage could only be a good thing. She knew she had made an immediate impact, and she was happy and excited about what was to come of her future at Melvins. After meeting with Melvin, she was escorted back to the mid level part of the club where Simone had some more words of encouragement for her.

"Girl you done met Melvin already, he doesn't just ask to meet anybody. Shit half these girls ain't never had a conversation with the nigga. You should be proud, and keep killing it. You stand to make a lot of money here if you stay consistent."

"Thank you Simone for everything you have done to help me, I really appreciate it" Raspberry replied.

Raspberry also had to thank Candice for introducing her to Simone. She had finally found her way so to speak around the area, and word was traveling fast about just how good she was on stage.

Like high school, many admired her beauty and the way she carried herself. Each night she performed she got more and more comfortable on stage, it was like a second home to her. It was where all eyes were on her, and she was noticing herself changing.

Another night at Melvins and another packed house as some of Melvin's dancers who were on early graced the stage. Melvin's office sat almost right above the stage off to the right where he could see out on the club. He also had cameras in different corners of the club. Including near the bar. There was plenty of security throughout the club, Melvin ran a tight ship. The women always felt safe and hardly ever had any problems. A lot of the women witnessed Raspberry's rapid rise and weren't a bit pleased by it. How could a new chick come in and just make more money than a few of the women put together a night. It was almost like high school all over again, as a teenager Desiree dealt with hate and jealousy. And now as a grown woman she was dealing with the same thing at her place of business.

Raspberry felt the hate and got the stares, but she was only focused on getting her money and being successful as she could be. Something would happen to shift her focus to something else other than the women she was working with. And the jealousy towards her. After finishing up her set one night, Raspberry decided to sit at the bar for a little and have a drink. While doing that she noticed a man that looked really familiar coming towards her, it was a man that was frequently at Melvins and he had spent a lot of money on Raspberry.

"Hello beautiful, I'm Malik. Can I buy you a drink " ?

"Sure why not. I'm Raspberry" Raspberry replied.

"Oh I know who you are, I have noticed you since the first night you hit the stage. You seen how much money I spent on you, Im just glad Im finally able to meet you up close and personal. You look like a natural up there, no disrespect" Malik said taking a sip of his drink.

"No disrespect taken, I'm glad you enjoyed it and I appreciate all the money you've spent on me. I'm actually new to this, I have never been a dancer before" Raspberry replied.

"Really ? That's surprising, and speaks to how talented you are. You look great up there honestly."

"Thank you, what are you a talent scout or something"? Raspberry asked looking curious.

Malik just laughed a little and replied. "No not at all, I'm just a customer like everyone else that comes in here. But I also personally admire your beauty. And I was wondering if we could see each other outside of this place sometime? I see you so much more than just a dancer at a strip club, you feel me. I think we can have something special one day." Malik said.

"Oh really ? And what makes you say that, we hardly know each other. Let alone being involved with each other" Raspberry replied.

"I just think you're special, and I have interest in you. Maybe we can go for dinner sometime so we can talk some more and get to know each other better" Malik said as he ordered them both another drink.

"I will have to give that some thought, I'm sure I'll see you around soon. I will let you know, I have to go" Raspberry said as she walked away.

Something told Raspberry that Malik was anything but just a regular customer at Melvins, the way he dressed and the fact he had a gold Rolex watch on his wrist said anything but. It was an unwritten rule in the exotic dancer field to not date men that were considered customers to them at their profession. But Raspberry couldn't deny she had an attraction for Malik, he was indeed a tall dark and handsome man. And he carried himself very well. So there was definitely some interest there from the start, Raspberry was still somewhat skeptical about him period. So she decided to have a conversation about it with Simone.

"Simone can I ask you a question" ? Raspberry said.

"Sure girl, what's on your mind" ? Simone replied.

"Well I met this guy, and he said that he had noticed me from the very first night I was on stage here at the club. He wants to take me out, and he is an attractive man and seems nice. But that rule of not dating the customers continues to stay on my mind" Raspberry said.

"Girl rules were made to be broken at some point and time, if you really dig him and he wants to take you out go for it. You only live once" Simone replied.

"Have you ever dated anyone from working at Melvins" ? Raspberry asked Simone.

"I have dated a few guys, difference with me is I had a few stalkers that were too much and I had to get rid of them. Wasn't as easy to do at first, but Melvin had to flex his muscles and get a few of them to leave me alone. Plus I got my gun license and mama stay packing, other than that it was cool. Look girl, just take a chance and see where it goes, you never know" Simone said.

Raspberry agreed and was willing to do just that, but before she did she wanted to do a little more homework on just who Malik was and his intensions. That would be a little difficult being that not too many people in the area knew Malik. Malik was originally from Miami but his business ventures brought him to the Maryland area not too far away from the main campus at the University of Maryland. Raspberry really didn't know what Malik did for a living, he was pretty private about a lot of his business. The fact that Malik was so interested in Raspberry, gave her an opportunity to find out what he did for a living. So after another great set at Melvins Raspberry did the usual, sat at the bar and basically got free drinks from the various men at the bar. That is until her next set, in between giving a few private lap dances.

While sitting there, Raspberry noticed Malik from a distance sitting at a table near the back of the club. So she got her drink and decided to go to his table.

"Why hello there beautiful, glad you decided to come and join me. Once again a great performance, you keep me coming back to this club for real.

"Oh I do, do I" ? Raspberry said smiling.

"Of course baby, I come to see you" Malik said greeting Raspberry.

They both sat and watched some of Melvin's other dancers hit the stage. As they watched, Raspberry couldn't help but to ask Malik what he did for a living.

"So I noticed the Rolex the last time we talked, and now you drinking champagne. You must have a really good profession" Raspberry said looking curious.

Malik just smiled and replied, "I do a little bit of everything, in due time you will see what I do."

"In due time ? Oh ok if you say so big spender" Raspberry replied.

"If you still around in the near future, you can live a great life being with me. I'm willing to give you that. It all depends on how bad you want it. Let's start with dinner and go from there."

"Ok it's a date, looking forward to it." Raspberry replied.

After talking to Malik again and spending more time with him, Raspberry's concerns changed to optimism. Maybe this could work, maybe Malik might be the man for her. Only time would tell. Meanwhile back in Baltimore, Anita was being charged with shooting one of the men that fateful night. She couldnt be charged with his murder because after an autopsy was performed it was determined that her gun didnt fire the fatal shot. Which Anita already knew. The Baltimore Police were very frustrated that they had no leads on who killed Deanna and the other two men that were found dead in the house.

No other weapons were found besides Deanna's, Anita's, and the man Anita shot. Anita stuck to her story and never wavered. She would take the years for her part in the robbery and shooting one of the men. But there was no way she was giving up Francisco or Chaos, who hadn't been seen or heard from since the murders. The murders hurt Francisco's business somewhat in the Baltimore area, he took most of his workers off the streets for two reasons. He didn't want the police questioning any of his workers on the street, even though many of them had no clue of what really happened. Secondly, he knew the rival crew would seek revenge for some of their crew that were killed by Chaos. The police had no idea that Chaos was even involved, not a lot of people knew him in the Baltimore area because he was only brought out as an enforcer. When he was brought out, more than likely someone had to be killed. Or if he was there for muscle.....meaning for protection. Francisco wanted him with the girls that night because he wanted someone he could trust. And more importantly someone he felt was experienced enough to handle the job and get it done. Some of the few people Francisco still had on the streets were rounded up and questioned anyway, but none of them flinched.

A few of them got charged with possession of a substance but nothing more serious than that. Deanna's parents were not happy about the fact they were no leads in the case as far as the killer or killers were concerned.

Raspberry and Malik continued to spend time together but hadn't got intimate yet, until one night they were at a party in a hotel. Leaving in the elevator things got hot after the kissing inside the party which resulted in Malik and Raspberry having sex in the elevator. It was a fantasy of her's and this was the night to chase that fantasy with a man she was very much into. It was intense and a very passionate episode between the two. Wasn't much foreplay, they were beyond ready to feel each other as he thrust inside her. She let off a slight moan and grunt as her entered her vagina. It began fast and rough, continued in rhythmic fashion as they both climaxed and were in the corner of the elevator. Wondering how they could have such a passionate episode so quickly? Malik had stopped the elevator so they could, and they both were glad he did afterwards. Their clothes a mess but they didn't care as they stepped out the elevator both laughing as some people who were about to get on looked on.

It was a great and exciting night, and Raspberry was somewhat happy for the first time in a while. Since her sister's death, she had been very closed up and to herself outside of Melvin's. She was of course still grieving. Back at her dorm room, Raspberry had arrived late night after being out with Malik. Getting up from her sleep as Raspberry walked in.

"Damn girl, it looks like you had a great night" Candice said.

"It was nice, we had fun. We have a lot of fun together, things are going great right now" Raspberry replied.

After making the money at Melvins she made, Raspberry had saved some money to buy a car. Upon mentioning it to Malik, Malik decided he would buy her a car. She was overjoyed with the fact that even though she had saved her own money, Malik stepped up and wanted to buy her a car. And that's exactly what he did, one day he took her out for breakfast and said he had a surprise for her. It was a brand new black Honda Civic and Raspberry loved it. Back at Melvins later on that night, Raspberry was dressed in another one of her sexy outfits as she danced across stage. Money littered the floor beneath her feet as always. After the set, Raspberry was getting dressed in the dressing room downstairs and thinking maybe she was growing out of her dorm. She needed more space since her life had changed somewhat.....since she's been with Malik.

So with some of the money she saved, she decided to get her own apartment off campus, she was even happier to do that. Something she could call her own. Her roommate Candice was sad to see her go since they developed such a unique bond, but she knew herself that Raspberry's life was changing. When she moved it was not only just that change, but other things were changing too. Her motivation towards school was there, but not as much. She found herself having to will her own self to go half the time. With the earning of money, it made her drive to make it off the charts. She loved being able to buy what she wanted, something she wasn't used to growing up on Baltimore's West Side. It became her desire, and she wasn't stopping anytime soon. Plus she was dealing with a man that had a little money, and he didn't mind spending it on her.

Raspberry noticed a change at the club amongst the other women, their jealousy and envy were not so hidden anymore. Each time she went in a room the other women were in, she felt uncomfortable. Like she was being watched and talked about. She knew it and she felt it. So from that point on she pretty much kept to herself even more and made her money. Her apartment was finally in order after moving off campus and she loved the space she now had. After not knowing too much about what Malik did for a living, Malik decided that it was time to be honest with Raspberry because their relationship had gotten more serious than expected. So they met for lunch so Malik could tell her.

"Things have gotten serious, I don't know if any of us expected this at first. But I trust you, and I think we may have something here. So I want to be honest with you and tell you what I do, but I need your word that whatever I say to you is between us and us only. No matter what." Malik said.

"Of course Malik, not too many people even know we're together" Raspberry replied.

"I run an Escort Service, and I sell cocaine wholesale. I just wanted you to know in case some shit pops off, but like I said you must keep this to yourself. I could give you the life you want, and you don't even have to be involved in this shit at all. Just be my Queen and do your thing. And let you King lead while you follow. You dont have to do much, and eventually I want you to quit Melvins" Malik said.

Raspberry just sat there and stared off into space a little and thought about what she was just told for a few minutes before she responded.

"I figured you were hustling or doing something. The Escort Service threw me off a bit, but if that's what you do that's what you do. I want no parts of the drug game, my mother is a recovering addict and I personally hate drugs. As long as you keep that away from me, we are good. I'm a little intrigued by the Escort Service though. And I don't plan on leaving Melvins anytime soon" Raspberry replied.

"Why wouldnt you ? Im going to be making enough money for the both of us. I dont want you working at no club forever. Not my girl. I was going to ask you just how comfortable you were with dancing being with me and all. I could make us both a lot of money, if you just quit Melvins and help me with this Escort Service" Malik said eating his lunch.

"That depends on what type of jobs I will have, and you know I'm not quitting Melvins. So if you can give me a job that fits around my schedule at Melvins and work around what I got going on. I'm down." Raspberry replied.

Malik agreed that he could and Raspberry had created another avenue for her to make money on her own terms, this further validated her as a person of power. She worked out deals for herself on her own, and she was about to learn more about what direction her life would take in the future. She realized more than ever how powerful her beauty was.

Life was going great, Raspberry was even able to send money home to her mother to help out from time to time. Not too long after that, she learned some news she was hoping not to hear. After twenty four years of marriage, her father wanted a divorce from her mother Denise. Raspberry now twenty two years old wasn't totally surprised, she knew her parents had issues. But thought they could work things out considering they got through her mother's drug addiction and their own daughter's death. Maybe her father had enough. Although he himself had his own personal demons like alcoholism, mental abuse, and physical abuse to name a few. In retrospect some of those things drove Deanna to the streets, which eventually led to her death. Her death was a huge blow to an already broken family, the only positive in the family was Desiree being in college and hopefully in a few years getting her degree. With everything that was going on with Desiree's family of late, it drove her harder to succeed. Desiree was still grieving her sister's death.

One day she was on the phone with her mother. And what was supposed to be a good positive conversation, was anything but. "Hey mom, how's everything going ? I sent you a hundred and fifty dollars" Desiree said to her mother.

"Hey baby, not so good. Now I don't want you to worry, I want you to stay focused on your school work. Your father has asked for a divorce" Denise replied.

"Wow, just like that ? I mean I knew yall were having problems, after all yall been through he's just going to give up like that"? Desiree said sounding disappointed.

"And that's not the only problem. He's planning on selling the house. I can't afford this house and the up keep Desiree, so I'm going to have to move" Denise replied.

"I'm going to come home mom" and before Desiree could say another word, her mother interrupted. Desiree said.

"No you're not, I'm going to stay with your Aunt Angela. We have already talked about it" Denise said.

"I just can't believe this, all this is happening so fast. I thought after Deanna's death maybe the family would be closer" Desiree said angrily as her voiced cracked and her emotions showed.

"I know Desiree, but life sometimes deals you a bad hand. If anybody knows that, I do. I been through a lot in my life and I know I'm not no angel but I tried my best to make it work with your father. I also found out that he was cheating, so I have no effort to give to this marriage any longer. It's for the best Desiree" Denise replied.

"Well I'm still sending that money, and will seen more when I can. Especially now that you will be living with Aunt Angela. Call me if you need anything, I will be home in a week to get my things from the house. Tell Aunt Angela thank you from me for letting you stay with her. As soon as I can mom, I'm going to get you your own apartment" Desiree replied.

Desiree's parents splitting up bothered her. But what bothered her more was finding out now that her mother had no place to go, and her mother having to move in with her Aunt Angela just outside of Baltimore. Raspberry felt even more driven after finding that out. Her focus on getting money got even more intense. And her focus on school had lessened even more. Raspberry was on her way to Melvin's, when she got there she got there a little earlier than usual. Upon getting there, she saw Simone talking to Malik. Something she thought was strange since she didn't know that Simone knew Malik. They didn't see her and she didn't say anything, she just walked downstairs to the dressing rooms. That night she thought about it, but didn't say anything to either Malik nor to Simone. Maybe they did know each other, I mean Simone had been at Melvins for a while now. It was something she kept in her memory bank. It was another good night for Raspberry as she danced her sexy body across stage to another packed house, Malik looking on from a distance towards the back of the bar.

Later on that night Malik and Raspberry sat in a Diner and had something to eat as they talked in between eating.

"I just thought about something baby, we should go to Atlantic City after your last class tomorrow before Spring Break" Malik said taking a sip of his drink.

"That would be nice, but I don't know. There's a lot of money to be made at Melvins. And with my mother having to move out of our home back in Baltimore. I have to get this money right now" Raspberry replied.

"Come on baby you're going to always get money at Melvins, let's go have some fun spend some money and time together. Some of my money, and enjoy ourselves" Malik said.

It was very tempting, Raspberry had never been to Atlantic City. And Malik was treating so why not. So she decided to go, they stayed for two nights but it seemed like they were there longer. They did a lot of things in that short time, including having passionate sex in their high rise hotel suite. Even having sex on their high rise suite balcony. They had one of the finest suites they could offer. Malik took her shopping, they popped a few tags and ate at one of the finest restaurants in the city. After a great time, they arrived back in College Park and Raspberry went back to her apartment. Upon entering her apartment, it had been ramshacked. Furniture was turned over, drawers opened. And clothes were thrown everywhere, as if whoever that did it was looking for something.

Money and jewelry were stolen, and she was extremely upset. Who could've done this to her ? She lived in a fairly decent neighborhood and not too many people knew her after just recently moving there. As she picked up the things that were thrown all over the floor while wiping tears from her face. She also had a feeling of being enraged, she had grew tired of people taking advantage of her and taking her kindness for weakness. She needed to assert herself more than what she was, and she was confident that one way or the other she would find out who robbed her apartment that day.

Raspberry was contemplating whether she was going to tell Malik or not, about her apartment getting robbed. She knew if she told him he would be even more angrier than she was. So for the moment she kept it to herself but was feeling the loss because her money and jewelry were stolen. She really didn't want to ask Malik for any money, so she just decided to work some extra hours at Melvins in between her classes. School was getting even more challenging for Raspberry than ever. Meanwhile Malik was continuing to spoil Raspberry and trusting her even more. He had gotten so comfortable and spent so much time with Raspberry that he began taking her with him on money runs when they were together. She would wait in the car while he went in each business and collected. But more importantly she would pay close attention to each stop. A lot of the people Malik did business with also knew Raspberry from just being around him. Raspberry was still curious to know who robbed her apartment, but still hadn't said anything to Malik. But something told her that she would find out who robbed her apartment somehow some way.

Later that night she was about to go on stage at Melvins when she saw Simone off to the side talking to another woman. Raspberry noticed the watch and bracelet on Simone's wrist. It looked very similar to the watch and bracelet that was stolen from her apartment. She disregarded it and proceeded to go on stage for her set. Simone for one of the few times watched Raspberry as she was on stage. After coming off stage, Raspberry ran into Simone.

"Nice set as usual" Simone said with a smirk on her face.

"Nice watch and bracelet Simone, I had a set just like it. But they were stolen from my apartment" Raspberry replied as she walked past her on her way to the dressing room.

Simone had a puzzled look on her face after Raspberry said it. But never responded to Raspberry. Later that night Malik wanted to speak to Raspberry about something and it couldn't wait.

"I been thinking baby, I really don't want you to be dancing forever. Why don't you come with me and help me with my Escort Service. It's more money and less work. I really don't want you doing this anymore." Malik said.

"I don't know about the escort thing, I love what I do. I love being on stage. I am interested in the escort thing, but I want to ease into that instead of just diving in. But I definitely dont want to stop dancing" Raspberry replied.

It was something her and Malik disagreed on and Malik knew it. But that didn't stop him from pushing the issue and being persistent about not wanting her to dance anymore. He didn't want his woman to keep dancing. Raspberry over the current days noticed that she wasn't on as much as she was used to. So she decided to talk to Melvin about what was going on with her time slots.

"Look I dont bullshit nobody so I'm not going to bullshit you. Your boyfriend Malik came in here and asked me if I could cut some of your time slots" Melvin said.

"What ? I can't believe he did that" Raspberry replied surprised.

"Well believe it, cause he did. I'm going to let you handle it, and I'm assuming you don't agree with him" Melvin said taking a puff of his cigar.

"No I dont, I definitely dont. I will handle it, don't worry about it. Won't happen again, thanks for telling me Melvin" Raspberry replied.

Raspberry was furious Malik had went to Melvin. It was her job, a job that she had before she had even met Malik. Before she could call Malik and give him a piece of her mind, she looked outside and saw Simone talking on her phone. As she leaned out the door to get Simone's attention she heard apart of her conversation.

"No Malik I don't think she knows, we good. When are you picking me up tonight" ? Simone asked as she held her phone.

Raspberry quickly put her head back inside and closed the door. She now had confirmation who had robbed her apartment, and who was setting her up. But why would Simone and Malik be setting her up ?

It was something Raspberry would undoubtedly try her best to find out. Things had changed as far as Raspberry's future. It no longer included Malik, she had other plans for him. She had seen Simone being bold enough to wear her watch and bracelet in front of her. The picture was becoming more and more clearer as to what was going on. Instead of flipping out and breeding drama, Raspberry had another way. She had thought long and hard about this situation. She didn't want either Simone or Malik to know that she knew what they were doing. As hard as it was not to flip out, Raspberry wanted more than just revenge. She continued seeing Malik and didn't even mention that she knew about him going to Melvin.....at least not yet. Raspberry was very much inside Malik's circle, she found out he had other businesses such as laundromats and car washes. He even let her collect at a few of them. But the part of the business Raspberry wanted was the Escort Service. She hinted to Malik that she wanted in on the business, but the condition was that she could still dance at Melvins.

Malik finally agreed, and from that point on Raspberry decided to take a leave of absence from school. Much to the disappointment of her mother. After Raspberry told her, she explained to her mother she had a plan and not to worry she would return to school at a later time. After finding out what Simone and Malik did, Raspberry knew she had to be more observant of her enemies. Her plan was taking shape. One day Raspberry decided to go to the library and went to a computer to look up a human's neck. Closely looking at the screen and carefully reading. Later that night she was to meet with Malik to do her first job as an escort. Malik only dealt with high end customers in the escort business.

Wouldn't be long before Raspberry was hustling between the Escort Service and dancing at Melvins. The money was great and she was living the life she enjoyed. And she was finally able to get her mother an apartment like she had promised her. Raspberry had built her base in the escort world like she did in the exotic dancer world. And she no longer needed Malik as much as she once did. She watched and learned the business, the next plan of action was to put it into action. So Raspberry had talked to Malik about getting together with him at his home but she didn't want anyone to know, because to the outside world they had broken up and was just business partners now. Malik agreed to keep their meeting between themselves as the night arrived. After Raspberry's apartment was robbed she kept her distance from Malik on a personal level, they were no longer involved intimately. She told him things were moving too fast and she needed time, but she did want to continue doing business with him. After letting him know she wanted to see him, she insinuated that she was missing him and wanted to get together. That was music to Malik's ears. He was beyond excited to see Raspberry because he never wanted them to stop seeing each other on an intimate level in the first place.

Raspberry had come to Malik's house in a beautiful and sexy dress that literally had nothing on underneath it. After hanging out together for a little while, laughing, drinking, and ultimately having sex. Malik and Raspberry lay together on a blanket in front of his fireplace just enjoying each others company.

"Baby why don't you lay back in the chair and let me give you a massage" Raspberry said hugging Malik and giving him a kiss.

"You know what ? That shit sounds so good right about now. You come your fine ass over here and give me that massage" Malik replied.

So as Malik lay relaxed with his eyes closed, behind him Raspberry slowly and quietly put on some gloves and pulled out a straight razor.

"Keep your eyes closed baby, I have a surprise for you. But you have to keep your eyes closed" Raspberry said kissing Malik softly on his cheek.

At that moment, Raspberry leaned Malik's head back a little further and opened the straight razor. With her right hand she placed the blade on his neck and came across with enough force to kill any man. Blood quickly shot out of Malik's neck as he grabbed his throat moaning and gurgling in his own blood in pain and dropped to the floor. Raspberry just looked as she backed away and watched him bleed out. After Malik's last breath, Raspberry began cleaning any blood on her and washed the blood off the razor.

She quickly got her things, but before she left she staged it as if it was a robbery. She went in Malik's wallet and took about two thousand dollars out of it and put it in her purse. She went near his safe and made it look as if someone was trying to get in it. Pushed furniture around and opened drawers. Then she was off into the night. She had done something she could have never imagined doing, and for some reason she felt no remorse for it.

The news of Malik's death had spread fast throughout the area, and the way he died was even more puzzling. Someone had actually had the heart to slit the man's throat in his own home. The police initially thought it was a robbery, and it may still had been a robbery. But there was no forced entry. It had to be someone who knew him, and that could've been a number of people being that Malik had his hands in a lot of businesses. A lot of people could've wanted him dead, he had money and was definitely a target for anyone who was jealous and envious of him. The police questioned a few people within his circle, including Raspberry.

"Hello I'm Detective Roberts, and your name is" ? Detective Roberts asked.

"My name is Desiree" Raspberry replied.

"Ok you know why you're here right" Detective Roberts asked.

"Yes, Malik was killed and yall trying to find out who did it" Raspberry replied.

"Where were you on the night in question" ? Detective Roberts asked.

"I was home at my apartment" Raspberry said crossing her legs.

"When was the last time you seen Malik? Word is you two were involved in some sort of fashion" Detective Roberts said.

"About a week and a half ago, we weren't together anymore. We broke up about two weeks ago." Raspberry said.

"And what happened the last time you two talked, where were you two at when the two of you last seen each other" ? Detective Roberts asked.

"We were at my apartment, he wanted to talk and make sure there were no hard feelings about the break up" Raspberry replied.

"And was there" ? Detective Roberts asked

"No not at all, we had a unique relationship. We were lovers as well as friends. There were never no problems if we seen other people" Raspberry replied.

"Oh so like an open relationship huh" Detective Roberts asked.

"No.... more like when we're together, we're together. When we're not together, we're not together" Raspberry replied.

After answering a few more questions, Raspberry was free to go home. She didn't crack at all answering questions for Detective Roberts. In her mind she was thinking her future plans would raise even more eyebrows. And no one would know it was her.....no one would even suspect it was her.
Page 44

While Raspberry was new to the Escort Service world. She met and befriended a beautiful Latina name Isabella. They had only worked together for a short time through Malik's Escort Service. And with Malik dead now, Raspberry was looking to capitalize on what he left behind. Isabella and her had a unique friendship and Raspberry told Isbella that they could both continue the Escort Service on their own.

"You are serious aren't you" ? Isabella asked as she stared at Raspberry.

"I mean what else do you have right now" ? Raspberry asked Isabella.

"Yes you do have a point, but where do we start" ? Isabella asked.

"I can get you in at Melvins, that's a start. That will get you a following, you're beautiful and sexy. It shouldn't take long for you to be in high demand. But you must report to me, and we must keep this between us" Raspberry replied.

Isabella agreed and Raspberry planned to say something to Melvin about having Isabella join the team. Meanwhile the police was still investigating Malik's murder, with no leads and no murder weapon. All they knew was Malik's throat was slit from ear to ear. From the looks of Malik's house which was covered in blood throughout the living room where his body laid, and money missing from his wallet. Someone had clearly tried to get in the safe, and furniture was moved around. The police initially thought it was a robbery, maybe at the hands of a rival drug dealer. But once again there was no forced entry. So to police, it was someone Malik knew who may have murdered him.

Could it had been an associate of Malik's, and was it about money ? Was that why money was stolen and someone tried to get in the safe ? A lot of questions, but not enough answers as police questioned some more of the women who had worked for Malik. After questioning most of the women, there still was really no leads. Raspberry decided to take a drive, a drive to the Washington, D.C. Virginia border. More specifically the Potomac River bridge. It was late at night as she pulled alongside the median on interstate 95 standing overlooking the water. When she pulled out the straight razor she had bought a few weeks prior to Malik's murder. Along with the gloves she had on that night, and threw them both in the river. She stood there for a few more minutes and watched it hit the water before she got back in her car and proceeded to head back to College Park. The next day Raspberry had asked to speak to Melvin. So Melvin agreed and after hearing from Raspberry about a new prospect she had in mind, he was eager to talk to her.

"So who's this chick you talking about" ? Melvin asked.

"Her name is Isabella, Spanish chick Puerto Rican. Very beautiful and sexy. And more importantly will bring some more money in here" Raspberry replied.

Melvin just stared at Raspberry for a minute before responding. "And what do you want out of this deal, because I know you want something" Melvin replied.

Chapter Three
"Coming Into Her Own"

Melvin agreed and the rest is history. Isabella and Raspberry developed a pretty good friendship, as Raspberry got Isabella on at Melvins. Simone was not too happy about the fact Raspberry had put someone on without her knowing. And her going over her head straight to Melvin. Simone was also getting somewhat jealous of Raspberry's rapid rise, even though she had put Raspberry on. She didnt believe she would be so good so fast. One night Raspberry was getting dressed when Simone came in the dressing room.

"So you went over my head to put a Puerto Rican bitch on I see. See you forgetting who put you on Miss Raspberry. You bad....yeah you're beautiful. But I can pull the plug on your ass if I want to." Simone said getting in Raspberry's face.

"How you going to do that ? Melvin is not going to get rid of me, I've brought a lot of money to this place. Listen I appreciate all that you have done for me, but I don't owe you anything" Raspberry replied.

"Just don't ever do no shit like that again, consider that your warning" Simone said walking away from Raspberry. Raspberry just stared as she walked away and shook her head.

Despite the initial issue with Simone, Raspberry was able to get Isabella into Melvins and she worked the nights Raspberry didn't work. While Raspberry met with some of the women she made contacts with while working for the short time she did for Malik at his Escort Service. She also bought a gun and began going to the range. She figured she needed to, being in both the businesses she was in. It was only smart to do so. She used some of the money she had took from Malik's house. She took about two thousand dollars from Malik's house, with that money she would build her own small Escort Service, that was the plan. She still very much wanted to remain at Melvins, that was her front job. She needed that because people knew her for that in the area, she didn't like drawing attention to herself unless it was on stage. Otherwise her life was kept quiet and she didn't like being around a lot of people unless it was about business.

Raspberry would go to the range three times a week, in the little bit of free time she had. And she had free time in between her two hustles because she was a single woman. Men were definitely hitting on her, but for the most part she just thank them for the compliments and kept moving. She was totally focused on getting money and progressing in both fields. After the two men she was with, Ricky and Malik were no good for her. She had grew tired of the girlfriend thing, plus after knowing Malik had something to do with her apartment getting robbed she could no longer trust men like she once did. Although she was very much open to dating, it just had to be someone who could capture her attention much different than she had ever felt before. And also someone more trustworthy. She believed when that time would come she would know it.

Page 46

Isabella continued to do her part at Melvins while Raspberry got her Escort Service off the ground. She had three women from her days working for Malik that were ready to join her team along with Isabella. Raspberry had the ladies networking from in and around the Baltimore and Washington D.C. area. Where their customers ranged anywhere from doctors to lawyers to congressmen. They did private parties at local hotels in and around the area. Business was booming, Raspberry was cashing in more ways than one. And making the best out of her plan. Before you knew it, some people that were skeptical about doing business with her who were associates of Malik, now were seeking her out to do business.

She still wanted to maintain a low profile even though the name Raspberry was heavy in the area. One night after hitting the stage at Melvins, Raspberry spotted a man that got her attention that was sitting at the bar, he was with another dude talking when Raspberry sat right next to the both of them.

"Hello gentlemen, how are you two brothers doing tonight" Raspberry asked.

The one that Raspberry was eyeing responded back. "We good beautiful, may I buy you a drink. And oh yeah they call me Stone, and your name" ?

"My name is Raspberry." Raspberry replied.

"Oh yeah, you looked great up there. How could I forget that bad ass body and beautiful face. So let's get up outta here and go somewhere we can have some one on one time" Stone said getting closer to Raspberry. As Raspberry just smiled.

"It seems to me you want my other type of business, see I run an Escort Service. Maybe you can give me a call sometime and I can introduce you to one of my girls, because I'm not an escort. So whenever you're ready you can use this card" Raspberry replied handing the man her card.

"Wow I thought we had some type of connection the way we were staring at each other" Stone said sounding confused.

"Baby you're handsome, I wouldn't have approached you like this if you wasnt" Raspberry replied as she looked at him with her bedroom eyes. I

If that wasn't enough to convince Stone, I don't know what would. Stone continued having drinks with the man that was with him. Raspberry left the bar and went down to the dressing room until her next set.

Stone was confused and somewhat disappointed that he couldn't take Raspberry home that night. She knew exactly what she was doing, she used her beauty and sex appeal to lure men and she knew it would work everytime. Not only for herself but also for her business...because thats just what it was. Just business. But what she also did was dangerous, because she was advertising her business at Melvins. Something Melvin told her never to do in which she agreed. It was part of their agreement. If Melvin would have overheard her conversation with Stone, it wouldnt have been good for her.

A few nights later, Simone was off to the side of the stage watching Isabella dance, as she took sips of her drink. She was still a little upset and grieving over her friend Malik's death. She was also still angry at Raspberry for going over her head and putting Isabella on. Isabella stayed clear and out of the way of Simone after Raspberry told her that Simone wasn't too happy she was at Melvins. She worked strictly through Raspberry and Melvin. After talking with a few of the women Simone decided to call it a night.

"I see yall tomorrow night, make sure yall asses are here on time or I might get my sexy ass up there on stage for yall" Simone said laughing as she walked out the door and proceeded to the parking lot to get her car.

She got in her car and started to drive down the street en route to her apartment. After driving a few minutes she noticed something was wrong with her tire, so she decided to pull over to the side of the road along a wooded area. A few miles away from Melvins.

After pulling over she got out of her car and proceeded to check her tire. Which was on the passenger side of the car. As she was checking her tire she noticed she had a slow leak, she could hear it seaping out of the tire. So as she is looking at her tire, a car pulls over alongside the road right in front of her. She couldn't see who the person was walking towards her because of the lights and the reflection. It was really dark outside.

As the person approached her closer, she looked up and saw a gun barrel and let off a scream. But it was too late. Boom !!...then another two shots. Boom boom !! The person shot Simone at point blank range in the face. After she immediately dropped to the ground, the person shot her two more times at close range in the chest and stomach. With the car blocking the view of what was going on, and very little cars on the road at the time on a late night. There were no witnesses in plain sight. The person got back in their car and drove off. Simone lay there dead on the side of the road, she was found about an hour later. Car was still running. News spread fast as shockwaves hit the area, especially at Melvins. And Raspberry's roommate Candice was devastated. Simone was her first cousin, and like a sister to her. Raspberry stayed away from Melvins. But she did call Candice and gave her, her condolences. She stayed away from Melvins to avoid the media circus that was going on there, and she told Melvin she was sick. Not knowing if there was a serial killer targeting dancers from Melvins. He agreed it was best for now, as he himself was upset about Simone's murder because they had grew close over the years she had worked for him. He closed down a few days in the wake of Simone's murder.

A lot of the women at Melvins was scared to death, because they thought there could be a serial killer targeting dancers. The women had no idea, and were paranoid. Melvin tried his best to ease their fears but they were still there. Simone used to dance herself for Melvin, and had been there for the last five years. She had brought Raspberry into the game, and gave her the name Raspberry. The police were searching the area for evidence, the murder took place a few miles away from Melvins in a wooded area. Simone was found on the side of the road with her car still running. She had a gun shot wound to the face which was fatal.

There were a lot of rumors and theories about what happened to Simone, either way the outspoken emcee of Melvin's Bar and Lounge was gone. Four days later Simone's funeral was held in her native Washington, D.C. A packed church said their farewells to the once little girl who grew up in Southeast D.C. Among the people there were all the women from Melvins including Raspberry. And of course Melvin himself. The women all dressed very nice, most of the women took Simone's death hard. She may have been a hard ass at times, but she made sure the women was on point and ready. Raspberry dressed in a beautiful black dress with black heels and shades. Her face behind the shades was a face of stone, no emotion as she sat quietly through the service. Melvin took Simone's death pretty hard, he had some good years while she was there. It was hard to imagine Simone not being apart of Melvin's anymore. Candice, Raspberry's former roommate was uncounselable. Simone and Candice weren't only just cousins they were like sisters. Simone's death made Candice take a leave of absence from school. After getting back to College Park a few days went by after the funeral and Melvin needed a new emcee for the club. Someone who was a leader with a strong personality, and who better fit that description than Raspberry. Who had more than came out of her shell since being at Melvins.

So Melvin decided to talk to Raspberry about taking the position as his head dancer and emcee. Melvin figured he would ask Raspberry because she had such a great following and she was a leader. But Melvin still had a lot on his mind after returning to College Park, but he had to get himself together because his business had to go on. The next day it was back to business as local authorities continued to investigate Simone's murder. Initially there were no leads, the only thing police knew was she was shot with a 9mm three times. Her car was almost out of gas when she was found. After being left running until authorities got there and were able to search for evidence. Her family was totally shocked after Simone had fought so hard to escape the violence of her neighborhood in D.C.s Southeast, to become successful in her own right. She had been in trouble early on in life and was sent to live with her aunt when she was fifteen just outside of College Park, Md. After finishing up school in College Park she was working at a retail store when she met Melvin at a party, the rest was history.

Even though her and Melvin never were romantically involved, Melvin grew to counting on her with not only the club but in his personal life also.

They were true friends, and Melvin was devastated over her death. In the meantime Raspberry's Escort Service was doing well, and she was about to get a promotion at Melvins. A few days later Melvin called Raspberry to his office. Raspberry knew what was coming her way.....it was apart of the plan.

"Hello Raspberry, I'm sure you know why you're here. I need someone to be my head dancer, my emcee. You brought me Isabella, and you been loyal. So I will let you decide on what you want to do, the offer is on the table. I know you got that Escort thing going on, but I can pay you more money than you can make doing that. So the decision is yours" Melvin said.

Page 49

Raspberry didnt waste any time in deciding, it was what she wanted. Plus it being more money, it was a no brainer for her.

"Of course I will do it, and I'm honored that you asked me to be the head dancer and emcee" Raspberry said as she smiled at Melvin.

"I'm glad you're happy about it and glad you accepted my offer, can I ask you a question though"? Melvin said sounding curious.

"Yeah why not, what is it" ? Raspberry replied.

"Do you know who would do such a thing to Simone ? I mean shit I know she had her ways. But to murder her like that. She didn't deserve that.....she just didn't deserve that" Melvin said shaking his head.

"I know you and Simone were close, and I feel bad about what happened to her also. But no I'm sorry I have no clue who would do that to her" Raspberry replied. Melvin still visibly upset about her murder sat back down at his desk and stared off into the distance.

"I'm going to get out of here, call me if you need me. And thanks again for the promotion" Raspberry said walking out of Melvin's office.

Raspberry had orchestrated Simone's murder and did it flawlessly. By first putting a few small holes in her tire. She knew Simone's car so she knew which one to get. She also knew what side, the passenger side so she would be on the other side of the car where no one could see her. Raspberry had drove that road in between Melvins and her apartment plenty of times to know the route down to a science. That's why she calculated that once she hit the wooded area she would have to pull over. Raspberry was not too far behind her. Once Simone pulled over, she pulled in front of her car with her lights on so Simone couldn't see who was coming. That is until it was too late.

Once Raspberry approached her, she pointed her 9mm directly at Simone's face and fired. Killing her instantly. To make sure she was dead, Raspberry walked over to her and fired two more shots. One in the chest and one in the stomach at close range. She left her lifeless body lay in the wooded area alongside the road, with her car still running. She felt no remorse because she seen Simone as an enemy, she knew Simone and Malik had set her up. Simone had boldly wore her watch and jewelry in plain view so she could see after robbing her apartment. Her heart had turned cold, throughout the trials and tribulations in her life people had taken her kindness for weakness. And after killing two people who had crossed her, as sick as it sounded. She felt empowered. She felt like taking the ultimate thing from them, which was life. Was the ultimate satisfaction for crossing her. The mind of a monster in a female body, Raspberry was just that. She thought out her plans and executed them the way she liked, and she was always two steps ahead of the enemy.

Page 50

Raspberry decided to go on a road trip back home to Baltimore, she was going back home to visit Anita before she was to be sent to another prison. Anita had requested to see her, so Raspberry came from College Park. Upon entering the prison, Raspberry was in awe as she was nervous and scared straight being in a prison for the first time. She was taken to a waiting room where Anita would meet her behind a glass. Sitting there waiting for Anita, Raspberry had thoughts of her sister that she missed so much. It had been almost two years since her murder. Suddenly Anita walks in and her and Raspberry lock eyes then smile at each other.

"Hey Desiree, glad to see you" Anita said as she sat down across from Raspberry.

"Hey Anita, you look well. Hope you taking care of yourself in here" Raspberry replied.

"I'm maintaining, doing the best I can. I called you down here so I could talk to you about the night

Deanna was killed and who really was involved. I don't want you to take this to the Police, I just wanted you to know for you and your family. You do what you feel is best with the information I give you. Me and Deanna were sent to rob this East Side Baltimore crew, we were sent there by Francisco. Francisco runs everything, he was the boss. But the man that was with us that night, and the man that fired the fatal shot that killed Deanna goes by the name of Chaos. He is Francisco's right hand man and enforcer. He also threatened my life if I told anyone this. He said he could touch me inside or outside these walls. I believe he could too, but I just didn't feel right without telling you this. Its already been over two years now. You know how close me and Deanna was." Anita said.

"And you have no idea where these guys may be" ? Raspberry asked.

"No not really, the last time I saw or heard from Chaos was when he dropped me off the night Deanna was killed" Anita replied very quietly.

"I need to find these men" Raspberry said as she stared off into space for a moment.

"If you find Chaos, you will find Francisco. And vice versa, they're pretty much always together. Only thing is, I don't know where to tell you to start to look for them. They could be anywhere" Anita said.

"It's cool, I have my ways. And don't worry, the Police will not know this. Your secret is safe with me. There will be some money put in your account here, thanks again for what you just gave me. And take care of yourself, if you need anything contact my mother. She will get in touch with me" Raspberry said getting up from her seat about to leave.

"I'm not doing this for money Desiree, I'm doing this because I loved Deanna like a sister" Anita said.

"Yes I know that. But look.... everybody needs money. Even you. So that's my personal thank you from me. Take care" Raspberry replied before leaving the prison.

After leaving the prison and on the ride back to College Park, Raspberry felt relieved somewhat that she had found out what really happened that night to her sister. And who was responsible for her death. She was thankful that Anita gave her the information she did and let someone know the truth about that night. Now Raspberry's mission was to somehow find Francisco and Chaos. It wouldn't be easy, but Raspberry was up to the challenge. She owed her sister that, no matter how much Deanna was in the streets she didn't deserve to die the way she did. So Raspberry was going to do everything in her power to try and locate Francisco and Chaos. Once she located them, she would handle the rest. But where would she start ? Not knowing if Francisco and Chaos were anywhere in the area. Which she highly doubted, since they were on the run for the murders of her sister and two other men. She figured the only person that knew all the hustlers and players in the area was Melvin. And she didn't even know if he knew them or not, but it was worth a try. She didn't have anything else to go on as of yet and she had nothing to lose.

Raspberry was looking forward to her first night as emcee and head dancer, she was excited about the opportunity. She had a lot of things going on with the Escort Service business. And now locating Francisco and Chaos was another task on her agenda. But of course she had some help, Isabella had became a good and trusted friend of Raspberry's. And in the process became a asset to Melvins, which in part helped to get Raspberry promoted. Adding another beautiful and sexy woman to his stable only helped Melvin. And he appreciated Raspberry for that. It was business as usual at Melvins, and he was very pleased at the increased business he was getting since Raspberry had took over for Simone. He had weekly meetings with his head of dancers, and for the last five years that person was Simone. This would be his first meeting with Raspberry as his emcee and head dancer.

"I'm very impressed with the increase in business, and you bringing Isabella on board, she's doing well" Melvin said taking a puff of his cigar.

"Thanks for the opportunity, and I told you she would be good for this place. But now I need a favor from you, I need to locate some people you may know. Or know of. A guy by the name of Francisco. He moved weight and was heavy in the streets in Baltimore when I was younger." Raspberry said.

Melvin just looked at Raspberry for a few minutes and responded, "No that name doesn't sound familiar to me at all. Of course I didn't fuck around in Baltimore too much. D.C. yeah, but not Baltimore too much."

"Ok well if you hear anything about him, or where he might be. Please let me know." Raspberry said.

"Can I ask why you want to locate a drug dealer"? Melvin said looking confused.

"He's an old friend of mines, sort of a friend of the family's" Raspberry replied. Page 52

After Raspberry left Melvin's office, Melvin began thinking and was really curious why Raspberry wanted to know the whereabouts of Francisco. After thinking about it for a brief moment, Melvin just brushed it off and excused it as maybe being the truth. Raspberry of course was not going to tell Melvin the real truth about why she wanted to locate Francisco. But she needed somehow to find someone who did know where he might be. Meanwhile Raspberry was enjoying the fruits of her labor, her Escort Service was doing very well and she was getting paid well at Melvins. She sent her mother Denise money home every week, ensuring that she was well taken care of. Her mother was still not happy about her dropping out of college, that was all her mother truly wanted was her daughter to graduate from college and live out her dreams. After all she had been through, that was the one bright spot in her life. But Raspberry had came too far and had done so well financially that there was no changing her mind at the moment. Her dreams had changed since being in high school. Life had changed and so many things had happened. For the moment her mother was enjoying the financial rewards from her daughter's labor. In Raspberry's mind school was on the back burner for now.

She had moved her mother out of her Aunt Angela's house and into her own apartment in a decent neighborhood in Baltimore. Between the money she had stolen from Malik after she killed him and the money she had stashed from Melvins and the Escort Service. Did wonders to change her life around. And also got her business off the ground. Raspberry continued going to the range when she had free time, she was obsessed with being a marksmen. She still kept the same gun she had killed Simone with, unlike the straight razor she used to kill Malik. Which she threw in the Potomac River. She kept the 9mm because she had also used gloves when she killed Simone to avoid leaving any prints on the gun. All other prints that were on the gun were carefully wiped down. She never let anyone know she had a gun, really never let anyone know she would frequent the range. When she went she went alone. All anyone knew was she was an Exotic Dancer at Melvins. Excuse me, the head dancer at Melvins. And she was glad that's all most people in the area knew about her. The next night at Melvins was another packed house, Raspberry and Isabella were both dancing on this particular night. After Raspberry's set she went to the bar and mingled with the crowd like she normally does. And like always, men surrounded her and seeked private dances from her. She did a few, but there was a man that was there the whole time as each man fought for her attention to get a private dance. He just watched from a distance, and didnt say much.

Each time they would glance at each other and each time their eyes would meet. After a few of her private dances he was still sitting at the bar. There was something about him that intrigued her, so she decided to spark up a conversation as she sat down at the bar next to him.

"Hello I'm Raspberry" Raspberry said extending her hand in the man's direction.

As he turned towards her, he extended his hand and replied. "Hello my name is Stevie."

"I never seen you in here before, is this your first time at Melvins"? Raspberry asked.

"Yeah actually it is my first time here. I'm not from the area, I'm down here visiting a friend of mines. I'm from Lancaster, Pa." Stevie said.

"Oh so you from Amish Country, isn't that what's up there ? You live on a farm " ? Raspberry said as she laughed.

"I see you got jokes, hell no I dont live on no damn farm. Lancaster has a city, that's where I'm from. Maybe you should come see for yourself sometime, it's only a little under two hours away from here" Stevie replied.

"Hmmm...maybe one day, who you here with"? Raspberry asked.

"I'm here with a friend of mines, he's back there getting a lap dance where me and you should be at. This is only my second time in a strip club so I might as well get a lap dance from somebody as sexy as you are. Plus I figure thats why we both made eye contact and you came over here" Stevie said smiling.

Raspberry just smiled and replied, "So do you still want that lap dance." ?

"You already know beautiful, lets do it" Stevie said as Raspberry took his hand and led him back to the private room for his lap dance.

And most times thats how things went at Melvins, most times it was just business. Raspberry appreciated men like Stevie and other men who kept it professional and business like. She had recently dealt with a few stalkers that some of Melvins security had to handle. Sometimes Raspberry liked to seek out her potential customers. There would be times she would make eye contact with someone in the crowd, and know at some point in that night she would be giving him a lap dance. And of course she loved the attention the men were giving her in and outside the club, but from a distance. She also loved her space, and more times than not she kept her club life seperate from her personal life. Isabella for a while didn't know where Raspberry lived, and she was the closest person to her from the club. It was just how Raspberry was and how private she was.

Her seeking out certain men was something she liked to do from time to time. And it wouldn't be any different a few nights later when she was heavy into her set gliding across the stage looking beautiful as always. And taking her top off to expose her beautiful round breasts. Looking out Raspberry knew who the regulars were, those faces were familiar. Most times she would first go over to their tables, a few. And then she would locate a new face and go all out. Once again she delivered, leaving the men speechless and in awe at the way she moved on top of them as they sat in their chairs. The crowd loved it as always, and had seen Raspberry do it plenty of nights. But to them it never got old thats why they kept coming back for more. After Raspberry left the stage, Isabella was on next to close the show. It was one of the rare times they both danced. As Raspberry sat at the bar, she heard a voice behind her say. "Hey beautiful can I buy you a drink" ?

She turned around and it was a brown skin handsome man with a bald head and freshly groomed beard. Washington, D.C. hustler by the name of Tricky.

"Sure I'll take a Long Island Ice Tea. And who may you be sir" ? Raspberry asked looking into the man's eyes as they made eye contact.

"My name is Tricky, I been here before a long time ago. I see Melvin still owns this bitch huh" Tricky replied.

"Yes he does, so you know Melvin" ? Raspberry asked.

"Oh yeah. Me and Melvin go way back to our days in D.C. I just havent been here in so long. And definitely haven't ever seen you in here before, shit I would've been back by now" Tricky said smiling at Raspberry.

"Thank you, and thanks for the drink" Raspberry said.

"Where is Simone ? She usually be loud walking around here talking all kinds of shit" Tricky said in a joking manner.

"Sorry to tell you but, Simone is dead. She was killed a few months back" Raspberry replied.

"Wow...really ? Can't believe that, does anyone know what happened? The Police have any leads" Tricky asked concerned.

"No not that we know of, I guess the investigation is ongoing" Raspberry replied.

"Hows Melvin ? Haven't seen him in a while, we need to chop it up. Is he here" ? Tricky asked.

"No not at the moment, but I will tell him that you stopped by when he gets back in" Raspberry said.

"Ok you do that beautiful, and maybe next time I can get your number too" Tricky said as he smiled at Raspberry, and she smiled back without responding.

She agreed to do so and Tricky was gone. It was always interesting to Raspberry the different men that she would meet at Melvins. Isabella hadn't spoke to Raspberry in some time, and she wanted to catch up so they had lunch together.

"What have you been up to mami, you been on the go. I cant catch up with you anymore, except when I see you at Melvins" Isabella said in her very strong Spanish accent.

"I know girl, I just been busy trying to build everything up. We both going to take a break soon and go to some place warm for vacation." Raspberry replied.

"Yes that sounds so good mami, but you think Melvin is going to let us both be away from the bar" Isabella said.

"He'll survive, he has all these years before we got here. But anyway I met this guy the other night name Tricky. Said he's from D.C. and he used to roll with Melvin back in the day. Another nigga that knows Melvin" Raspberry said.

"Tricky from D.C. ? I know Tricky. He used to sell guns, my brother Hector used to do business with him" Isabella said.

"Hmmm....so he sells guns"? Raspberry asked looking curious.

"Well he used to, I'm not sure if he still does or not. But don't tell him I told you that, I don't want nothing to do with that. Tricky has a reputation for being a little crazy, a loose cannon" Isabella said.

"Dont worry Isabella, I won't" Raspberry replied.

The fact that Raspberry knew Tricky sold guns was something that made him more interesting to her, she could benefit greatly from him if she was lucky. It was something she definitely was willing to take a chance on, and sooner rather than later. Raspberry was out and about shopping when she spotted a woman who looked familiar to her. When she came a little closer she realized the woman was her former roommate Candice. As she walked up on her, she said.

"Candice, hey how you doing." Raspberry said.

"Hey Desiree, it's been a while. Girl you look good, and them shoes. Melvin must be paying you really nice now, they say you're the head dancer and emcee now. Melvin has been real good to you huh......"? Candice replied.

Raspberry just smiled. "Enough about me, how have you been" Raspberry asked.

"I have been up and down emotionally, it's been five months since Simone has been gone and it's still very fresh in my mind. You should know, you went through this with your sister's death" Candice replied.

Raspberry just looked at her for a minute and replied, "Yes I do know. I know what you're dealing with isn't easy. And I hope things get better for you. It was nice seeing and talking to you, and take care I gotta get going" Raspberry said as she walked away.

"Nice talking to you too. And I miss seeing you in class. Are you ever coming back to school" ? Candice replied asking.

"Not anytime soon, but one day possibly. Take care Candice" Raspberry said walking away.

Raspberry and Candice encounter was somewhat weird being that they hadn't seen each other since Simone's funeral. Candice seemed like she was somewhat bitter about Raspberry's rise, so Raspberry kept the conversation short.

The next night Tricky was back at Melvins and looking for Raspberry. But before he could find her, he seen Isabella.

"Hola mami, how are you ? You still fine as a muthafucka Isabella" Tricky said as he seen her by the bar.

"Hello Tricky, its been a while. Haven't seen you since my brother Hector was out. What brings you to Melvins" ? Isabella asked as if she didnt know he was looking for Raspberry.

"I'm looking for Raspberry, and if Melvins bald head ass is here. I will talk to him too" Tricky replied.

"Well I dont think Raspberry is here yet, but I will let her know you are looking for her" Isabella said.

"I'll just wait for her over here at the bar" Tricky said as he continued to wait for Raspberry as he ordered drink after drink.

After about twenty minutes Raspberry finally arrived and joined Tricky at his table.

"Well hello, and how is Tricky today" ?

"I'm good, just wanted to know if you would like to go out somewhere and we can see each other somewhere besides this bar. Maybe some bowling or to a movie" ? Tricky asked.

"That sounds nice, dinner especially. Now can we be honest with each other and talk a little business" ? Raspberry replied.

"What type of business we talking about ? You must know something I dont" Tricky replied

Unbeknownst to what Raspberry was talking about, or at least that's the way he acted.Raspberry put it all out on the table.

"I know you sell guns Tricky, and I'm far from the cops so your secret is good with me" Raspberry said as she took a sip of her drink.

Tricky just stared at Raspberry for a moment smiling and replied, "So you saying thats supposed to mean ? You trying to blackmail me or extort me or something ? You open your mouth about my business and I will kill you, I promise you that."

"You don't have to threaten me, relax Tricky. This is about business, maybe we can help each other" Raspberry replied.

Tricky just shook his head. "What do you want ? Or should I say what type of business are we getting into" ? Tricky asked sounding curious.

Page 57

"Look I have an Escort Service and I need to supply my girls with guns. It's a very dangerous business" Raspberry said.

"You got some balls. And let me guess, Isabella told you about what I do? You might as well tell me now, I know thats who told you. Her brother Hector used to buy shit from me. Bitch never could keep her mouth shut. Ok I'll keep in touch, and will let you know when I get a shipment in. I'm out" Tricky said as he got up and left.

"That's fair, thanks. Looking forward to doing business with you" Raspberry said as Tricky was leaving.

While Raspberry waited for Tricky, she decided to pay her mother a surprise visit at her new apartment. Her mother Denise was very surprised to see her daughter home.

"Hello beautiful, what are you doing here? I was actually just waiting on your call" Denise said fixing things up as Raspberry walked in the apartment.

"I wanted to surprise you for once, since I always tell you when I come home" Raspberry replied.

"Very nice surprise, always good to see my daughter home. I guess I can make your favorite meal since you're staying."

"Yes that would be nice mother, so how's everything around here" ? Raspberry asked.

"Everything is going well around here, have you decided to go back to school yet" ?

"No not really mom, I have a lot of things going on right now between my jobs. I know you like living here in this nice apartment, I have to keep grinding to keep us living like this" Raspberry replied.

"Desiree you know I never been a materialistic person, and we don't come from money. A roof over our heads and food to eat is all we ever needed. Plus I never asked for this apartment, I would've been fine with your Aunt Angela" Denise said as she walked towards the kitchen.

"I know mom, but since I have been making good money I thought it would be better to have your own nice little spot. And I got the extra bedroom for when I come home" Desiree said smiling.

"So in other words this apartment was more about you being comfortable and me having my own ? Girl you know you cant fool me, but I must say I do appreciate what you did. But I really would appreciate you going back to school and getting your degree" Denise replied.

"Mom I promise you when the time is right for me I will go back to school and get my degree" Desiree said as she helped her mother out while she cooked. Denise just put her arm around her daughter Desiree and gave her a hug and kiss.

"Desiree you have always made me proud, and I know you will make me proud by getting your degree" Denise said.

After eating dinner that Denise had prepared for them, they decided to go out to the Cemetery to visit Deanna. It was the first time Raspberry had been out there since the funeral. It was an emotional moment for her and her mother.

On the drive back to College Park Raspberry had a renewed spirit after spending time with her mother and finally visiting her sister's grave. It was like she had finally come to terms and accepted her sister's death after the years since her murder. And she had to be honest with her mother about her not planning on going back to school anytime soon which upset her mother. But her mother knew it was ultimately her decision. And now she had made a promise to her mother when she made the money she wanted to make she would return to school and get her degree. Back at Melvins, Isabella was downstairs getting dressed for the night when Raspberry walks in.

"Hello mami, how's things going"? Raspberry asked.

"Everything is going ok, how was your trip home" ? Isabella asked,

"It was nice, got a chance to spend time with my mother. And I also finally went to my sister's grave, I hadn't been out there since we buried her. It was just too hard at the time. But me going today, helped me to move on and basically accept it" Raspberry replied.

"Wow mami I could only imagine, I always thought my brother Hector would get killed in the streets. The life he was living. I just hope when he gets out he can stay outta these streets and out of trouble. I'm glad you got some closure mami, and I'm glad you're in better spirits" Isabella replied.

After a overnight stay back home in Baltimore, Raspberry was back to business and had a meeting with Tricky planned after he decided she gave him an offer he couldn't refuse. Tricky was willing to provide Raspberry with as many guns as she wanted. For her business and her personal use. But of course Tricky didn't know that at the time. Tricky was also like Raspberry, all about money. Increased sales and the fact he had such a good personal relationship with her made him take the chance and trust her. As soon as Raspberry bought her first two guns, she then planned on getting rid of the 9mm she had for the longest. The same 9mm that killed Simone. She decided to take a another drive, this time even further to a Virginia bridge late at night to dispose of the 9mm. She then got back in her car and drove home. Meanwhile her and Tricky's personal relationship began to take off.

After initially being skeptical about Raspberry. It was only a matter of time before he couldn't resist her beauty and sex appeal. Just them being around each other doing business, Tricky's attraction for her grew stronger. They began having a sexual relationship. To most mixing business with pleasure wouldn't be the smartest thing. It was just the opposite for Raspberry. She used her beauty and sex appeal often to get what she wanted, and it worked everytime.
Page 59

The next day Isabella made her way to the club, but before she got there she parked her car a little ways from the club and got out. When she got out, Tricky came behind her with a gun to the back of her head.

"Why the fuck you tell Raspberry I sold guns for" ? !! Tricky yelled.

"Tricky chill, she told you that" ? Isabella replied.

"She didn't have to, it wasn't hard to figure out. I don't even know this broad like that yet, and she already know my side hustle" Tricky said letting Isabella go.

"I just said it because she asked about you, she said she was interested in you. It was only casual conversation, I didn't know she would try to use it to her advantage" Isabella replied sounding worried.

"You real fucking lucky I happen to like her a great deal. Because if I didn't, you both would have problems. Regardless of me being cool with your brother or not. Next time somebody ask you about me, just say you know me. And leave it at that. I assume she dont know about us" Tricky asked looking directly at Isabella.

"No I couldnt tell her that, she seemed really interested in you when she first met you. Besides I have no problem with yall being together" Isabella replied.

"Oh I know, because you and I both know I do what I want. Just remember what I said.....be easy" Tricky said leaving as Isabella went on her way a little frightened.

She had never seen Tricky act that way towards her before. And she didn't want to see it again. Isabella paid Raspberry a visit, after knocking on the door she walked in her apartment. She immediately got to the point.

"Why did you tell Tricky what I told you about him ? He wasn't too happy and knew that I had told you" Isabella said looking for answers.

"So what, I just figured why not get straight to the point. I needed guns and he sells guns. I'm sure he won't complain when he takes my money. He's just angry I have leverage over him. I have plans for Tricky, so don't worry" Raspberry replied.

"Don't worry ? The man held me at gunpoint, I feared for my life and you're telling me not to worry."!!

"Listen to me, Tricky is not going to kill you. There's too much money out here for him to get. For him to risk it all going to jail for killing your ass. If he really wanted to kill you, he would've done it already. I promise you will be safe and Tricky will not lay a hand on you. Since you gave me the information, I owe you and you are safe with me. Besides Tricky wants some of this ass, he aint going nowhere" Raspberry said smiling.   Page 60

Tricky was making money hand over fist, and supplying not only Raspberry with guns, but also his regular customers. Tricky was also moving a huge amount of cocaine and heroin, he had people working for him in the Baltimore and D.C. areas. As well as a few cities on the West Coast. Business was booming and Tricky was happy that it was, along with his growing relationship with Raspberry. She was never around any of his drug business, Tricky always ran a tight ship in that area of his businesses. He didn't trust a soul, didn't have too many business partners either, just a few soldiers that would do anything that he asked them to do. Raspberry had a feeling that Tricky at least knew of Francisco. And maybe even knew Chaos, and did business with them both. Both organizations did business within the same area, the Baltimore/D.C. area. She didn't want to ask Tricky if he did know them to tip him off of her intentions, she just watched and observed all she could when she was with him. Raspberry's Escort Service was still going steady and bringing her income she needed, and she continued to work her nights at Melvins.

Isabella was still somewhat nervous and scared about her telling Raspberry about Tricky's profession. From that point on, Isabella tried to stay out of Raspberry or Tricky's way. She feared them both to a certain extent. In Isabella's mind, what could Raspberry do to stop Tricky ? Isabella had saw first hand what Tricky was capable of when he had hustled with her brother Hector. Even as crazy as her brother was he never crossed Tricky. Tricky was originally from Harlem, New York. He then moved to Southwest D.C. when he was fourteen and was raised there until he became a man. He had a few properties within the area, but all were outside of D.C. in Suburban Maryland. D.C. was where he was known for his reputation in the streets. He had a beautiful home in Clinton, Maryland. A place where he could breathe from grinding in them streets, he loved that because no one knew him there. He had several cars. A BMW, a Chevy Tahoe, and a late model Cadillac. All in which he kept at his residence in Clinton, Maryland. After dating Raspberry for the last three months, she finally got to see where Tricky resided.

"Wow this is beautiful, only you live here" ? Raspberry asked looking around and looking amazed at Tricky's home.

"Yes just me, of course my kids are here when they visit. I have two kids, two boys. They live not too far from here with their mother. I set her and them up with a nice apartment. I had to get her and my kids out of D.C. It just wasn't safe for them to live there anymore, especially with my reputation and some of the jealous and envious enemies I have there" Tricky replied.

Raspberry was getting a better understanding of Tricky, his life and what he was all about. That was great for her, and great for her plan for him. She was getting information that would eventually help her in the foreseeable future. She just listened and asked careful questions that wouldn't seem suspicious. All the while gathering as much information as she could about Tricky, she was playing chess and she was playing for keeps.

Page 61

Raspberry was getting closer and closer to making her move on Tricky. She had built a nice inventory of guns after buying a few from him. She claimed the guns were for her girls at the Escort Service. The only female Raspberry trusted was Isabella, and even Isabella she didn't trust fully. But she had a common interest with Isabella, they both did what they had to do to make their money. Wiithout jeopardizing their integrity and respect as women. Some may think being apart of an Escort Service was demeaning for a woman, but the girls that worked for Raspberry did it with class. Their clients were not everyday people that had no promise. Their clients were doctors, lawyers, and business owners from Fortune 500 companies. Even some important local politicians from around the area. They did parties, they did whatever the money called for them to do. They were never on street corners, and they made great money. And even though they were making great money, it never stopped their hunger for more. That's what Raspberry liked about Isabella, her drive to want the better things in life. Raspberry didn't do the Escort thing at all, she just put it together and ran it. She set her lady friends up with men who had money and power, that alone intrigued the women.

Raspberry had a group of three women working for her. Besides Isabella who was working at Melvins as well just like Raspberry. She made sure the women were well compensated for their services, she was very fair with them. That's what ultimately made them happy to work for her. When Raspberry had killed Malik and took what she could from his house, among the things she took was some heroin. She never liked or indulged in any drugs, she drank occasionally usually after her performance at Melvins. She just knew she had to get rid of it as soon as she could, she had it since she killed Malik. She thought long and hard and remembered she had a cousin in Baltimore name Shameek. Who was heavy in the game with heroin. Which was the number one drug being sold in Baltimore, because of its large number of users. She was far from a drug dealer, but she needed to get rid of it and make herself some extra cash in the process. She wasn't real close to her cousin to actually trust him, but she was willing to give him a shot. And at the same time see where she stood with him, and test his loyalty to her.

She had no other person in mind when she thought about who could move it. She just knew she had to get it to someone who was experienced at selling heroin. Because she couldnt keep it. So she decided to go see her cousin Shameek in Baltimore. After making her way back home to Baltimore and searching for her cousin's whereabouts. She finally caught up with him on a Baltimore street corner.

"Hey cousin, surprised to see you back in B More, thought you was the college girl heavy in them books at the University of Maryland. And I'm surprised to hear what you want me to do, you always was the good one in the family. How's college treating you" Shameek asked.

"Everything is good and going well, I just got this from someone and you know I don't deal in drugs. You know my mother is a recovering addict. But I just don't want to hang on to it any longer, and I could use the extra money. So I figured this was your line of business and you can help me move it. You can have half off the top, just have my half after you get rid of it" Raspberry replied.

"Look you know you brought this shit to the right person, I got you cousin. Call me in about two to three days. I will give this to a few of my best soldiers, and it's nothing" Shameek replied sounding real confident.

And why wouldn't he be, he controlled his area which was in Southeast Baltimore. He was making a lot of money and he had enough soldiers that no one would dare bother him or his business in that area. He was very much feared in that part of town. Raspberry didn't really trust him, but he was all she had. Plus he was family. In a sense Raspberry was testing him to see just how loyal of a person he was despite the fact they were family. She always felt the best way to find out a person's loyalty and intentions is to put them in a situation, she created the situation and now she was about to find out just what type of person Shameek was to her.

Meanwhile back in College Park, Tricky was eagerly awaiting Raspberry's return from her trip back home to Baltimore to meet with her cousin Shameek. Tricky didn't know that Raspberry had met with Shameek, she told him she was visiting her mother. She didnt want Tricky moving the heroin because she didnt want him to know that she had it. After getting back, Raspberry was home at her apartment when Tricky had came over after hearing she was back.

"Glad you're back, so how was your trip ? How's your mother" Tricky asked.

"It was nice and my mother is fine, did you get any more guns" ? Raspberry asked getting to the point.

"Slow down and relax, we will talk about that later. I want you to come to my place tonight, I have something nice planned for us. Dinner with candlelights and a good romantic mood, some soft music. And after some hot and sexy dessert" Tricky said pulling Raspberry closer to him and putting his arms around her.

Raspberry just looked at him and replied, "Ok sounds good. I need to go home shower and change. I will be at your place around 8".

She was a little surprised Tricky came on so strong as she arrived back in town. They had kept their distance from each other for a little while. She sensed that he missed her, and she missed him too. Regardless she would be prepared any way the night turned out. Isabella was told she was to see Melvin in his office, she didn't really know why as she nervously went to his office.

As she knocked on the door Melvin asked who it was then proceeded to tell Isabella to come in.

"Hello Isabella, have a seat beautiful. I called you up here to ask you a few questions and to ask a favor of you. First off, how do you know Raspberry" ? Melvin asked.

Looking a little confused by the question Isabella replied. "We met about a year and a half ago and we been friends ever since. Why do you ask" ? Page 63

"Oh yeah. Well I need you to do me a favor and keep your eyes and ears open if you hear about her doing anything strange or out of the ordinary. I need you to report to me, you will be well compensated for it. I promise you that. I have some suspicion that she may be involved in something. Possibly someone's murder. So do we have a deal"? Melvin asked extending his hand towards Isabella's.

Isabella was somewhat shocked and also torn between her loyalty to Raspberry and her job at Melvins. If she didn't agree, would he fire her? There was a lot of things going through her mind in just those few minutes Melvin had talked to her. She decided to play it safe and take Melvin's offer.

"Yes, if I see or hear anything I will report to you. But whose murder may she be involved in ? I just dont believe Raspberry would murder someone. As long as I've known her, she's been a very driven woman thats about her money. But yes Melvin, if I see anything I will report to you" Isabella replied.

After Simone's death, Melvin had grew suspicious of Raspberry. He watched her demeanor at Simone's funeral, how she showed little emotion for a woman that put her on at Melvins. And how cold she was when he spoke of Simone. He had no proof of her doing anything, but he was real weary of her. He certainly didn't think at first that she was capable of murdering Simone, but maybe she knew who did. Either way Melvin was still grieving over the loss of his friend Simone. And he wanted answers, trying to find out who murdered Simone.

The pressure of doing what Melvin said was weighing on Isabella, and that was right after he just told her. She tried her best not to show it. And she didn't want to tell Raspberry Melvin's intentions. In fear of her saying something to Melvin, and the whole thing blowing up in her face. Her job could be on the line, and she couldnt afford to lose her job at the moment. Isabella was beginning to like Melvins and was getting used to her position there. So for now, she would continue on as normal as she could without letting either one of them onto what she was really doing for Melvin. After talking with him, it did make her think about Raspberry and who she really was. To her knowledge she was a woman of her word. But Isabella had only known her for a little over a year. So she believed Raspberry was who she said she was. And until she seen anything different, that's what she went by. The next night Raspberry was to spend a romantic evening with Tricky. After postponing the night they had planned, because she had been tired from her trip to Baltimore the previous day. She didn't know what to expect, Tricky said he had a surprise evening planned for the two of them.

So Raspberry put on a nice pair of jeans and a blouse, it didnt matter much what she had on. She always looked beautiful. With her flat stomach, full hips, and nicely shaped thick round ass. Any pair of jeans she wore, always stuck out. She knew Tricky would love the view from all around as soon as she came through the door. They looked amazing on her, and more importantly. She bought the outfit to wear to Tricky's home. She was excited about the night ahead and eager to see what Tricky had planned for them. Page 64

As Raspberry arrived, Tricky was waiting for her at the door.

"Hello beautiful and welcome once again to my home. Come in and make yourself comfortable, you want anything to drink"? Tricky asked.

"Oh most definitely, it's been a rough week. Remy on the rocks for me, you know what I like" Raspberry replied smiling as she took her coat off and made herself a little more comfortable like Tricky said.

"Well leave that rough week shit at Melvins, it's our time now. Let's make a toast to the beautiful business relationship we have and the beautiful personal relationship we have" Tricky said.

"Yes, I will drink to that. Cheers" Raspberry replied.

"I figured since we have been doing some great business together, we deserve a night like this" Tricky said sitting beside Raspberry on his couch.

"You are definitely right, we do deserve this. And it's been a pleasure doing business with you, and a joy getting to know you personally too" Raspberry replied.

The lights were dim and Tricky had candles lit doing his best to set the mood for a passionate night between the two. He had dinner prepared for them while they sipped their drinks, Raspberry enjoyed it all. It had been a long time since a man had did that for her, not since Malik. Even still she wanted to enjoy the moment for what it was, they began getting close and the passion between them was undeniable. They had chemistry that was so obvious that they both climaxed at the same time. It was a great night, and as the two of them laid there in bed together. They once again talked business.

"So when do you expect the next shipment in" ? Raspberry asked.

"Not sure just yet, but when it comes you will know. I know you don't need no more guns already. Don't get me wrong, I'm not complaining I'm always looking to make money" Tricky said.

Raspberry just laughed a little and replied. "No its just good to know in case you need me to help you move them".

"Woman you're definitely one of a kind I tell you. You amuse me, you know that? The fact that you are a woman and you talk the way you do at times, with a man's mentality. It's kind of cute, because you are sexy as hell" Tricky said smiling.

Raspberry just smiled back as they continued to talk until Raspberry left because she had to meet with some of the women that worked for her in the morning. It was indeed a special night between them, but Raspberry still had her eyes on the prize and her

mind focused on her ultimate plan.
Page 65

A few days had passed and Raspberry decided to call her cousin Shameek to see if he was good on his word of moving the product she had gave him. Plus she wanted her money.

"Hey Shameek, did you do what we discussed" ? Raspberry asked.

"We got a problem cousin. Spot got raided and they took all that shit. Including some of my shit" Shameek replied.

"Ok so what does that mean? We need to work something out right ? Because I need that money, that was the purpose of giving it to you. I remember you telling me that it was in the right hands, and I couldn't have brought it to a better person than you. Right"? Raspberry said.

"Listen I know what I said, and sometimes this type of shit happens. I told you it was some of my shit too. A few of my peoples went down for that. Sometimes you take a loss in this game, consider it a loss. Besides you not built for this game anyway. I gotta go, I hit you another time" Shameek replied hanging up the phone.

Raspberry just looked at the phone somewhat shocked and shook her head in disgust. She never really believed what Shameek said. She felt that Shameek was playing her for a fool being that she wasn't familiar with the drug game.

She was planning on finding out just how much of a lie Shameek was telling. She already had in mind how she was going to do it too. Meanwhile she got a unexpected visit from Isabella at her apartment.

"Hey chica, what's going on ? I was in the area decided to stop by" Isabella said.

Raspberry upon letting her in replies. "Oh yeah, who you know over this way ? And everything is fine." Raspberry replied.

"Just in the area, my car just got serviced. How's the other girls working out ? I might want to pick up some more clients" Isabella replied.

"If you say so, where is all this coming from ? I thought you was happy with the money and spot you had at Melvins" Raspberry asked.

"Oh I am mami, I just want some extra work" Isabella replied.

They both talked a little more and Isabella left so they both could get ready for the night. Raspberry was a little curious to why Isabella wanted more work. But it left her mind with little thought. Later on that night to a packed house at Melvins, Raspberry took to the stage and decided to try something new. She came out in an outfit that no one had ever seen her in. A very thin one piece night gown that you could obviously see through to her near flawless body. From the time she hit the stage the men in the crowd were in awe.

Chapter Four

"Appetite To Kill"

Raspberry was in her zone, and at her very best when she was on stage. Her body was so sexy, that even after falling back from the scene for a while. She was still the main attraction whenever she hit the stage. Isabella was next to hit the stage. After coming off stage, Raspberry passed Isabella smiling and said, "Do your thing girl" as she went back stage.

Isabella was somewhat caught off guard but continued on to do her set. After the night was over, Raspberry had asked Isabella to go out to breakfast. It was the early morning hours of the next day. She had something to discuss with her, a favor to ask and a new client for her also.

"I got this cat in Baltimore that's a mid level dealer, and he needs a fine sexy woman like yourself to entertain him for a little while. He got in touch with me, and since you wanted a client I got you one. You know just until I say. You will definitely get paid for your services, but it's not a traditional way of our business. He's not to know that you're being paid to entertain him. It's like you two are going to meet on the street. Once he sees you, he'll almost certainly try to holla at you......any normal man with any kind of vision that sees your fine ass would. From there, you go with the flow and come back to me for further instructions. You understand" ? Raspberry asked.

"Yes I do, wow you really have this planned out huh" Isabella replied.

Raspberry just looked at her, and they both continued to eat their breakfast. Isabella was now asked to do two different things by Raspberry and Melvin. Two people who held her life in their hands so to speak. Her source of income and her well being. She was very much torn and had no way to turn and caught in a tight situation. She wanted very much to remain loyal to Raspberry, but she also felt obligated to give Melvin what he needed. Getting as much information as she could to what Raspberry was doing. In her mind she wasnt going to cross Raspberry. She would give Melvin bits and pieces, but not everything. But now Raspberry had directed her away from herself and onto a client in Baltimore. A few days later in Baltimore, Shameek and a few of his crew were outside of a corner store. When Shameek spotted a beautiful Latina walking down the street. His people also spotted her and began to try to get her attention. Shameek immediately stopped his people and walked across the street to talk to her.

"Hey beautiful, what's your name" ? he asked.

As she stopped and turned around she replied smiling, "Hello my name is Vanessa."

"Well hello Vanessa, excuse my silly ass friends over there. They don't know how to treat a lady of your caliber" Shameek said staring at her.

"Oh is that right ? Hmmm...ok. Well you stopped me" ? Isabella said.

"Yes. I stopped you because I think you're beautiful and I would like to take you out sometime" Shameek replied.

"Thank you, and that sounds nice. I would love to. Here's my number" Isabella said.

"Ok cool, cant wait to see you soon. I will call you. Until then beautiful, keep it tight" Shameek said.

Isabella had to keep reminding herself that she was Vanessa around Shameek, and not Isabella. Melvin was growing increasingly impatient with Isabella's inability to get information about Raspberry even though she was trying. No one was to know about her thing with Shameek, so Isabella tried her best to play it cool and follow through with what Raspberry said. She had to get back to College Park so she could work at Melvins that night. Raspberry had promised Isabella that she was safe from Tricky or anybody else for that matter. So she made sure she kept her loyalty to Raspberry. It was business as usual. Melvin was frustrated because he wasnt getting any information on Raspberry as quick as he would've liked. And for now there was nothing he could do about it. But that didnt mean it would stop him from continuing to be on the prowl. Tricky got his new shipment in, and he didn't tell Raspberry. For some reason he didn't want her to know at the moment. And didn't want her buying anymore guns at the moment either. When she asked he would say that there was a problem with the shipment and it was dropped. After a while Raspberry got the hint and figured Tricky didn't want her buying anymore guns. Raspberry noticed a change in Tricky, and began to think something was going to happen between them. She didn't know exactly what was going to happen at the time, but she could feel something brewing. It was almost like the trust that

Tricky had in Raspberry was shifting, which in turn made her trust him less.

She hadn't touched base with Melvin in some time so she decided to meet with him in his office.

"Melvin you been kind of distant with me lately, what did I do to make you be that way towards me"? Raspberry asked.

Melvin just stared at Raspberry and replied. "Nothing in particular, you been busy and I been busy. You're still Raspberry and you still work for me so we're still good" Melvin replied.

"Oh ok.....because you just seem distant for me being your head dancer. I figured we would communicate a little more than we have been. I mean I remember you communicating a lot with Simone about things going on with the club" Raspberry said.

"It's nothing personal. You know if you have anything to discuss with me, my office is always open to you.....to all you girls" Melvin replied.

After meeting with Melvin, she and him had a better understanding of each other and life went on as usual. Meanwhile Shameek was eager to speak to Vanessa and get to know her better. He also wanted to take her out. So he decided to call her.

"Hola mami, this is Shameek. You know the guy you met the other day, how are you" ? Shameek said.

"Oh hello Papi, I'm fine. I was just thinking about you. How are you"? Isabella replied.

"Im good beautiful, just wanted to know when you wanted me to take you on a date. When are you free"? Shameek asked.

"I'm free on Thursday" Isabella replied.

"Ok that's cool with me. Thursday it is, I will see you then beautiful" Shameek said as they both hung up the phone.

Shameek and Vanessa were both excited to see each other, and now they had a date set. Tricky wanted Raspberry to come to his house and discuss some business. He wouldnt tell her to what extent until she got over there. Raspberry didn't know what to expect so like most times she carried her gun on her with the silencer. She had noticed the change in Tricky, plus him not telling her about the shipment didn't seem right to her. She didn't know what she was walking into, but she was ready for whatever. Upon arriving at Tricky's house, Raspberry had some jeans and a shirt on with her gun in her back. The silencer was in her pocket. After knocking and Tricky letting her in. She had a seat on his couch.

"I know you wondering why I have you here, well I have a surprise for you" Tricky said.

"Another surprise huh ? Sounds exciting, I'm ready for my surprise when you're ready to give it to me" Raspberry replied smiling.

"Ok you sit right there beautiful, don't move. I will be right back" Tricky said as he went in another room.

Raspberry sat on the couch as Tricky went in the other room, but she quietly followed behind him until she could see in the room to see what he was doing. As she looked in the room, she saw Tricky grab his 357 out of a drawer. She quickly and quietly ran back to another room and hid as she pulled out her gun and quietly screwed on the silencer.

"Raspberry.....beautiful. Where are you ? I got something for you" Tricky yelled as he loaded the gun.

With no reply and complete silence in the house, Tricky began going through the house looking for Raspberry.

"Where are you, you shady bitch !!! You didn't know I knew you was trying to set me up......huh ? Come out here and face me, so I can blow your fucking brains out !! You can join your sister. Yeah I know about your sister, about her murder. You're about to suffer the same fate bitch, come on out and stop hiding" !! Tricky continued while still walking through the house searching for Raspberry.

Walking through the house, there was no Raspberry in sight. Did she leave ? Was she hiding in the house watching Tricky ?

Tricky continued walking through the house as he walked past Raspberry. She was hiding behind this corner. As he walked past, she got behind him and raised her gun. Fired one shot to the back of Tricky's head, he immediately dropped to the floor. She then stood over him and pumped two more bullets in his chest. She immediately staged the scene in his home like it was a robbery. She went through drawers in his bedroom and recovered three grand in cash. She also attempted to break open the safe. Knocked drawers over and clothes everywhere to make it seem like a struggle. Raspberry then quickly got out of there and into her car, and went home.

The next morning Raspberry lay in her bed thinking about what happened the previous night, and how did Tricky find out about her sister because she never discussed her sister with anyone. She had no clue, but she was relieved to have made it out of Tricky's house alive after he was planning on killing her. She was glad she was thinking on her feet and took her gun with her that night. And how did Tricky figure Raspberry was setting him up ? So many questions but no answers. When she saw Tricky in his room getting his gun, she was somewhat shocked but quickly got herself prepared to defend herself. She had no idea why Tricky wanted to kill her, it definitely threw a curve ball into her plans for him. She cared about Tricky, but she did notice a change in his behavior towards her. She was fortunate she did, or else she might have never seen it coming and suffered the same fate as her sister. She knew eventually that someone would find Tricky, but she was hoping it would take a little more time to find him being that he was a busy man.

As she sat there, her phone suddenly rang.....it was Isabella.

"Hey mami, have you heard about Tricky? His children's mother and his children found him dead in his house, shot three times !! I can't believe it, I have to call my brother" Isabella said sounding concerned.

"Wow....really ? I was just with him a few days ago" Raspberry said softly weeping.

"Mami are you ok ? I know you and Tricky were involved, do you need to talk I can come over there" Isabella said.

"No I will be fine, I will call you later. And don't tell anyone we were involved. That was our business and our business only" Raspberry replied.

Isabella agreed to keep it to herself but wondered why Raspberry made such a point about it. Either way Isabella was shocked at the news about Tricky. Her brother and him although weren't necessarily friends, did business together and were often around each other. From her living with her brother for a little, she came accustomed to seeing Tricky and being around him. She would miss his presence in the physical form, although the last time she seen him it wasn't pleasant between them. Isabella felt bad now about telling Raspberry about what Tricky did. Could that had been a reason he was killed ? Raspberry did say she had plans for Tricky. Isabella was shocked and confused.

Melvin wanted to talk to Raspberry as soon as possible, he had seen her and Tricky together before. He didn't know to what extent their relationship was, but he seen them several times inside the club talking. So he told Raspberry to come to his office.

"I'm sure you know why I have you here" Melvin said as he started pacing back and forth around the room.

"Actually I don't know why I'm here, but I'm sure you will tell me" Raspberry replied.

"I have you here because someone I knew was murdered a few nights ago, you know the man you been talking to Tricky" Melvin said staring at Raspberry.

"Yes I know, I have been taking it hard myself. Very tragic and unfortunate, I'm really going to miss him. He was a good person. Always treated me with respect" Raspberry said sounding upset.

"When was the last time you was with him" ? Melvin asked.

Raspberry looked at Melvin and said. "What does that matter to you ? Our relationship was between us and it will stay between us. We were friends and went out for breakfast a few times."

"You work for me, I knew Tricky personally. Although we weren't necessarily friends, we hung out together a few times back in D.C. And always was on good terms. I would like to know what happened to the man" Melvin replied.

"Why would I know what happened to him ? I was with him earlier that day and he was fine. I went back to my place, woke up the next morning to the news he was murdered."

"Shit just seems funny, I don't know. The shit with Simone, and now Tricky. These are people I know" Melvin said confused.

"Do you think someone is after you Melvin ? Is that why these two murders have you paranoid" ? Raspberry asked.

"No one is after me. And even if they were, I got something for they ass if they come for me. I just want to know what happened to these people." Melvin said.

"Well I think you should let the Police do their jobs. Trust that they will find out what happened to them" Raspberry replied.

After getting no where with Raspberry, Melvin decided to do just that for the moment. Let the Detectives do their jobs. Meanwhile back in Baltimore, Shameek was getting ready for him and Vanessa's first date. And very much excited about spending time with the beauty. Vanessa was also excited about seeing Shameek, they had talked on the phone a few nights before and the anticipation was building.

Shameek picked Vanessa up at a location in Baltimore and he took her out on a date. They went to eat, and later walked along the Baltimore Harbor at night. As the city skyline towered over them. Meanwhile for Raspberry it was business as usual, that is until one day Detective Nelson stopped by Melvins. Approaching the bar Detective Nelson had asked one of the bartenders could he speak to Melvin. The bartender after making a call instructed Detective Nelson to Melvin's office.

Upon entering Melvin's office Detective Nelson said, "Hello I'm Detective Nelson and I'm here investigating the murder of Travell "Tricky" Andrews. Are you familiar with who that is"? The Detective asked.

"Yes I knew Tricky, he was an associate of mines. I was very sad to hear about him being murdered" Melvin replied.

"Yes very unfortunate, do you know the last time he was here ? Because I was told he would frequent this place from time to time. And who was he with"? Detective Nelson asked.

"Yeah he was here a few weeks ago, wasn't particularly with anyone but he was here watching the ladies perform" Melvin replied.

"Ok well you don't mind if I talk to some of the ladies that work here" the Detective asked.

"Of course you can, you can speak to anyone you want. I would like and hope that you guys solve this case and find Tricky's killer" Melvin replied.

After leaving Melvin's office the Detective talked to a few of the ladies that were there, which none of them were Raspberry or Isabella. The Detective then left and said he would return to interview the rest of the ladies another day, as the investigation continued. As soon as the Detective left, Melvin quickly picked up the phone and called Raspberry. Raspberry was home at the time when she heard the phone ring.

"Hello." Raspberry answered.

"Yeah, this is Melvin. That Detective was here a few minutes ago asking questions about Tricky, and the last time he was here and who he was with. Look I know you and Tricky was fucking around, and that's yall business. When the Detective asked who he was with I didn't say shit, for two reasons. I'm not no snitch, and I was looking out for you. But I also want the Police to solve this murder, so if you know anything you have to tell me now" Melvin said.

Raspberry paused for a minute and replied. "Why would I know anything about Tricky's murder ? Yeah we used to see each other and I will tell the Detective that myself. I have nothing to hide Melvin, but you....you starting to make me feel uncomfortable. That's the second time you have accused me and questioned me about this situation. I work for you, make my money and mind my business. I don't bother anyone around there. And somehow you been questioning me a lot lately" Raspberry said sounding annoyed.

Raspberry wasn't too happy about the way Melvin came at her, but she also knew Melvin was still grieving Someone's death. Raspberry had money to make and like any other time, she was not going to let something petty stand in the way of that. Isabella had got to the club a little early and Melvin had already gave her the heads up about the Detective coming by and probably returning to interview her about Tricky's murder. Isabella was very nervous about it, she really didn't want to say anything. She actually didn't know what to say. She didn't want to incriminate anyone, including herself.

"Look you need to get yourself together and do what we discussed. Tell the Detectives anything you know about Raspberry. Now is your time to do it and get justice for Simone and Tricky. I just think she knows something about both murders, and remember our deal and I'm holding you to that. If Raspberry knows anything about Simone or Tricky's murder her ass is mines. You just remember our deal" Melvin said as he walked away.

And just like clockwork Detective Nelson came back by Melvins, and the first person he interviewed was Isabella.

"Hello I'm Detective Nelson, and your name is" ?

"Isabella." She replied.

"I have you here because I'm investigating Tricky's murder. Did you know Tricky personally"? Detective Nelson asked.

"Yes I did, he was an associate of my brother's. I knew him from my brother" Isabella replied.

"And your brother is" ? Detective Nelson asked.

"My brother is in jail, he can't help you with anything. He was locked up when Tricky was killed" Isabella said visually annoyed.

"When was the last time you seen Tricky"? Detective Nelson asked.

"I seen him here, a few weeks ago." Isabella replied.

"Was he with anyone that night" ? Detective Nelson asked.

"There's a lot of women in here, he was with damn near all of them at some point and time" Isabella replied.

"Even you Isabella? He been with you too" ? Detective Nelson asked.

Isabella just looked at the Detective and replied, "I told you before, I only knew him through my brother."

"Ok, thank you for your time" Detective Nelson said.
Page 73

The next to get interviewed was Raspberry, who had just came in the club after Isabella was questioned.

"Hello there, I'm Detective Nelson and I'm investigating the murder of Travell "Tricky" Andrews. I hear you and Tricky were pretty close. When was the last time you seen him" ? Detective Nelson asked.

"I knew Tricky from coming here to the club, and we went out to dinner a few times. He was a nice guy. And the last time I seen him was in here, a week ago" Raspberry replied.

"Was he with anyone when you last seen him" ? Detective Nelson asked.

"I didn't see anyone but him" Raspberry replied.

"Ok thank you, that's all I need. Enjoy your night" Detective Nelson said.

"You too Detective, you enjoy your night also" Raspberry replied smiling.

Walking down the steps Raspberry just smiled, and almost busted out in an all out laugh. But quickly straightened her face up as she walked in the dressing room. Upon walking in, Isabella was the only other person in the dressing room.

"Well hello Isabella, did you get questioned too ? I'm assuming you did, being that you knew Tricky better than I did" Raspberry said giggling a little.

Isabella didn't know what to say at first.

"Yes he talked to me, I told him I only knew Tricky through my brother and that's true. He asked if I knew anything about Tricky, I said no" Isabella replied.

Raspberry just shook her head.

"You know Isabella. If they dig deep enough they may find that you know more than what you're saying. But I leave that up to you. Anyway did you handle what I told you to handle" ? Raspberry asked.

"Yes I'm on it, but this driving back and forth though"......Isabella replied.

"Listen, when all this is over. Me and you going to be rich. And you won't ever need for any money. So just hold on a little while longer, I have something planned for that soon" Raspberry said interrupting.

After talking to Raspberry, Isabella had a certain calm about her. Raspberry had that effect on her. She got refocused on what she was supposed to do quickly.

Back in Baltimore Shameek continued to talk to Vanessa and their relationship grew, He had grew very fond of her.

Vanessa couldn't spend the time Shameek wanted to spend with her because she didn't live in the area. She would come see him when she had the time to. In between her job and all. Regardless of it all, Shameek loved every minute of the time he did spend with her. Back in Clinton, Maryland and College Park, Maryland the investigation was ongoing. As Detective Nelson interviewed the last of the people he needed to complete his part of the investigation at Melvins. Another night had arrived, Isabella and Raspberry were both on the bill to a packed house as usual on a Friday night. This time Raspberry went first and decided to let Isabella close the night. Most women who worked at the club didn't like to follow Raspberry. It was too much pressure, because she was always a crowd favorite. Isabella was up to the challenge, she had developed her own following at Melvins.

And she herself looked amazing in this short skirt with a sexy almost see through top, and of course her heels. Her body was beautiful, she had curves in all the right places. As the crowd watched her dance, Melvin couldnt help but realize how much the crowd loved Isabella. Melvin had made his way downstairs to the bar area for a drink. Raspberry herself watched from back stage and enjoyed Isabella's set. As long as Isabella was loyal to her, Raspberry always wanted her to win. She saw Isabella as a valuable asset to her future plans, as long as she maintained her loyalty. Isabella was loyal to Raspberry for two reasons, she feared her and she respected her. Plus she appreciated the fact that Raspberry had put her on at Melvins. She had no idea what Raspberry was capable of. But she knew that she was always about her business. She also knew that people around her were being killed. And Melvin the club owner wanted Isabella to spy on Raspberry, because Melvin had become increasingly suspicious of her. Isabella had no clue whether Raspberry knew or had anything to do with Simone or Tricky's murder. She didn't have any proof. And that's where she was supposed to come in at, Melvin wanted her to find out any way she could. She was still torn between what Melvin wanted her to do and what Raspberry wanted her to do. They both conflicted each other, and she soon would have to make a decision either way.

For the moment she just tried to make them both happy by doing what she could for the both of them. Without it looking obvious to either of them. Either way she was caught in a bad situation. Raspberry hadn't talked to her mother in a while since visiting her about a month ago. So she decided to call her.

"Hey mom, how's everything going ? Did you get that money I sent you" Raspberry asked.

"Hey baby, yes I did get it. Thank you. And everything is ok, how are you doing down there ? How's your job going" ? Her mother Denise asked.

"Jobs going well mom, glad to hear you're doing well. I hope to be coming home soon to visit. But until then, you take care. And if you need anything, don't hesitate to call me" Raspberry said.

"Ok baby I will, and you take care of yourself down there" Denise replied.

Page 75

It was back to business for Raspberry as she continued to do her thing at Melvins. And getting a piece of her side hustle which was running her Escort Service. Both places supplied her with a comfortable lifestyle, one that she could live well and take care of her mother. Raspberry did want to go back to school and get her degree, but for the moment she was occupied and doing the things she loved. Using her beautiful body and natural sex appeal, along with her classy way of doing business to make a living.

She was also ruthless and a cold blooded killer. As witnessed to how she murdered Malik, Simone, and Tricky in cold blood. She had an appetite to kill, and came too far to turn back now. She had moved forward with her plans and was eager to execute them. Anyone in the way of her pursuing success was a target and in grave danger. Problem was they would never know it. Because up until this point, no one had a clue of what she was capable of doing and just how ruthless and cold blooded she was. But many would soon find out. Melvin was the only one suspicious of Raspberry, but he had no proof. He himself didn't think she was capable of doing such ruthless acts, but maybe she knew who did. Either way Melvin was keeping a close eye on her through Isabella. Back in Baltimore, Shameek was steady grinding doing his thing in the cocaine and heroin business. He had a lot of East Baltimore and was moving West as well, his organization had become stronger. One of the strongest crew's since Francisco and Chaos crew, that ran most of West Baltimore a short time back. As Francisco moved his people out of the Baltimore area since Deanna's death, Shameek's crew capitalized on the new vacant blocks that were left behind.

His business was everything to him, and he was hands on with it. He also was head over heels for Vanessa. They had started getting serious and Shameek couldn't be more happier. He had stepped down as being so much into the day to day operations. And let his top soldiers have more of a leadership role. Shameek was quickly catching feelings for Vanessa, he made sure Vanessa was well taken care of once she became his lady. He let her drive a few of his cars, in which he had three. She was enjoying herself and enjoying the affection of a man that was crazy about her. One night at Shameek's house the two were enjoying a quiet evening at home when there was a knock on the door. He was surprised because he had told his boys that he didn't want to be disturbed while he was spending time with Vanessa. They knew when he was with her, he was not to be disturbed unless it was a real emergency. So it was just the two of them at Shameek house.

Shameek walked slowly towards the door and looked through the peep hole and it was blocked. He then asked who it was to no answer. He proceeded to turn around to a small drawer in the hallway, just before you get to the front door and pulled out a 9mm Ruger. Already loaded and walked towards the door to open it. Once he opened it, he felt a gun press to the back of his head as he opened the door. Vanessa had set him up. At the door was a lone gunman with the gun pointed right at Shameek's face. Shameek quickly dropped the gun as the gunman at the door came inside the house.

"What the fuck is this Vanessa"? Shameek yelled as he moved back into the living room.

"Shut the fuck up and direct us to the money, and I mean all of it" the gunman said.

"I ain't giving yall shit, what yall two bitches robbing me" ? Shameek said in disbelief.

Pointing the gun towards his face the gunman said, "I'm not going to tell you again." !!

Shameek then went in his bag and took out a few wads of money and tossed it to the gunman.

"I know there has to be more, where is it" !!! The gunman said.

"That's all that's here, so fuck yall bitches. Yall got what yall wanted, now get out of my house. And yall both dead bitches walking after this is over. My goons are coming, believe me" Shameek said before getting interrupted by the gunman as Vanessa stood behind Shameek with her gun on him.

"I told you to shut up didn't I" ?!! The gunman said.

Just then, Shameek attempts to back hand Vanessa, and the gunman immediately fires two shots hitting Shameek in the chest with both of them and killing him. The two women then grabbed the money and ran out of the house to a car that was outside.

Shameek lay in a pool of blood on his living room floor, shot two times in the chest from an apparent robbery. News began to spread fast about what happened to Shameek. His crew stood outside his house on the street as investigators combed the area for evidence. His crew was shocked and extremely angry and saddened. And how could this have happened to a man that was running an organization with a lot of protection from his crew. Shameek damn near had the whole city of Baltimore. How could this happen to a man of his stature ? When he was only hanging out with his girlfriend at home. The main question everyone wanted to know was, where was Vanessa? She hadn't been heard from since she was at Shameek's earlier that night, she was definitely a person of interest in the case. The only problem was, no one from Shameek's crew remembered what she looked like exactly. Shameek kept her away from his crew and that lifestyle. When they were together it was just them, he wanted it that way and she was more comfortable that way. She was the last known person with Shameek, and now he was dead. And she was nowhere to be found. Page 77

Not too many of Shameek's people even knew who she was, they just knew that she was Spanish and that she had been seeing Shameek. And her name was Vanessa. His house was somewhat out of order, at least in the living room where he was found. The police were still at Shameek's house trying to piece together any clues they could find in helping them solve the case. They were no leads as of yet. Back in

College Park, Raspberry and Isabella had just got back from Baltimore. With a bag of money and the same clothes they had on at Shameek's house. Yes, Raspberry had set Shameek up by using Isabella as Vanessa. Being that Shameek had never seen Isabella, she was the perfect person to use to set him up. It was easy for her and Isabella agreed to do it. But after actually going through with it, Isabella had second thoughts. And was somewhat shocked that Raspberry had shot and killed Shameek. As they both sat in Raspberry's apartment, Isabella was visibly upset.

"You killed him, I thought we were going to just rob him and get your money back. I don't want to be involved with killing and I don't want to go to jail. I just want to dance and do the side thing with the Escort Service" Isabella replied.

Raspberry just sat there and paused for a moment. Then replied. "You know that dude Shameek was someone I knew personally. He helped decide his own fate more than anything. It had to be done because of his lack of respect for people and people's shit. I needed you and asked for a favor. You agreed and you will get paid for your work. But this stays between us, and only us. After tonight we can not talk about this again" Raspberry replied.

Isabella really didn't know what to say, after seeing Raspberry murder someone. She was scared outta her mind to say anything otherwise than what Raspberry had told her. She could see now what Melvin was so suspicious about. What transpired at Shameek's house was a total shock to Isabella. But she always thought in the back of her mind that Raspberry may have been capable of doing such a thing.

She had no idea she was going to kill Shameek, but she knew now that she meant business. And she was also curious as to know if Raspberry had killed Tricky also. She definitely didn't put it past her after seeing what she seen. She agreed to keep her mouth shut about what she had seen and to never mention it again. She feared Raspberry, now more than ever. She was now really confused as to what she would say to Melvin. She definitely couldn't give him the information he really wanted. But she had to give him something. Isabella remembers Simone being at odds with Raspberry because of her being put on by Raspberry. And she also remembers what ultimately happened to Simone. Did Raspberry really kill Simone and Tricky? She had a lot of questions but didn't dare to try to find the answers.

Page 78

Melvin was sitting in his office when the phone rang.

"Mel what's going on ? I was thinking about coming down there soon. I know its been a while since I been through, I been laying low. But I do want to come this weekend. Hope you have some better looking women than the last time I was down there" the man on the phone said.

"Chaos, what's going on man. I haven't heard from you in a while. And hell yeah man, I got some gorgeous women down here. And business is booming" Melvin replied.

"That's good man, I just been away for a while. Out the mix so to speak but I'm back now. Think I might make a trip down there" Chaos said.

Yes Chaos. The same Chaos that fired the fatal shot that killed Deanna, Raspberry's sister. Melvin did know him and Francisco, he had known them both for about five years. And had done some business with them in the past. Raspberry had been seeking Chaos and Francisco after finding out from Anita what really happened the night her sister was killed. She described her relationship between her, Chaos, and Francisco as being people she knew to Melvin.

Melvin had no knowledge of Raspberry's sister getting killed, it was something she didn't share with too many people.

"Well come on down man, would love to have you here. Just let me know what day this weekend and I will set you up in V.I.P." Melvin replied.

"No doubt, more than likely Saturday. I will hit you Friday night...... stay up and keep hustling pimp" Chaos said before hanging up.

Isabella was still somewhat shook up about what she had seen Raspberry do to Shameek. And little did she know, that Shameek was Raspberry's cousin. Isabella knew she had to get herself together quickly because she had to dance at Melvins that night. But before that night, earlier that day Raspberry stopped by Isabella's place.

"Hey what's going on, came to see how you was" Raspberry said as she came into Isabella's apartment.

"I'm fine mami, just relaxing before tonight" Isabella replied.

"Listen, I hope you got your mind focused on what you have to do. One slip up looks funny to anybody that knows you well. We did what we had to do, and we got the money. You will get your cut" Raspberry said.

"I'm good and I will be fine. Dont worry" Isabella replied.

"Oh I'm not worried, but you should be if you dont get your mind right" Raspberry said.

She was not about to give Raspberry any reason to believe that she couldn't be a trustworthy and loyal person to her.

That next day Shameek was laid to rest in his native Baltimore, Maryland. Shameek was Raspberry's cousin on her father's side. They were first cousin's. Raspberry's father Robert was Shameek's mother's older brother. Raspberry didn't attend the funeral. Day had finally turned to night as Raspberry was in her usual position as head dancer and emcee. Isabella was on the bill as usual and as always the place was packed. Amongst the people in the crowd was a stocky bald head man with a goatee that was in the V.I.P. area. Raspberry noticed him because he wasn't a familiar face, but somehow she wanted to get closer. And she wanted him to see her. So she went over near the V.I.P. area. The man was sitting with a few other guys and some of the dancers who were over there mingling. Raspberry went over to him and introduced herself.

"Hello I'm Raspberry, welcome to Melvins." Raspberry said.

"I'm Chaos, and this isn't my first time here at Melvins beautiful. But definitely glad to meet you" the man replied.

Raspberry almost passed out as she was now face to face with the man she had been quietly searching for. The man that took her sister's life. That was his name, Chaos.

It had been almost five years, and she was now face to face with him for the first time. After just standing there staring at him, he then checked to see if Raspberry was still alive.

"You ok beautiful" ? Chaos asked.

"Oh yeah, I'm sorry. Was just stuck in thought a little, do you need anything" ? Raspberry replied.

"No we good right now, but you definitely can stay close. Especially close to me" Chaos said winking at Raspberry before she walked away.

She was still in shock herself about finally seeing Chaos, he was just as Anita had described him. Raspberry didn't think she had seen Francisco. The night went on and Chaos found himself over near Raspberry again.

"So we meet again beautiful, we need to see each other outside this club. Somewhere nice, like a getaway. Would you go away with me" ? Chaos asked.

Raspberry smiled and replied. "Maybe if I get to know you, I just don't go away with anybody. You could be a serial killer for all I know" Raspberry said as they both laughed.

"But no seriously, here's my number. Call me sometime so we can do that......that getaway I mean" Chaos said before leaving the club.

Deep inside Raspberry was overjoyed, after wondering where Chaos was all these years. She didnt have to look any further as now she had his own personal phone number. And was eventually going to go away with him, it was too good to be true. Melvin was there as Chaos was about to leave the club, they talked for a brief moment and then Chaos left. It was a interesting night to say the least.

To most people who would not only see but meet the person that was responsible for their loved one's death, would probably not be able to keep their composure. When Raspberry first seen Chaos, she had no idea it was him. And once she realized it was him, she was glad she didn't have to look anymore. Her search was over. From that point on Raspberry knew exactly what she wanted to do and what she had planned for Chaos. But first she had to get to know him, which wasn't going to be easy. But she was committed to doing just that, and she already had a great start by having his number. Isabella was told to see Melvin in his office as soon as possible. Melvin was expecting some information from Isabella about Raspberry. Isabella was nervous because she really didn't know what to tell him.

"So what's going on ? It's been a while since we last spoke. So I know you got something for me" Melvin said looking at Isabella.

"I really don't have much Melvin, she hasn't been doing anything in particular or anything suspicious. Just working here and doing her side thing with her Escort Service" Isabella replied.

Melvin just looked at Isabella, then walked closer to her. "Listen, don't feed me that bullshit. I know you and her is thick as thieves and you know more about her than you're leading on. If I happen to find out that you do know more than you're telling me, you're finished here" Melvin said as he walked away.

"I'm telling you Melvin, that's all I know" Isabella replied.

"Yeah we'll see, you can leave now" Melvin said frustrated as he sat back down in his chair.

Melvin wanted so bad to force Isabella's hand, but he really didn't have much leverage in doing so. All he could do was threaten to fire her. But he couldn't get rid of her, she was one of his best dancers and biggest money makers. Even though he knew that deep down inside, he still wanted Isabella to think he really would get rid of her if she didn't get the information he wanted her to get.

Meanwhile Raspberry was about to call Chaos for the first time.

"Hello Chaos, this is Raspberry from the club" Raspberry said.

"Hey what's going on, I'm glad you called" Chaos said.

"So what brought you to Melvin's that night"? Raspberry asked.

"Just a night out on the town, I been to Melvin's a few times and had some good times so I decided to stop by again" Chaos replied.

"So where you from and what do you do" ? Raspberry asked.

"I'm from Jersey City, New Jersey orginally. But I been in the Baltimore/ D.C. area for a while now" Chaos said.

"And where are you from, may I ask" ? Chaos asked.

"Me....I'm from Annapolis. Went to the University of Maryland for a while. But dropped out for a while, thinking about going back some day" Raspberry replied.

"Oh ok....and I work in construction, contract work and real estate. Me and my partner are in business and have been in business for years" Chaos replied.

"Ok.....interesting. It's nice to meet a man that has something going on for himself, that's very attractive" Raspberry said.

"You're very attractive to me also, when I see you on stage it's like I'm in another world. I been to plenty of strip clubs all over this country. And there are many women who can control that stage and captivate your mind while they're doing it. But you, you're special" Chaos said.

"Thank you very much, it's good to know I have that effect on some people. At the same time that's apart of the job, and I enjoy every minute of it. So do you plan on returning to Melvin's to come see me dance again" ? Raspberry asked.

"Not only will I return baby, but I plan on being a bigger part of your life than I am now. And hopefully more" Chaos replied.

"Oh really ? Hmmm....I love a confident man, I think it's so sexy. Maybe we can start with dinner" Raspberry said.

"Anything you want beautiful, you say the time and place and I'm there" Chaos replied.

They talked a little while longer and set a date for their first actual date. Raspberry was experiencing a range of emotions. Being flattered, appreciative, sexy, angry, enraged at the fact that she had not only stood face to face. But she had started a courtship with her sister's killer. It was something she never would've imagined that she could have done at the time her sister was murdered. Or in recent years for that matter. The few times Raspberry was around Chaos she would often times just stare at him. He would love to think that it was because she was so attracted to him. But in reality it was just the disgust that she had for him, and being patient enough to execute her plan successfully without letting her emotions get in the way.

It was apart of who she was and how she executed her plans, she watched you. Most times when you least expected it or noticed it. She used her beauty and sex appeal to get what she wanted, and often times preyed on her victims. She would seem shy to some, but decisive to all. Chaos was blown away by her beauty, and like most people she seemed like a great person to be around. Her personality was seductive and her spirit was genuine and also free. She lived life and she made the most of her opportunities. After committing her first murder, she felt like she couldn't stop. She was making money and there was a quiet respect that went unsaid when it came to her. She loved the fact that she had total control over most things that had to do with her life. She was proud that she had that power. Page 82

Raspbery had gotten away with murdering four people up until this point. Malik, Simone, Shameek, and most recently Tricky. And Police had no idea that she was behind all four murders. Most people never knew what Raspberry was capable of, because she showed little emotion. And no one but Melvin even suspected that she could have been responsible for Simone or Tricky's death, let alone Malik and Shameek's murders also. It was always a mystery so to speak with her. She did what her sister and Anita failed to do just five years prior, being successful in a home invasion robbery. It was something she wasn't necessarily proud of, but in her mind had to be done. Unfortunately it was a relative. Someone she had trusted and they had to pay the ultimate price for stealing from her. The average person would've maybe felt some sort of remorse, especially it being a family member. But to Raspberry that made it even worse on her cousin Shameek's part. And the reason why he had to pay the ultimate price. In the game he was in, it was an envitable outcome for many. She now had her sights set on Chaos, a man that personality wise had been very sweet to her since the day they met. They did things together, and had been seeing each other for about two weeks now.

He showered her with gifts, and planned to take her anywhere she wanted to go. But she wanted to take it slower and get to know Chaos for who he was. And to get enough information she could from him, so she could use it against him in her plot for revenge. She had yet to see Francisco for the first time, but she knew it would come as her and Chaos got closer and more serious. She waited patiently as always. In the meantime she would enjoy all that was done for her by Chaos. Melvin was one person that noticed how much time Raspberry was spending with Chaos. So much so that Melvin had a conversation with Chaos about just that. Melvin and Chaos met for dinner and a drink at a restaurant in Downtown D.C.

"So what's going on man, you and Raspberry getting serious man" ? Melvin asked.

"You still nosey as hell Melvin, yeah man we getting closer. Things are going good between us, why you ask" ?

"Well before you even met her officially, she was asking about you and Francisco" Melvin replied.

"Asking about me and Francisco? How the hell she know about us"? Chaos asked sounding confused.

"I said the same shit when she asked me. But then I just brushed it off. But I kept it until I saw you" Melvin said.

"Ok thanks for the information, I'm definitely going to see what this is about" Chaos said sounding anxious.

He couldnt wait to see Raspberry so he could ask her a few questions about her inquiring about him and Francisco. And also how she even knew of them. After talking to Melvin, Chaos became weary of Raspberry.
Page 83

Chaos continued to stay low key for the most part living quietly in a Northwest D.C. condo. He and Francisco still had a lot of money and was still doing their thing in the hustle game, mainly selling crack cocaine. Francisco didn't live in D.C. he preferred to live in Virginia which wasn't that far away. About an hour and a half drive, maybe two from Chaos. They split up to avoid being tied together as one entity, only those in the streets knew they built an empire together. When they would meet to discuss business, it would be at various locations to not leave a pattern for anyone to follow. Including their enemies and law enforcement. If either of them was caught, they knew to keep their mouths closed. No matter what they had sworn to each other that if one got caught, they would never give the other up. One would take the weight for the both of them. It was something they had sworn way back when they both first got into the game. They lived by that code and they would die by it. Never give your man up to no one. It was also how they were able to get away with so many things they did. They were very smart and both looked out for one another. Best friends since they were kids back in Jersey City, New Jersey.

Throughout the years that they hustled together, which included a few prison stints by them both. They never let the money or women come between them and let it break the friendship and bond they had for so long. It was basically them two against the world, that was their mentality. The people they had working for them they treated very well, and they knew if they ever got busted that they were to never mention Francisco or Chaos name. They were to take whatever charges they faced. In their early days of hustling there was one person that worked for them that got busted on a possession of a decent amount of cocaine. And was facing some serious time. That worker decided he was going to give Chaos and Francisco up, before he could do so he suddenly disappeared. He went missing for weeks before his body was found in a dumpster at a apartment building in Jersey City. There was no evidence tying Chaos or Franciso to the crime, but many people around the city figured that they had been responsible for the man missing. And eventually being killed. Police couldn't tie either of them to the murder so they never had to worry about any murder charges.

A few months later Chaos and Francisco moved South to Baltimore where they set up shop in West Baltimore. And quickly became a major force in the Baltimore drug trade. When Francisco met Deanna and Anita, he saw himself and Chaos. Only difference was Deanna and Anita were females. He loved their work ethic and truly believed they would be top earners in his organization. And they were for the time they worked for him. But he also seen their excitement for action. That's why he decided to send them to do the home invasion robbery. He had faith that they could get it done, he felt that they were more than ready to successfully do the job. Unfortunately we seen how that worked out for Deanna and Anita.

Deanna was killed and Anita ended up in jail for many years to come, taking the charges associated with Deanna's murder. Anita was sentenced to twelve to fifteen years for her role in the home invasion robbery. And for shooting a man. The case was still open with no leads or recent developments. Chaos who essentially murdered three people that night, got away and disappeared into the night. Chaos knew he made a crucial mistake that night by just shooting once he got out back and could hardly see anything. That crucial mistake ended in Deanna being accidently shot by Chaos, and shot by the other man also. Chaos fired the fatal shot that took her life. But was it really an accident ? Anita seemed to think that her and Deanna was set up by Francisco and Chaos. Chaos himself had a short memory when it came to situations like that, it wasn't the first time he had killed someone. He was not only Francisco's partner but also his enforcer. Whenever Francisco needed work to be put in on the street he turned to Chaos.

Chaos loved to put in work. He had so much built up anger from his childhood that he just naturally fit the mold of a loose cannon. Violence just came naturally to him, it fit him well in his line of business.

Coupled with the life him and Francisco end up living hustling. He was naturally the man to see when you wanted somebody handled. So Chaos really didn't feel any remorse for Deanna's murder, he hardly knew her. They were only around each other a few times including the night Deanna died. As bad as that night was, Chaos and Francisco never talked about it again. Chaos decided to call Raspberry and told her to meet him at a restaurant in Downtown D.C. He naturally got to the Downtown D.C. restaurant first and waited on Raspberry to arrive. She finally got there and they embraced each other with a hug.

"So I brought you here to talk to you about something I heard. And I wanted to know if it was true. Did you ask Melvin about me and my homie Francisco" ? Chaos asked.

"Yes I did, I was curious because I had heard both yall names in the wind. Can't remember where, but I was just curious as to who you both were" Raspberry replied.

Chaos just stared at Raspberry and Raspberry stared at him, he then responded. "So you mean to tell me after hearing our name in the wind so you say. You didn't remember who told you about us ? Hard to believe, but I will trust you're telling me the truth."

"Listen baby, does it even matter ? We're here now and we're happy, why let he say she say come between what we have. Let's move forward, just heard about you and was curious" Raspberry said coming closer to Chaos hugging him and kissing him.

They began to kiss and eventually have sex later that day back at Chaos place. That's usually how it was, Chaos couldn't resist Raspberry. Often times when men weren't happy with her, Raspberry would literally throw herself at them. Once again using her sex appeal to distract them so she could get what she wanted. It was no different this time. Chaos was very much into Raspberry and she knew it. But he also remembered what Melvin had told him. Regardless, it felt like Chaos couldn't stop himself from falling for Raspberry. Page 85

After a night of wild sex, the next morning Chaos and Raspberry lay cuddled in each others arms in Chaos huge king size bed.

"You know you was right about that bullshit with Melvin, it is he say she say. Can't believe I almost let myself get caught up in it" Chaos said as he kissed Raspberry's forehead.

"It's cool baby, it's only right you are skeptical about anyone at first. We've only been seeing each other for a little over a month now, so I understand" Raspberry replied.

Chaos always felt a calm mood and attitude when he was with Raspberry, it was one of the reasons he was so into her. She made situations that seemed stressful for him seem ok and not as bad as they seemed. Chaos was used to seeing a situation and acting on it, she made him think about things. He was naturally a angry and high energy intense person. That calm she had brought to his life did wonders for his overall being. And it didn't happen overnight, it took time and thought to have Chaos trust her and feel comfortable around her. Even though they were only dating for a little over a month, Chaos felt like he knew her all his life. It didn't seem long enough for him to have that type of trust in her, but he did.

It was the kind of relationship they were building, and Raspberry had to constantly remind herself that Chaos was the enemy. The same man that took her sister's life. It was something she battled with the whole time she dealing with Chaos. But her main focus was to keep her composure and stick to her plan. After having a great night with Chaos, Raspberry returned to College Park to her apartment to relax for a few hours before reporting to work at Melvins. It was another night that Raspberry and Isabella both were hitting the stage to a packed house as usual on the weekends. Raspberry was closing the show, she hadn't seen Melvin since Chaos had told her about what Melvin had said. So as she was walking from the dressing room downstairs through the hallway. And the stairs to the main stage, she seen Melvin walk towards her.

"Hello Raspberry, do what you do as always. It's a packed house and a lot of money to be made out there, I'm sure you gonna get it too."

"As always boss, thanks for your encouragement" Raspberry replied with a smirk on her face as she walked on stage.

Raspberry wasn't too happy that Melvin told Chaos that she had asked about him and Francisco. Especially when Raspberry asked Melvin if he knew them years prior, and he said no. She knew for the moment she had to take this one on the chin because Melvin was a necessary evil. He was apart of her cash flow, but she was definitely on notice for him. And getting tired of him in the process.

As soon as she walked on stage she decided to try something different this particular night. As the music dropped for her to dance she immediately went in the crowd and did her entire performance out in the crowd.

Chapter Five

"Business Never Personal"

It was something that Raspberry didn't do a whole lot, and something Melvin didn't necessarily like the women doing. Mainly because of their safety. Melvin just watched from a far and shook his head in disgust. It was personal because it was his responsibility to protect the dancers. But as far as business was concerned, it was a great night. An epic night. Raspberry had a twist to her performance that had the place on fire. And set yet another standard that she had already established before and no one could match. Also in attendance that night was Chaos, who had came from D.C. to see her. Isabella herself was in awe watching Raspberry, and seeing her defy Melvin's rules was something to see also. None of the women dare go against anything Melvin said, they all knew they were expendable. All except Raspberry. She knew the influence she had on Melvins Lounge, she knew that since she became the head dancer and emcee. Business was better than ever. Melvin was caught in a tight situation, he couldn't get rid of Raspberry if he really wanted to. It would hurt business tremendously, which would also hurt his pockets.

Instead Melvin would try to figure out another way to get Raspberry. He was suspicious of her and didn't trust her but dismissed it as a necessary evil for the moment. One thing he didn't want to do was ruin any potential earnings over something personal. Unless he had proof, which he didnt at the time. It was always about business with him, never personal. After an amazing night and performance from Raspberry. Isabella asked Raspberry out to breakfast to talk. Since they hadn't talked in a little while.

"I wanted to tell you how amazing that was the other night, and the fact you broke that rule Mami your dance was flawless" Isabella said sounding excited.

"Thank you, I don't know I just felt like doing something different. Really wasn't about no rule. I may work at Melvins, but when I dance I dance for me and mines. To put money in these pockets" Raspberry replied putting her hands on each thigh towards her pockets.

"Oh I feel you Mami, I do the same. I just know a lot of these women here are scared of Melvin. Including me. You had the guts to stand up to him and say I'm doing it my way, I admire you for that. That took heart and we all noticed it. But anyway I wanted to ask you how the Escort Service was going" ? Isabella asked.

"It's going as good as it could be, why are you asking ? You wanna work" ? Raspberry asked sounding curious.

"I was honestly thinking about it, I will get back to you and let you know" Isabella replied.

"You know you dont want to work. Talk to me when you're serious, you know I dont play no games with my money" Raspberry said.

Page 87

Raspberry never believed that Isabella really wanted to be back in the Escort Service business. She had complained many times before about doing something different, but never made the complete transition to become an escort. Plus she was real comfortable at Melvins with a good following. The Escort Service was no longer serving her, that was one of the main reasons Raspberry got her on at Melvins. She really liked Isabella, because as far as she knew Isabella was very loyal to her. But of late, she had been somewhat weary of Isabella. She knew she couldn't trust Melvin after what he did. Her and Melvin's relationship was strictly business. The other women at Melvins were not a threat at all to Raspberry personally or professionally, so in her mind they were never a factor. After being at Melvins for sometime now, Raspberry was still the main attraction. Something that she had been able to maintain since she had first arrived. Meanwhile Chaos had been dating Raspberry for a while and felt it was time for that trip he had promised her. So he decided to meet with her for lunch in College Park.

After meeting at a restaurant and being seated, Chaos began to tell Raspberry what he had planned as a surprise.

"I know you wondering why I called you down here, well I know you remember me saying I wanted to take you away on a trip. Well I got two tickets to Vegas for the weekend, beautiful five star hotel. We can take in a few shows, see Vegas and hit a couple clubs. Great time baby, let's just go. Leave all this shit behind, Melvin will be ok for a weekend without you" Chaos said.

Raspberry smiled and just looked at Chaos for a moment. "I've never missed a weekend and the money I will be missing" Raspberry said looking unsure.

Chaos interrupting. "If you worried about the money, I can take care of that. Just go with me, you never been to Vegas and said you wanted to go. The time is now baby, come on lets go. Life is short and you never know if we will ever get this opportunity again. I got your salary while your gone" Chaos said trying his best to convince Raspberry.

After sitting there for a few minutes thinking about it, Raspberry replied. "Ok I will go, I do really want to go to Vegas. And thank you for inviting me, should be fun" Raspberry said smiling.

"No need to thank me baby, this is what I always wanted us to do. And of course we're going to have a great time. You're special to me, and I want to show my appreciation for you" Chaos said.

They continued eating their lunch and talked more about their upcoming trip. Raspberry was excited to go on a trip, it had been a while. It would be weird not being at Melvins on the weekend, but on the other hand it would be nice to just get away for a while. She hadn't had a getaway since Malik and her went to Atlantic City for a weekend. Back when her and Malik were dating. It would be nice to get away from the everyday grind at Melvins, so she decided to take Chaos up on his offer. And she was excited about going.

Page 88

The flight to Las Vegas was nice. Raspberry and Chaos flew first class out of D.C. and landed in Vegas to their five star hotel at The Luxor. Raspberry had finally arrived in Vegas and was beyond excited.

"Saw so many pictures of this place, and I'm finally here" Raspberry said in awe.

"Yes baby we here, after we check in it's time to hit the strip and party" Chaos said sounding excited even though he had been to Vegas already a few times.

He was excited for Raspberry, excited her first time in Vegas was with him. And he would have fun giving her a tour and showing her around the city. Back in College Park Isabella was asked to fill in for Raspberry as head dancer and emcee for the weekend. But before she did that, Melvin wanted to talk to her. So as she sat in Melvin's office, he had that talk with her.

"So what's going on Isabella, you have no new information for me about this bitch" ? Melvin asked.

Isabella just stared at Melvin, and replied. "She really doesn't let me know too much about the Escort Service or anything else for that matter. Being that I'm no longer involved in it. But I did ask her to put me back on so I could get some information for you" Isabella said.

"You know my patience is weighing thin with you and your inability to follow the orders I gave you. It's simple shit you can't get done. You are around her more than anyone, and you don't know shit !!! Just get out of my office, and you don't have too much more time to get this shit done Isabella" !!! Melvin said angrily.

Isabella was upset and now was feeling the pressure of giving Melvin some type of information about Raspberry. He was forcing her hand and her back was against the wall, she didn't know what to do. Meanwhile Raspberry and Chaos were having a great time in Vegas, eating at some of the finest restaurants and partying at some of the hottest clubs in the city. Chaos spared no expense as he was spending money like it was nothing, and Raspberry enjoyed every minute of it. Chaos believed showing Raspberry a life with no limits of spending would further impress her about him. He was a partner in a drug empire with a childhood friend of his, the money was endless for them. They still had their operation in Baltimore and also had business all over D.C. Not to mention in Texas and California. Chaos was showing Raspberry just how much he liked her.

She was spoiled already, by not only Chaos but other men that wanted her attention. Raspberry had too much pride and independence to let a man spoil her too much, it wasn't something she wanted to get used to. So she kept the spoiling to a minimum, and was more concerned about how she could make more money creating business opportunities through Chaos. Just like she did with Tricky, and Malik before him. She gave him what he wanted from a woman's standpoint dealing with a man. Physically he was gone off of their sex life, they both were to a certain extent. Their chemistry was obvious. Page 89

And so the trip went on, fun filled days club hopping evenings and passionate late nights. By now it was Monday morning and they were flying back to Washington, D.C. Both happy that they had such a great time, they both were on cloud nine. But it was back to reality and back to Melvin's for Raspberry, but before she did that she met with Isabella to get caught up on things.

"So how was the trip Mami ? I know yall had a great time out there" Isabella said sitting down crossing her legs.

"It was nice, had a great time. Vegas was definitely off the chain, have to go again sometime soon" Raspberry replied.

"That's great, glad you had a great time. Anything else interesting happen while you were out there" ? Isabella asked. Raspberry just looked at Isabella and laughed a little.

"Like what ? You want to know about our sex and how it was ? How many positions he put me in ? Damn girl." Raspberry said as they both laughed.

"I'm sorry Mami, didn't mean to come off like that" Isabella replied.

"Anyway, enough about me. What's been going on at Melvins since I left" Raspberry asked.

"Same old same Mami, the people were wondering where you were. We told them you needed a break which you did. You didn't miss nothing Mami" Isabella replied.

Later that night, it was Raspberry's first night back and she was eager to get back on stage. As she came into the club Melvin was standing near the door when she came in.

"So how was your trip"? Melvin asked.

"It was nice, had a good time. Much needed getaway for sure. But now I'm back and have to get to work, excuse me" Raspberry replied walking past Melvin.

Melvin just watched as she walked right past him and he shook his head. Melvin knew he wasn't one of Raspberry's favorite people. But he also knew that they had to coexist for the sake of the business, and more importantly for both of their pockets. Raspberry was back, and no one enjoyed it more than the crowd at Melvins. They were happy to see her back where she belonged, and once she hit the stage the excitement was at a level it was when she had first hit the stage years ago at Melvins.

It was another great night at the club for Raspberry, as Isabella watched from backstage. Isabella was still in awe of all the love Raspberry got and how she controlled a crowd, it was something no matter how long she had danced she could never do fully. Isabella developed a nice following but didnt have the effect Raspberry had on the crowd. It was something she had never seen from any of the other women except Raspberry, she herself even tried to mimic her and still didn't have the effect she did on the crowd. That's when Isabella realized Raspberry was just that good.

It didn't matter to Raspberry about the lost lives, to her those people were in the way of her rise and they had to go. She had a keen sense on when and what to do to her victims, even the timing of their demise. Chaos told Raspberry he was going to be out of town on business for a few days, so she could concentrate on herself and do what she had to do. And that's exactly what she did. Going all in at Melvins and at her Escort Service. She was now down to two women for her Escort Service. One of the women decided she wanted to do something else with her life. The opportunity for Isabella to land a spot was now on the table, the opportunity that Isabella was waiting for. So it was only natural for Raspberry to offer it to her most trusted female companion. Raspberry never really discussed anything about her Escort Service to Melvin, only that it existed. All he knew was she had a few women working for her, and that's all he needed to know.

She only told Melvin about her Escort Service in the first place, to make a deal with him for putting Isabella on. She never really talked about her personal life to Melvin, but she did mention some things to Simone. Who she later found out was closer to Melvin than she originally thought. So being how Simone and Melvin were close, he could've knew more than he was leading on. She did tell Simone that she was from Baltimore, never mentioned much about her sister to Simone. Although Simone knew that her sister was murdered, she didn't know the full details. Her roommate Candice which was Simone's cousin, Candice knew a good bit about Raspberry's personal life. And right before she killed Tricky, he mentioned some things about Raspberry's life she hadn't told him. So she decided to meet up with Candice, that's if she could find her. They hadn't been as close since Raspberry left school, they seen each other on and off over the years. And now Raspberry was searching for her old roommate to get an explanation as to how Tricky knew the things he mentioned before Raspberry killed him.

So Raspberry decided to drive around campus hoping to see Candice, she looked for about fifteen minutes before she seen a female that looked like Candice. She hadn't seen her in a while so she wasn't too sure if it was her or not. As she drove closer the female turned around, and just as she thought, it was Candice.

"Hey Candice how you been"? Raspberry asked.

Candice looked for a minute and replied, "Desiree" ?

"Yeah it's me girl, it's been a while" Raspberry said.

"Wow...yes it has been. I haven't seen you in like six to seven months. I haven't been to Melvin's since Simone was killed, reminds me too much of her" Candice said looking off into the distance.

Page 91

"I can understand that, and I'm sure you miss Simone. I know I do, she was the one that gave me my start. Thanks to you too" Raspberry replied.

"You know they still haven't found her killer, it's been over two years now" Candice said sounding disappointed.

"Yeah that's ashame, let's hope some day they do. I can only imagine how hard its been on your family, but I'm sure they will eventually find who did it. Anyway I came here to ask you how did you know Tricky ? And how did my name come up in yall conversation" ? Raspberry asked.

"Tricky is dead aint he ? I heard he got murdered in his own house. I knew Tricky from coming to Melvin's before, back when Simone first started. We talked here and there and eventually became friends. So this one night he was asking me about what was going on at Melvins lately, I had saw him somewhere I can't remember. And he asked me if they were any new dancers, I said yeah there was. That was a little while after you started. I mentioned you and told him how you was my roommate and you were looking to come up. He asked me about you, and I just told him a few things about you. Where you were from and so on" Candice replied.

"I was just wondering because he knew about my sister. And you know I don't talk about my sister to too many people. I only told you because you were my roommate at the time and the only person I could talk to" Raspberry said not sounding too happy.

"I understand, and I'm sorry if I did anything wrong. I was sad to hear about Tricky being murdered, and at his own house too. Just sad" Candice said.

"Yes very unfortunate, he was a good dude. But you know the game he was in, that was bound to happen sooner than later......sorry to say" Raspberry replied.

"Did you and Tricky have a thing or something"? Candice asked.

"No I just knew him from the club. A few lap dances and short conversation. Nothing major, but he never mentioned that he knew anything about me until one night we were together" Raspberry replied.

They talked a little while longer, reminiscing about the times they had when they were roommates. It was a good time. Seeing Candice after so long and getting a situation straight that had Raspberry puzzled since she had killed Tricky. She also knew after that day to keep Candice at a distance. And to continue to keep her personal business to herself. She was just hoping that Candice didn't tell Simone any of what she told Tricky. The reason why ? Because if Candice told Simone, nine times outta ten Melvin knows. In which Melvin could tell Chaos, which would completely destroy Raspberry's plans for Chaos.

She had to be even more careful from here on out, and she had to somehow find out just what Melvin did know. She figured since Chaos hadn't said anything to her, that he must not know. Although he could be holding on to it to get her set up. Page 92

It had been a little while since she had a moment like this thinking about her sister, it wasn't the first time and sure wouldn't be the last. Each time she had her moment, she got herself back together and focused on what she had to do. It was the story of her life since she was young. Dealing with what she had to deal with at home growing up with her father being demanding as he was. Speaking of her father, she hadn't heard from him in a long time. A little after her sister passed. He had felt guilty for what happened to Deanna's death. So much so that he had completely disconnected himself from his estranged wife and daughter. Raspberry never got any calls from him, she didn't know where he was. Neither did her mother. Raspberry herself never let it bother her, she was independent from the time she stepped on campus and never looked back. She could deal with not speaking to her father, especially this long. But deep down inside it still bothered her. It reflected on the relationships she had with men moving forward in her life. First with Ricky, then with Malik. Followed by Tricky and most recently Chaos. She was definitely more concerned with business when it came to Chaos. She was just being patient and waiting for her opportunity to get her ultimate revenge. She used men to satisfy her needs and get what she wanted. And if a few women got in her way they were casualties also. Ask Simone.

She hadn't been to the range in a while so she decided to go and get some work in. Raspberry had somewhat of an obsession with being a marksman. She had been so busy running around with Chaos and being at Melvins she lost focus on herself and what she enjoyed to do when she wasn't on stage. The days without Chaos did her good, the break was refreshing and she got back to business. She asked Isabella to be apart of her Escort Service again, giving her some extra work like she wanted. Isabella was happy to be in the mix again, now she could get what information she needed to give to Melvin. And she couldn't wait to let him know. Isabella stopped by the club on an off day to see Melvin. As she walked in his office he had his back to her looking toward the stage.

"You're here so I'm assuming you have something for me, don't you Isabella"? Melvin asked as he turned around.

"Yeah I do, I mean I have something. Raspberry put me back on at the Escort Service, so I should be able to get more information now" Isabella replied.

"So that's all you got"? !!! Melvin shouted.

"I mean it's a start isn't it ? I can get deep inside that part of her business and find some things out for you. Raspberry trusts me, please just let me prove I can do this for you" Isabella said.

Melvin stood up from his chair and walked over towards Isabella and whispered in her ear.

"You better show and prove, because if you dont you're finished." Melvin said.

Isabella slowly and quietly got up and walked out of Melvin's office. She always feared Melvin, and now she knew what she had to do and she had to do it fast. She knew Melvin meant business, and he was very serious about what he wanted. Page 93

Meanwhile Chaos had returned from his trip on business and as soon as he got settled in, he called Raspberry.

"Hey baby, I'm back in town. You get a chance to get caught up on your business" ? Chaos asked.

"Yes I did, how was the trip and is everything ok with business" ? Raspberry replied.

"The trip went well, and you know I don't talk business with my lady. But let's just say things are good" Chaos said as he winked his eye and smiled.

That was something Chaos and Francisco rarely did. Was to discuss any of their business with anyone but themselves. And partially to their workers. So to no surprise, Chaos kept his mouth shut. As much as Isabella wanted more information on Raspberry for Melvin, Raspberry wanted the same from Chaos. It was a cat and mouse game, and was sure to only get even more interesting as it continued to go on. Another day had came and another night was upon Raspberry as she was to be strictly the emcee and Isabella was on center stage tonight.

Chaos was also in the building this night, he knew Raspberry wasn't performing but he hadn't been to Melvin's in a little while. So as he came in Melvin's he was immediately escorted to the V.I.P. section and he was given a bottle of Champagne. As he was sitting over there enjoying the music and women dancing, Melvin strolled over to his table.

"Hey Chaos, what's going on ? Welcome back to Melvin's, you get your bottle" ? Melvin said sitting down.

"Melvin, what's crackin ? And yeah I got my bottle, thanks" Chaos replied.

"I wanted to talk to you about something" Melvin said to Chaos.

"Whats up" ? Chaos replied.

"How serious is your situation with Raspberry"? Melvin asked.

Chaos just paused for a second and replied. "Nigga why you keep asking me about me and Raspberry's relationship ? You trying to holla at her or something" ?

"No man, she works for me and isn't my type. I know she deals with you. Listen man, be careful. I don't fully trust her and have been suspicious of her for quite some time. I'm not hating, just making sure you're good. Remember she was asking about you and Francisco, she may have something up her sleeve. Im just looking out homie. Have fun and a good time whatever you're doing with her, just be careful" Melvin said getting up from the table.

"Suspicious of her in what kind of way man" ? Chaos asked.

"I think she has some information about who killed two people I was cool with. Simone and Tricky" Melvin replied.

"What makes you think some shit like that? The woman is harmless as far as I know" Chaos said.

"Just be careful man" Melvin replied before walking away.

Isabella had made a great impression on the crowd since starting at Melvins, but she never made the impact Raspberry made. That in part drove her to be the best dancer she could be. But she always felt like she was in Raspberry's shadow. So on this night, Isabella decided to do something different herself. Isabella pulled a man out of the crowd and put a chair on stage and told him to sit in it. After the man was seated in the chair, Isabella began giving him a private lap dance right on stage. One so intense and sexy that it drove the crowd crazy. She was flawless and sexy, Chaos amongst those in the crowd watched as her beautiful body moved across the stage. The man she gave the lap dance to was beyond excited. Raspberry looked on from backstage and just smiled, she loved it. The fact Isabella had stepped her game up, made things a little more interesting. She saw that Isabella had learned something from her legendary spot on stage. It was like a momma bear watching her baby bear come in to her own.

Coming off stage Isabella walked passed Raspberry.

"Did you like that Mami" ? She asked.

"Impressive, very impressive. I loved it" Raspberry replied smiling.

They had that type of relationship. They both knew they were the money makers at Melvins and the crowd loved them both. But they were also two people going in two different directions, and Isabella had a lot of pressure on her. She had to get information about Raspberry that could be used against her. In order to find out who may have killed Simone and Tricky. It was a favor asked by Melvin, it was crucial that it got done. Plus there was a potential reward in it for Isabella. She could do what Raspberry did to Simone by getting rid of her and claiming that head dancer spot. It was something she thought about. And then there was her loyalty to Raspberry. The person that put her on at Melvins, and also a person she feared after seeing what she was capable of. She was still torn, but she knew she had to do something soon.

After Isabella's set, Raspberry went up to V.I.P. to see Chaos.

"There she is, what's up baby" ? Chaos said clearly drunk after go through bottle after bottle since he had first arrived.

"Looks like you are up, been drinking heavy tonight huh" ? Raspberry replied.

"Why not, I'm paid. My homie Melvin always takes care of me when I come through here. It's a great time whenever I come through. But you know what ? Your girl.....that Spanish chick. She bad" Chaos said as he sat slouched down in the V.I.P. couch.

Raspberry just smiled and replied. "I'm glad you enjoyed yourself."

The next morning Raspberry got a call from her mother, she knew something was wrong by the time of the call being so early. And by the sound of her voice.

"Desiree I have some terrible news, your father had a massive heart attack and died. Where ever he was living at in East Baltimore, they found him early this morning that's why I'm calling you now. You have to come home baby" Raspberry's mother Denise said crying over the phone.

Raspberry was speechless for about a minute before she replied, "Ok mother, I'll be home."

Hearing her mother distraught did something to Raspberry. She felt bad, really bad. Although her father had eventually left her mother. He stood by her in some of her worst years throughout a twenty seven year marriage. She didn't have the relationship with her father that she would have liked, but deep in her heart she still loved him. And her mother Denise still loved him also. That was obvious. Denise needed her daughter home with her, she was really going through it. Raspberry immediately called Melvin and told him, but she also told Melvin not to tell anyone else about her father.

He agreed and Raspberry was off to Baltimore, on her way home again. The drive home she had time to reflect on her father's life, his relationship with both her and her sister. And his relationship with their mother. She thought about the few good times her and her father had, the good times they had as a family when her mother was home. When he would take her and Deanna to the park to play. The carnivals he took her and her sister to when their mother was away. She shed tears, her and her father's relationship hadn't been good over the last few years. Ever since her sister was murdered, her family hadn't been the same. After the little over an hour drive, Raspberry was finally home as she arrived at the apartment she had gotten for her mother.

"Desiree baby, you're home" Denise said embracing her daughter as she came in the door.

"Hello mother, it's good to be home" Raspberry said as she sat down on her mother's couch.

"Look I know you and your father didn't have the greatest relationship in these last few years, but he loved you. The few times I did talk to him over these last few years, he would always ask about you. How you were doing in school. He just felt really guilty after Deanna died, he thought you hated him" Denise said.

"Mom I know my father loved me. On the way down here I got some time to think and I forgave him for all that he did to us. I really did" Raspberry replied.

"I'm glad you did, because he loved you girls. Both of you very much. And I know he loved me, despite our ups and downs. Our marriage had some good years" Denise said.

As much as Raspberry resented her father for all the things he did in the past, she now missed the good things about him. And all the good he did for her and her sister. She had come to terms with it and finally forgave him. She decided to take her father's advice, the same advice he gave the family just about four years prior when Deanna was killed. Page 96

Try to stay positive and always remember the good memories. As usual there were people who knew Robert Knight that came by Denise's apartment to pay their respects to the family. Although Robert and Denise were seperated, they never officially got a divorce. They had talked about it, but never officially did it. So Denise was still in charge and power of attorney over Robert's estate. Robert Knight was living with a girlfriend, while she was at work he had a massive heart attack. And was found by a neighbor and good friend. After hosting people at her apartment, Denise and her oldest daughter Desiree started to plan Robert's funeral. The same task Denise performed just over four years ago for her youngest daughter Deanna. Raspberry did what she could to help support her mother and get them both through this difficult time. Denise also had her own sister Angela help her with some things. She lived not too far away from her. Meanwhile back in College Park Isabella was getting prepared to once again fill in for Raspberry. She was more than capable and ready to do whatever she had to do. She felt like this was her chance to get her feet wet and prepare for what she envisioned as her future. She was more than ready to take over the reigns from Raspberry for good.

It was another night at Melvins and almost showtime as Isabella came into the dressing room and some of the other dancers were downstairs too. But before she got dressed, Melvin came downstairs in which he doesn't do much and instructed everyone out of the dressing room but Isabella. After the women left, Melvin came towards Isabella and told her to sit down as he did also.

"So now is your time to shine, you must make the most of this opportunity. You could be my future head dancer and emcee" Melvin said looking at Isabella.

"This isn't the first time I stepped in for Raspberry, I got this Papi" Isabella replied.

"That's good to know. And oh yeah, here's a little added incentive. If you get the information I need you to get on her, and she goes down for one of these murders. Then it's your show. You take her spot, I promise you that" Melvin said taking a sip of his drink.

"So you're thinking about the possibility of her not being here anymore ? I mean that's just crazy to think about, the impact she has on this crowd" Isabella said.

"Listen, I ain't ask you that. I'm saying that the shit can happen and you need to be ready to step up if you want that spot" Melvin said angrily.

At that point Isabella knew the seriousness of the situation, Melvin really wanted Raspberry's head. But right now she couldn't spend too much time thinking about it, she had a crowd to control and keep happy without the bar's biggest star. She had done it before, but tonight had more riding on it. With Melvin letting her know that she could take Raspberry's spot. He saw an opportunity and like Melvin said, she was going to make the most of it. She had a quiet confidence about her. She was a little nervous despite doing this before. It was a packed house and Melvin believed in her. Would the crowd ask for Raspberry? And disregard her ? She didn't think so. And stepped

on stage with her confidence at an all time high.
Page 97

From the time Isabella stepped on stage she commanded the crowd like it was her own. As Melvin stood off to the side of the stage with a smile on his face. Instead of her opening up the show by introducing the first dancer, she decided to open up the show herself by taking off the shirt and short mini skirt she had on. Which exposed her thick thighs and ass down to her sexy boy shorts. The crowd although surprised, loved every minute of it. The crowd didn't know in the beginning of the evening if Raspberry would be in attendance or not. Because no one had even seen her come in. But they knew Isabella was performing so most of the regulars were there. It was still a good crowd and Isabella shined like she was supposed to. Much to the delight of Melvin who was eating it all up. He was telling anyone who would listen that Isabella was his protégé and the next big thing. Something that was very risky being that the fact Raspberry was the real person who brought Isabella to Melvin. Melvin didn't care, he saw blood in the water and he was ready to attack.

He was feeling himself and he was at odds with Raspberry so he did it out of spitefulness. Much to the surprise of some of the crowd who never seen Melvin like that before. Melvin was a little drunk and definitely not his business minded focused self. As two of his bouncers helped him up to his office. Isabella was definitely in charge of things now as she watched Melvin from up on stage. This was her moment to show and prove her leadership. She had no other choice, so she ran with it and controlled the show for most of night. After a challenging night, Isabella was mentally and physically spent. She had survived her toughest night at Melvins without Raspberry and essentially without Melvin. And she did well, very well. Back in Baltimore Raspberry and her mother had put the final plans in place for her father's funeral. The funeral was the next day and Raspberry had a lot of thoughts going through her mind, and a lot of emotions flowed. She loved her father, and even though their relationship wasn't like it once was when she was younger. She was still going to miss him very much.

The funeral was here and Raspberry and her mother slowly walked in the funeral home where her father's funeral was. Amongst some family members and friends. Raspberry seeing her father laying in his casket was the first time she had seen him in over two years. And the last time she seen him it was from a distance and she didn't get to speak to him. It was definitely a moment that she would never forget for the rest of her life. She tried her best to remain strong for her mother who was taking her father's death pretty hard. After a moving service and a lot of love and support from family and friends. The day ended with Raspberry at home with her mother. She got through yet another loss of a loved one. A loved one of her immediate family which definitely made it tougher.

The next morning Raspberry was on her way back to College Park with a renewed focus and ready to get back to work. A lot of things had transpired since Raspberry left for her father's funeral and she had no idea what happened at Melvins while she was gone. Even though some things had happened, the people involved didn't really want to tell Raspberry what was going on. And more importantly what had happened while she was gone. Melvin went on a drunken binge and endorsed Isabella as his own new star in the making. Isabella took the show and made it her own. Something she said she would never do out of respect for Raspberry putting her on. So Raspberry returned to College Park and Melvins, along with her Escort Service. And hit the ground running. Isabella was anxious to let Raspberry know about how she moved the crowd, and she was also anxious to tell her about the way Melvin acted.

So while Raspberry was home after returning from Baltimore she got a phone call from Isabella.

"Hey Mami, didn't know why you took a leave of absence but glad you're back. Is everything ok"? Isabella asked.

"Hello Isabella, my father passed away that's why I was gone. Had to go back home to bury him" Raspberry replied.

"Oh I'm so sorry Mami, I lost my father when I was ten so I know what you're feeling. Is there anything I can do"? Isabella said.

"No I'm fine, thank you. So how has things been at Melvins since I left"? Raspberry asked.

There it was. Before she could lead into the conversation about Melvins, Raspberry had already done it for her.

"Well things went well. Melvin got drunk and a few of the bouncers had to take him up to his office. I had a great night though, they loved my set and Melvin.....he........was telling people I was his future star and head dancer" Isabella said sounding guilty.

"Oh really? That's news to me, never knew he was replacing me. I will have to talk to Melvin about that. But I am glad you did well and they loved your set. Isabella I always want you to win, because when you win I win. Its Melvin that has it out for me, I have been aware of this for some time now. But you just keep doing you girl, I can handle myself. Anything else interesting happen in this eventful weekend" ? Raspberry replied.

"No that's pretty much it, I just wanted to tell you before anyone else would. Since I was in the middle of it, I felt you should hear it from me first" Isabella said feeling relieved she had finally told her.

She felt a lot better after getting what she needed off her chest and being honest with Raspberry. And she defintely knew Raspberry could handle herself. She seen what she did to Shameek, and how flawless she was at handling a gun.

So in essence Isabella felt she was doing the right thing by telling Raspberry what really happened while she was gone. Of course that wasn't enough for Raspberry as she wanted to hear it from the horse's mouth himself Melvin. So she decided to go straight to

Melvin's office to see how things were between them currently. Even though she knew, she wanted to check the tempature so to speak. So as Melvin sat at his desk there was a knock at the door.

"Who is it" ? Melvin asked.

"It's me Raspberry" Raspberry said.

"Come in, what's going on" ? Melvin asked puffing on a cigar as Raspberry entered his office.

"I heard things were interesting while I was gone. And that you may have a new emcee and head dancer on the horizon. I thought maybe I would have been notified about this rather than hear it from someone else" Raspberry said.

"Hold on, I never said that there was going to be a new emcee and head dancer. I told Isabella she has the potential to be in that position, she does very well in place of you. She could hold shit down if she needed to and the business doesn't lose a step" Melvin replied.

Raspberry really had no reply for that, she just sat there for a moment staring at Melvin. And then said "Look Melvin, I know lately we haven't been getting along as well as before but I do my job well and I would hope you wouldn't be replacing me anytime soon. And about Isabella, we both know I brought her here to you just like Candice brought me to Simone. But see Simone took the credit for it, something she never really did. And then she got mad when I brought Isabella on, see the trend and jealousy. Melvin I never took you for a jealous and envious person, so let's keep it professional from now on. If you have an issue with me and would like to replace me. Just let me know first before my co workers."

"No let me tell you something, if I DO decide to replace you. And you can be replaced. Hell any of you women can be replaced, just know that I WILL let you know" Melvin replied.

"Don't be so sure of that Melvin, those men out there and some women from time to time. They don't come to see you. They come to see ass and titties, you have neither. But this is your place and you are the man so I will leave it at that" Raspberry replied leaving Melvin's office.

It was an interesting conversation between the two of them. Raspberry as usual using her wit to be respectful but still getting her point across. Melvin was obviously growing tired of Raspberry, and the fact she knew she had power at Melvins. According to the crowd that packed there every weekend. Melvin let anyone who worked for him always know he was the boss and he called the shots. With anything that had to do with his bar, he was to be notified first. Which was only right. Even to his most valued employees, he never wavered from his stance as the man. The women respected him, but not necessarily liked him. They made their money and his spot was the place to be in the area

Raspberry knew what she had to do now, it was already in her mind after talking to Melvin this last time. Melvin was somewhat of a bully around his place of business, a lot of the women were terrified to ask him a thing. What he said went and his word was bond, naturally how it should be if you own your own place. But his style was a little more to the extreme, he had instances where he screamed on some of his dancers for whatever reason. He had a strong personality and it was obvious from the time you started talking to him. But Raspberry was the only one who challenged Melvin's authority. So Raspberry would work around that, she had a plan in place for Melvin and the situation at hand. She remembered that her cousin Shameek had a right hand man that went by the street name "Blade" because he specialized in cutting and chopping people up. Shameek had spoke a little about him when Raspberry had brought the heroin for Shameek to sell. She had only seen "Blade" once before in person, and didnt know him too well. But she was thinking about getting to know him now.

But before she did that, she had to get in touch with Chaos. Who had became somewhat distant since Raspberry said she had to go back home. Raspberry never told Chaos where she was from, so he couldn't never tie her and Deanna together as sisters. Well she didnt necessarily tell him the truth about where she was from. She told him she was from Annapolis. So later that day she called him. Chaos was at home in his Northwest D.C. condo when the phone rang.

"Well hello there, did you forget about me"? Raspberry asked.

"Of course not beautiful, I let you do what you had to do and wasn't going to interrupt. I was handling business as usual, and I need to fly to Miami in two days" Chaos replied.

"Oh ok, I thought maybe we would spend some time, but thats fine" Raspberry said sounding somewhat disappointed.

"Don't worry beautiful, as soon as I get back I'm all yours. Only going to be down there for a few days on business, but I promise it's all about you when I get back. I'll bring you something back too" Chaos said.

"That would be nice, thank you" Raspberry replied.

While Chaos was handling business in Miami, Raspberry decided she would go back home to Baltimore and see if she could find "Blade". But she had to do it on her day off, because she had just came back from Baltimore burying her father. Ironically enough when she saw her schedule the next day, Melvin didn't schedule her off at all. Raspberry kind of figured that would happen. Her being gone for her father's funeral and all, but she thought that Melvin would at least give her the benefit of the doubt. She was wrong, so she would postpone that trip for another time.

In the meantime she just continued concentrating on being the best dancer she could be. While co-existing with a boss that wanted her head on a silver platter. It was another night and Raspberry was scheduled to work all week and the entire weekend. It had been a while since she had such a workload at Melvins, but she was game to do what she had to do. The good part about such a workload is the money that came with it. And anybody knew Raspberry knew she was all about her money. Isabella was on also, but not as much as Raspberry this particular week. The crowd was eager to see Raspberry since she had been gone for a little while. And she was excited about getting back on stage again. The first night back Melvin of course made her the headliner as Isabella went on right before her. So even though Melvin didn't get along with Raspberry, he knew deep down who his moneymaker was. So he stuck with the formula that made Melvins one of the hottest bars in the state of Maryland. He co-existed with her for the sake of business.

A packed house as usual, the weekend was here and Raspberry couldn't be any happier. She took to the stage with a focus seldomly seen as she was prepared to take her spot back. After her protégé Isabella had blew the roof off the place just a weekend ago. The crowd loved seeing Raspberry back at Melvins. She made the most of her set as she usually did and stepped off stage to a standing ovation. And a lot of money across the floor she was dancing on. Afterwards she went over to the bar and had a drink as regulars and other customers alike came over to greet her. And welcome her back after her little hiatus. It felt good to feel the love from the crowd at Melvins again, that she had sorely missed since being gone. It put a good bit of the pain she felt from losing her father towards the back of her mind. The whole situation let her focus more on the positives in her life. Being that now her father was gone she would keep more in touch with her mother. Instead of maybe calling twice a week. She now would call maybe three to four times a week. Her mother was alone in her apartment even though her Aunt Angela lived close by. She asked her Aunt Angela to check up on her mother from time to time.

Like her, her mother was still in the healing process since losing her husband. Before Raspberry had to go in that Saturday evening at Melvins, she called her mother to see how she was after not talking to her for a few days since she left to come back to College Park.

"Hello mother, how's everything going" ? Raspberry asked.

"Hey baby, everything is going as good as it can I guess. You know even though me and your father had been seperated for quite some time before he died. I really miss him. His presence. He would call me from time to time, even though he was with her. He was scared to call you. Can you believe that YOUR FATHER was scared to call YOU ? I know me either. But he was, and I guess he could never truly face you. Which is sad. But I'm glad you're doing fine up there" Denise replied.

At that point tears flowed down Raspberry's face as she tried to keep it together, she weeped and paused before she replied. "Mother I never hated him, we all had our ups and downs but I loved my father. I told you that. He was there for me and Deanna while you were away. I never forgot that despite the fact that he changed and eventually left you. And I don't blame him for Deanna's death. She was going to do what she wanted regardless, she didn't listen to any of us. But that was who she was. Like dad was who he was, and I know who my father was. It took me a while to realize that".

"You know that's the first time I heard you open up about the both of them since their deaths. But I'm glad you did, it's apart of the healing process. I want you to continue to take care of yourself, and call me if you need me baby" Denise said.

"Mother I will be fine, don't worry about me. And I will call you a little later this week. And if you need me call me. Love you always mother" Raspberry replied.

"Love you too baby, take care" Denise said hanging up the phone.

That next week rolled around and Raspberry found herself off for a couple of days during the week. So she decided to take the drive back home to Baltimore in search of Shameek's right hand man "Blade". But first she had to check with her two girls who were working the Escort Service, Isabella was also doing it part time. Things were somewhat slow with the Escort Service. And Raspberry didn't have the time to figure out why because she needed to get to Baltimore to find "Blade". So she just decided to handle that situation when she got back. On the ride to Baltimore like most times, Raspberry thought of her sister. But this time she not only thought of her sister but also her father. The ride is only a little over an hour, it seemed long to her when she was in her thought process. She arrived in Baltimore and drove around spots she had remembered where Shameek's crew had hung out. She rode around to several spots with no luck, a half an hour later still riding when she pulled up to this one spot and seen a few dudes that looked familiar. She parked and got out her car and walked towards a group of guys.

"Whats up yall, yall know where Blade is" ? she asked.

A tall dude out of the group stepped forward and replied, "Who the fuck wanna know" ?

"Are you Blade? I'm Desiree, Shameek's cousin" Raspberry said. The man just stood there looking at Raspberry for about a minute.

"Shameek is dead, what do you want with me" ? Blade asked.

"I know he's dead, he was my cousin. But I might have some information about his murder, that's why I'm here" Raspberry said.

"What information do you have ? And if you do, why you wait this long? It's been over a year now" Blade replied.

"I was terrified to tell anybody what I knew, I didnt want the killer to come after me" Raspberry said.

"Yeah I guess. You lucky you Shameek's family coming over here like this. What information do you have for me about the killer"? Blade asked.

"Well first of all, whatever you plan to do my name must not ever come up in this information I'm giving you. I want nothing to do with it, but I can help you set a situation up because I know this dude and his schedule" Raspberry replied.

"Listen, I don't need your help serving street justice sweetheart. I been doing this shit for years. All I need to know is who this muthafucka is and where he be at" Blade said.

"I don't doubt that you do, I'm just trying to help you do it and get away with it. Does that sound like something you're interested in" ? Raspberry asked.

"Of course I am, that was my homie that clown killed" Blade replied.

Raspberry exchanged numbers with Blade and told him she would be in touch, but she never told Blade who the killer actually was. In fear of Blade finding him and doing the job before Raspberry had planned for him to. So she decided to hold off until she put her other plan into action.

"I will be looking to hear from you real soon, don't keep me waiting too long....you hear" ? Blade said before Raspberry left.

"I won't, give me no more than a week" Raspberry replied.

She was on her way back to College Park and happy that she had found Blade. She was fortunate to remember where Shameek's people hung out at. It remained the same even after Shameek was murdered. Blade and a few of Shameek's soldiers looked all over the city for the Spanish chick Shameek was last with before he was murdered. They never found her. They hardly even knew what she looked like because Shameek didnt bring her around his crew much. He kept his personal and business life seperate. They almost went into an all out war with this other crew they suspected killed Shameek. But now with the help of Desiree, Shameek's cousin. They had a chance to locate Shameek's killer and get revenge after all. Raspberry was great at convincing people to buy into what she was selling. And her mind took you to a whole other level of thinking. After getting back in town, she called Chaos to come out to Melvins later that night to watch her perform. Chaos agreed to come so they could spend some time.

It was Friday night, and as usual the weekends were the busiest times at Melvins. Chaos upon entering was escorted to the V.I.P. section as always when he came to Melvins. A few bottles to start as he watched the dancers. Isabella and Raspberry hit the stage. First to hit the stage was Raspberry and she danced her sexy ass to the banging beats. As she danced she stared directly at Chaos.

The next day had arrived and Raspberry found herself in Chaos arms in his bed at his D.C. condo. Still unsure how they got there, they both had gotten drunk and were unable to drive home. So as Raspberry woke up, she woke Chaos up.

"How did we get home last night"? she asked feeling confused.

Waking up while yawning and stretching Chaos replied, "I got a car service to bring us home, I was tore up and I believe you was too. I hardly remember too much about last night."

"Wow, I never really got this drunk before, what was I thinking" Raspberry replied sitting up in the bed.

"Well there's a first time for everything, and we had a good time last night. And now we can have an even better morning" Chaos replied getting closer to Raspberry while kissing and hugging on her.

"Hold up, not right now. I have something to talk to you about. I always wondered what would happen if something happened to Melvin, would we be out of a job ? Would the club close? So I thought about running this by you. You ever have interest in owning a club"? Raspberry asked.

"No never thought about owning no club, not my thing" Chaos replied.

"It was just a suggestion, the club is a cash cow and Melvin makes a killing. So just imagine if you buy into it, and something happens to Melvin you take over. Just at least think about it, if anyone knows I do. I've been working there for a few years now to know how much money flows through there" Raspberry said.

Chaos just stared off into space, but Raspberry could tell he was thinking about it. And that's all she could ask for. After that talk, Raspberry had things she had to do so Chaos had a car service take them both back to the club to get their cars. It was an interesting night, and Raspberry for the first time ever lost control and drank way too much. It was something she never really did after seeing what alcohol at times did to her father. She was very surprised she let herself get to that point, it was a lesson to be learned moving forward. She had lost focus for a night, but vowed it would never happen again.

After driving home she decided to call Blade to check in with him about her plans and the information she was providing to him.

"Blade what's going on its Desiree. I just wanted to let you know I was being real when I told you what I told you. It's just going to take a little more time then what I thought. The information is from a reliable source who wants nothing to do with it and fears for their life. So I will keep in touch with you when I get any more information" Raspberry said.

"You better get this information soon, I don't like to sit and wait to handle what I have to handle. My homie Shameek deserves justice for the way he died.
Page 105

"No need to trip, I will have the information you need. You have my word" Raspberry replied.

Raspberry knew she needed to speed the process up, and she couldn't count on Chaos being ready to step in and take the club off Melvin's hands. Like she had planned. Chaos wasn't interested in owning a club. But she had to make this happen soon....real soon. Either way, she felt Melvin could be strong armed by the right people. At first she thought that right person was Chaos. And if not him, then definitely Blade. But she wanted to stick to her plan, and if it worked out it would benefit her and whoever did the strong arming the most. Her plan was to ask Chaos one more time before she went back to Blade. So she decided to meet with Chaos at a Washington, D.C.

restaurant. When she got there Chaos was already seated waiting for her, he got up once she arrived at the table and greeted her with a hug and kiss.

"So you sure you don't want to ever own a club ? I see the money that Melvin brings in, the investment could be huge for you in return. I see an opportunity for the both of us" Raspberry said as she took a sip of her drink.

"I told you, its not my thing. I don't know shit about running no club. And don't really want to. I hustle, and I'm the muscle. That's what I do" Chaos replied.

"Well look at it like this, you may not have to actually run it. And the return on the investment would be lovely. Imagine throwing parties there and holding down your area of V.I.P. with all your people's in there. And women everywhere" Raspberry said trying to convince Chaos to go for it.

"And let me guess, you're going to be the one that helps me with that" Chaos replied.

"I could if you let me, listen I wouldn't bring this to you without any plan of making you richer. Or if I wasnt serious, I know you're about your business and I'm offering you an opportunity here" Raspberry said. "

"Does Melvin have plans of getting out of the club business ? And does he know that you're shoppimg his club out here like this ? I'm just curious" Chaos asked.

"No he doesn't. I'm not even thinking about Melvin right now. I think he can be convinced to sell, if need be" Raspberry replied.

"For now I will say I will pass on that. Plus me and Melvin cool. And aint no way that man is going to sell that club. Its his life. I don't want the money and business to fuck up the friendship we have already" Chaos said.

Raspberry knew at that point she had to go in another direction, she was surprised Chaos would turn down such a potentially lucrative deal. She also knew now he cool Chaos and Melvin were. And was she worried about Chaos going back and telling Melvin ? No not really, because she kind of had Melvin and Chaos by the balls. Melvin needed her to make money, and Chaos was head over hills for her.
Page 106

A few days later she was back on the road to her hometown of Baltimore. She was planning to meet Blade at a Baltimore restaurant. She had everything planned out to how she was going to use Blade to take over Melvin's bar. After trying to do the same with Chaos, the second time let her know that he wasnt down with her plan. She knew that Blade wanted revenge for Shameek's murder badly, him and his goons tore the city of Baltimore upside down searching for his killer. And more importantly searching for the Latin female who was with Shameek the night he was killed. Raspberry quickly took the focus off of her protégé Isabella and onto Melvin. As they sat eating crab cakes, a Baltimore favorite.

"Hey what's up Blade, let's get down to business" Raspberry said as they both were enjoying the food.

"Shit.... hold on. Before we get started I just got the chance to notice how fine your ass is. Damn baby !! I should've asked Shameek to hook me up with you. When I seen you the first time, I was just bugged out how you came up on us. But I'm seeing now how good you look. I bet you have a man now.... huh" ? Blade said looking at Raspberry up and down.

Raspberry just smiled and replied. "Thank you, and yes I have a man. So now can we get down to business" ?

"Of course beautiful, whatever you want to do" Blade replied.

"Ok so this dude that murdered my cousin Shameek owns a club in College Park, his name is Melvin. And I actually work for him" Raspberry said as Blade interrupted.

"You what ? How the hell you still work for this nigga" ? Blade replied raising his voice as Raspberry looked at him and looked around as if to say keep it down.

"Let me finish, he owns a club. Now when I found out he was involved I wanted revenge also at first. But when I thought about it and said, what better revenge would it be than to take everything he owns and kill him. And you might ask how would I do that ? Well if he signs the club over to someone that you trust and has a clean record. Maybe they get the liquor license and he can run it as your front man. Meanwhile you making money hand over fist. I figure you and your goons can run up in there and get him to sign it over once you find a front man" Raspberry said.

"And for that, what do you get out of this ? Out of me strong arming this nigga to get his club. Even though I don't know the first thing about running no damn club. But I will say, your cousin and I used to dream about having a bunch of women dancing for us and giving us ass when we wanted it. Throwing money in the air making it rain. Now I will have my own place to do just that, if I decide to do this. And you're right, they would never give my ass a liquor license. But I believe I may know someone who might be able to be my front man" Blade said.

"Great. And to answer your question about what do I want. I would like to be a silent partner. I don't want much, let's say twenty percent" Raspberry replied.

Chapter Six "Time For Some Action"

"Twenty percent if what you said is true, and all this shit pans out. Look I have to go, but keep your phone close I will get back with you" Blade said as he finished his food and got up and left.

Blade seemed happy the wheels were in motion for the revenge he had seeked for his fallen homie Shameek. He couldn't wait to put work in as soon as Raspberry sent the word. Meanwhile Chaos was curious why Raspberry wanted Melvin out as the owner. He and Melvin although wasn't friends, they were associates who knew each other. And everytime Chaos came through he was treated very well at

Melvins. Melvin himself had warned Chaos about Raspberry. Instead of saying anything about it, Chaos decided to sit back and watch to see what happened next. Raspberry was about to head to the gun range when she got a call from Isabella.

"Hey mami, I need to talk to you. Melvin has been pressuring me to get information about you, he thinks you know about what happened to Simone and Tricky. Please don't say anything to him about it. I wasn't supposed to say anything to you and I don't want to lose my job or my life. I'm just scared and couldn't take withholding this from you any longer" Isabella said sounding worried.

"Ok slow down and relax. Don't worry about Melvin. He's not going to get rid of you because you and I both know we're the main reasons the bar is what it is. I told you that before. And don't worry, I won't say a thing to Melvin about what you just told me. See you need to learn how the game is played and once you do that you won't be as worried and surprised about the people above you. Melvin is a necessary evil right now at this point, but that's only temporary and not the permanent plan. I can't say no more but just hang in there, they're better days ahead for the both of us if you continue to keep your loyalty to me" Raspberry replied.

As always Raspberry brought a calm to Isabella when she seemed overwhelmed and afraid. It's one of the main reasons Isabella kept her loyalty to Raspberry. She always felt no matter what she was going through she could come to Raspberry and she would either handle it, or help ease her worries.

Raspberry was reassuring her that this time would be no different, and to stay focused on her grind while keeping her loyalty to her. Problem solved as Raspberry was on to the next situation that needed her attention. Which was deciding when she wanted Blade to handle Melvin for her. It was something she thought long and hard about, and more importantly carefully. The plan had to be flawless, there couldn't be any mistakes of any kind to raise suspicion towards any of them.

Raspberry trusted that Blade and his work was as good as it was advertised. In the streets his reputation spoke for itself. When he put work in, he put work in for real. Plus Raspberry knew how fierce her cousin Shameek was. And she knew he didn't keep nothing but the best muscle he could find around him and his organization. So she felt good about Blade handling it, and handling it the right way. Besides she had no other choice now, after Chaos didn't want to do it. Either way it had to be done, so she got the next best thing. And that was Blade.

It was no secret that Melvin and Raspberry's relationship had deteriorated over time, for a few reasons. For one Melvin hadn't been good with Raspberry since Simone was killed. Two he was in a sense jealous of her rise at his bar. Sounds crazy because Raspberry was working for him, and the more money she made the more money Melvin made. But after a while it wasn't about the money for Melvin, it was about the popularity and power. Melvin craved it while Raspberry naturally had it. The bar was name Melvins because although Melvin liked doing business behind the scenes, he also enjoyed the status of being the man. And he was the type that would let you know if you ever forgot who's club it was at the end of the day. Raspberry set up a day she knew that Melvin would be alone, and her plan was in motion. As she then made a call to Blade and arranged for him to come to College Park about an hour prior.

Blade came to College Park and met Raspberry at a pizza shop after they had went by Melvins so Blade could check out the location. They never got out the car just sat there while Raspberry explained the ins and outs of the club and some small detailed instructions. The stage was set and the plan was about to be put fully into action. Raspberry had met Blade at a pizza shop because she didn't dare trust him to know where she live. So she made sure he had no clue where she laid her head. Meanwhile after talking to Raspberry, Isabella felt a lot better about the situation she was in. And she was confident everything would work out. She did continue to make Melvin think she was still on the hunt for information on Raspberry. She had to, at least until Raspberry did what she said she was going to do and handle it. But the pressure that was once there wasn't as strong as before. She felt good and could concentrate better on being the best she could be at her job. She already had a buzz and was a crowd favorite. It was now time to elevate her game.

It was a Thursday evening and the club had a steady crowd, not as packed as the weekends but a nice crowd. Raspberry wasn't dancing this night but Isabella was the headliner. And as usual she took advantage of her spot in the spotlight for this night. She looked ever so sexy as her body moved across the stage, she was a seasoned vet and she never lost her hunger to show and prove. It was advice Raspberry had gave her once she put her on at Melvins, and not only did it come in handy. But it prepared her for what life was going to be like as a dancer. It was highly competitive and if you wanted to shine you had to work and earn it. From not only your customers but your peers. There was money to be made but that depended on how bad you wanted it. This was all tied into your appearance and performance, which her and Raspberry excelled in.

As the night progressed and came to an end. Raspberry would be the last one left with Melvin at the end of the night. The money was counted and taken out by his security team. Melvin never took the money made from each night with him. He always had three men who were armed take the money for the night before he even left the club. It was something he had done since opening the place many years ago. This particular night Raspberry went up to Melvin's office before he had came down and needed to talk to him.

"Melvin I have to go a little early tonight so I can't walk out with you, it's a situation with my mother I have to go" Raspberry said.

"Oh ok, that's fine, I got a couple of things to finish here before I leave. You go ahead, hope everything is ok with your mother" Melvin replied.

"Thank you, good night" Raspberry said walking out of Melvin's office.

She walked outside got in her car and drove off into the night. About ten minutes went past when Melvin came downstairs from his office. He made sure everything was in order and set the alarm.

After setting the alarm and stepping out the door and locking it. Melvin was confronted by three masked men armed with semi automatic weapons. One voice spoke.

"Open the door back up slowly, and don't say a fucking word or I will kill your ass right here on this street." !!

Melvin did what the armed gunmen said as he opened the door back up and went back inside the club and disarmed the alarm. Once inside the club, the gunmen spoke again.

"Now I'm here because you killed my homie Shameek, so now you got to die muthafucka. But before you die, you going to sign your club over to the man's name on this paper." The gunmen said.

Interrupting the gunmen Melvin replied. "Shameek ? Who the fuck is Shameek ? I don't know no Shameek. You have the wrong dude man, I haven't killed anyone in my life" Melvin replied.

"Just shut up bitchin nigga, and sign this paper right here right now" !! The gunmen said yelling.

"I can't sign my place over to no one, I built this place from the ground up" Melvin said pleading with the men.

"I'm not going to tell you again" the gunmen said pointing the gun directly at Melvins head.

Meanwhile Raspberry drove home from the club to her apartment feeling good and confident that her plan would be executed perfectly. She got home and went straight to her bathroom and took a long hot bubble bath. The next morning Raspberry got a call from Blade saying he wanted to meet with her.

So the two of them met at a spot in College Park. And once Raspberry got there, Blade ran the whole thing down to her, and how it went down.

"The nigga was acting a little stubborn about signing over the club, I gave him a little time. More time than I usually give people. Because I knew I needed the nigga to sign the paper. So there was some pain inflicted inside the club but it didn't get too messy. Got his ass outta there and let him feel some more pain, until I got his punk ass to sign over the club. Then I finished his ass off in Shameek's honor. Let's just say nobody will ever find his ass" Blade said sounding confident.

"Sounds like you did what you do and your work is clean. That's a great thing. Now we can concentrate on the next phase which is taking over" Raspberry replied.

"I just want the cash flow to start flowing, as you said it's a cash cow. You better be right. The club is now in my business partner's name. John Marks. He's a good front man as you know he has a lot of ties with some people that can get things done legally in Baltimore. The club is now mines" Blade said.

John Marks was a prominent figure in the city of Baltimore who had a side hustle with Blade, and formly had a business relationship with Shameek. Marks had his hand in a few pockets because he was a mover and shaker in Downtown Baltimore. He was able to get a liquor license that's why his name was signed on as taking over ownership of the club.

It definitely couldn't be Blade, he wouldn't have never been able to get a liquor license. So a new era at what was still called Melvins at the time was about to start. And the people that needed to know which was the dancers, had no clue. Isabella would be the first to find out about the new ownership. As she arrived at the club and started to go up to Melvin's office. She was stopped by a voice she heard below her.

"Hello there, I'm assuming you're one of my dancers."

"One of your dancers ? Where is Melvin"? Isabella asked looking confused.

"Melvin suddenly decided to sell the club and disappear, and now I'm in charge of this place. And before you ask, don't worry I'm a very fair man. I'm John Marks" he said extending his hand.

"You can't be serious, this has to be a joke. Melvin loved this club and loved what he was doing" Isabella replied.

"Well Isabella it is, he surprised you all and left. Said he didn't want his workers to know, he just wanted to be out of the business" Marks said.

"I can't believe it, just like that and he's gone ? He was just here a few days ago being himself as usual. Does anyone even know where he went" ? Isabella asked.

Page 111

As soon as Isabella got done talking to Marks she had to call Raspberry to see if it was really true. And she did just that.

"Raspberry, hey Mami. Melvin is really gone ? I just left the club and was talking to Marks, this Marks guy is really our boss now" ? Isabella said looking for answers.

"Yes he is Isabella. You ready for a new start? I hope you are, and I told you I got you and everything was going to be fine" Raspberry replied.

Once again Raspberry had came through on her promise to make things better for the both of them. Isabella definitely was relieved now of all the pressures she had been dealing with while Melvin was running things. And that made her feel really good. She also was a little confused and concerned about what happened to Melvin. She appreciated him for giving her a chance at his place. And she was somewhat still in shock to find out he just left and sold the club just like that. That was so not like Melvin to just leave without informing any of his employees. And selling his prized possession. Something he had built from the ground up, and slowly over the years made into an empire. Hard to believe that he would just leave like that and didn't look back.

In just over four years Melvins had changed drastically. Simone was gone, the outspoken and sometimes wild head dancer and emcee. And Melvin the orginal owner and founder was gone after owning the place for many years. At the moment the place was still called Melvins but was sure to see some changes in the near future with Marks now taking over. And Blade being a silent partner in the background. They were sure to put their imprint and input in the bar. As promised from Blade, Raspberry would remain head dancer and emcee and would also have more input on the bar herself as another silent partner. She would get her twenty percent stake in the club. She had ideas and was ready to share them with her partners to implement them. The plan worked perfectly, as Blade got his revenge along with a club to go with it. A front man to run it for him and a beautiful dancer that was loyal to him. Raspberry got rid of a headache in Melvin, who wanted to see her fall. And was quickly acquiring information about her trying to build a case against her. Because he had believed that Raspberry had information as to what happened to Simone and Tricky. And more importantly who may have killed them. Melvin believed that Raspberry may not of killed them, but she knew something.

Raspberry was finally free to do what she wanted and free to make whatever changes she felt was necessary to improve the club. She wouldn't have dared to even think about that if Melvin was still around. So the next day Raspberry and Marks met at the club and started to discuss the direction of the club moving forward.

"Welcome to a new era and time Raspberry" Marks said as Raspberry sat at a table with him.

"Yes that's me, nice to meet you" Raspberry replied as she ordered a drink.

"Now I have heard that you're a great dancer and I can believe it from the looks of you. I'm sure you have ideas and I'm here to make the ideas happen" Marks said.

" Is that so ? Raspberry replied.

"Yes. And I know Blade is from the streets, and comes off a little rough around the edges. But he's also a keen businessman and knows his stuff. Shameek taught him well before he was killed" Marks said.

"That's good to know that this business will be in good hands, and I'm only here to help the business even more myself. So first I was thinking of bringing in a few other women from my Escort Service here to add some new faces in the mix. Also change some of the routines we do, keep things more interesting" Raspberry replied as she walked and looked around the club accompanied by Marks.

It was a new and exciting time at the club for those who were glad Melvin was gone. Chaos was one person that still had no clue what was going on or where Melvin was. He would later find out from Raspberry that Melvin was no longer the owner of the club. He had signed the club over to someone else and disappeared. They seen each other later that day and met for dinner.

"So I guess you found someone to take the club from Melvin, because I know damn well he would never in a million years sign over his club to someone else. So did they kill him ? Where is he at" ? Chaos asked trying to find answers.

"I'm not sure if he's alive or where he is, I was told he signed over the club and left. Not sure where to, but he left" Raspberry replied as her and Chaos had dinner.

Raspberry knew good and well exactly what happened to Melvin. And according to Blade, no one would ever find him. But Raspberry definitely wasn't telling Chaos that at all, she knew Chaos was cool with Melvin and they were associates. The last thing she wanted to do was get Chaos involved and have him at odds with any of the new regime at the club that was planning on taking over. It was indeed a conflict of interest. So Raspberry never said a word to Chaos about it. Chaos himself was visibly confused and somewhat upset about Melvin not owning the club anymore. Raspberry had promised Chaos that he would still be taken care of when he came to the club, nothing would change. She didn't know whether that would make Chaos feel a little better from his uneasiness of Melvin leaving or not. But it was worth a try. She wanted to keep the peace for her sake and the sake of the club business, like she had promised Blade and Marks.

The next night arrived and it was the first night of a new era for the club, and the regular customers were about to get the shock of their lives as Marks approached the microphone to speak to the crowd for the very first time.

"Hello all and welcome to Melvins, I know you all may be wondering who I am. I'm the new owner and my name is John Marks. Melvin decided to sell the place and get out of the business. But for all of you that frequent here, not too many changes will be put into place. We want to keep most of the things the same the way you all like it" Marks said to the crowd.
Page 113

The crowd at Melvins didn't know what hit them when Marks addressed them before starting off the night, they were so used to Melvin running things that it was strange not seeing him at all that night. Most nights when he wasn't in his office. He would walk around the club greeting the customers and making sure they were taken care of. Also some of the regulars who knew Melvin well and would talk to him about any and everything. Would definitely miss him dearly. The bright spot about it all was Raspberry and Isabella was still there, and Raspberry said she wanted to add some new faces. Particularly the women from her Escort Service. It would take some time together for the crowd to get adjusted to the new way of things. And the first person to dance there under the new ownership, who else but Raspberry. And she started the new era at the club out with a bang, as she graced the stage in a beautiful almost see through piece that barely covered her ass.

The crowd quickly went from confused and in shock to being the crowd Raspberry was used to at Melvins. After a few minutes, she herself felt more comfortable as money was strewned all across the stage. It was business as usual at Melvins, and a great first night for Marks and Raspberry. Isabella closed the night out with a great performance also, and it made her feel a lot better about herself. And about the situation itself as a whole. So overall it was a great first night for Marks, he was all smiles and was looking forward to even better days ahead. At the end of the night, Marks wanted to meet with Raspberry in his office. Upon entering his office Raspberry says."You wanted to see me" ?

"Yes I did, have a seat. It was a great first night for us, definitely impressed with the business despite the sudden change. I know most of these people are used to Melvin and the way he did things. But me and you are going to make these people forget about Melvin entirely. And we're going to do that by making this place the hottest strip club in the state, and maybe on the East Coast period. I got big plans for this place. I need you to stay on your grind and keep those ideas fresh. The Latin chick Isabella is very beautiful, I got a chance to introduce myself to her yesterday. And I also want to say I'm happy with the help you have given me and Blade" Marks said.

Blade wasn't present for opening night, he chose to stay back home in Baltimore. He didn't want to be in the spotlight at the club. He just wanted to collect his money after it was all said and done for the night. Marks was in charge of getting Blade his money each night, and Blade trusted Marks fully with handling that. Along with any other club business that needed to be handled.

Page 114

As much pull as Marks had in Baltimore with the people within the community and government. He never thought to cross a man like Blade who was very dangerous. And had been accused of being apart of five seperate murders along with some assaults and robberies. Didn't do as much jail time as he should have done because no one would testify against him. So he only did about nine years for a few of those cases, none of the charges were for murder. Just assault and robbery charges. A four year stint and a five year stint, Blade had been in trouble for most of his life. So knowing that, Marks never crossed Blade and always made sure he got his money. The new start was going well at the club, amid rumors of what happened to Melvin. There were a lot of questions but no answers. And it seemed like people within the club had dropped even talking about.

It was a strange vibe and feeling around not only the club but the area, the community didn't know what to think. All they knew was Melvin was gone and no one had heard from him. The dancers didn't ask any questions just tried to stay professional and it was business as usual. Raspberry and Marks kept it that way and the others were to follow. Everything that was Melvin's was removed from the club, starting with his former office. Marks had his things moved into his new office, the transformation was sharp and quick.

Later on that day Raspberry and Chaos were out to dinner again, and talking about the club.

"So how's this new owner at the club, you get a chance to speak with him" ? Chaos asked.

"Yeah Marks is cool. He seems like he's about his business, he plans to make some changes to the club. And me being the head dancer I will have some input in the changes also" Raspberry replied.

"So I guess me not taking your offer, you offered it to someone else. And in the end Melvin suffered for it" Chaos said.

Raspberry just looked at Chaos for a moment and responded. "Chaos you know how business is, I definitely shouldn't have to explain that to you. You know all about that all too well. You will still get your V.I.P. treatment. I made sure of that. Just be optimistic, I am" Raspberry replied.

Raspberry believed it wasn't really about Melvin when it came to Chaos being uneasy about the new ownership at the club. It was more about him turning the deal down and Raspberry offering and finding another partner for the club. Chaos was beginning to feel like he was losing control and Raspberry was becoming more and more of a power player. He felt a little insecure about dealing with Raspberry period from this point on. But he most certainly wanted to continue their personal relationship. Raspberry did indeed meet with Marks, but she didn't want Chaos to know it. She told Chaos some things but not everything. She had to always remind herself what she was in this for.

Raspberry was clearly in a great position, she had got rid of Melvin without her having to do it herself. And without it having any ties to her. She believed Blade when he said they would never find Melvin. After she had convinced Blade that Melvin had murdered Shameek, she knew he would want to kill Melvin as soon as possible. But she made him wait and sit on it to let it stew to the point it would be handled as soon as she said the word. And it happened exactly how she had planned. She was a mastermind at making things happen the way she wanted for the most part. Of course she was far from perfect but was a deep thinker who carefully thought out ways to attack her enemies fatally. She had murdered four people and had a fifth set up to be murdered without anyone having any proof that she did so.

But now she had her sights set on Chaos, the man that fired the fatal shot that killed her sister Deanna. But she also wanted his boss and partner Francisco, who up until this point was in the wind and completely a mystery to her. Raspberry had never seen or met him. When her sister Deanna worked for him, she never brought Desiree around Francisco or Chaos. Deanna never even mentioned that she had a sister or talked about her family to Francisco and Chaos. It was all business. She didn't even know where Francisco was, Chaos hardly ever talked about him or their business. She had to figure out a way to get to

Francisco and his whereabouts. Which wasn't going to be easy because Chaos hardly ever brought Francisco up, let alone talked about him. But she was determined to do so regardless of Chaos doing it or not. She was going to find a way to force his hand. So after being given the day off by Marks, Raspberry was in D.C. at Chaos condo spending some time with him. When the conversation shifted to Francisco and as always Raspberry's wit got her what she was looking for.

"You know the Spanish chick you said you thought was so sexy ? Well she's a friend of mines and she's single. She asked me if you had any friends and I told her you have one dude you really deal with. She said to ask you about him" Raspberry said.

"You mean Francisco ? Not sure if Francisco is open to meeting too many new people, unless of course it's business. But she is sexy so I will mention it to him and see what he says" Chaos replied.

That was all Raspberry could ask for as she smiled and replied. "Ok, because she's a good woman and she just wants to have a good time with a good guy."

Raspberry was cool and content with Chaos mentioning it to Francisco. It was a start and a chance for her to get closer to Francisco and his organization. The night continued as her and Chaos enjoyed the evening at home sipping on drinks and watching T.V. while relaxing on Chaos comfortable couch.

The next day Raspberry headed back home as she knew she had to call Isabella when she got home to tell her what she had in mind. She needed Isabella once again to play her sidekick in her plan to get inside Francisco and Chaos organization. Isabella was loyal to Raspberry and in return Raspberry made Isabella's life easier. And often times protected her from the very dangerous people she was around. Eventually getting rid of Melvin who was putting pressure on her to get information about Raspberry while still keeping her job. Above anything Isabella felt like she owed Raspberry for all that she had done for her. So Raspberry wasn't too concerned about Isabella being on board with whatever she wanted her to do. She knew that would be no problem. Like her role in Raspberry's killing of Shameek, she was down for whatever when it came to Raspberry. This situation was no different, so as soon as Raspberry got home she called Isabella.

"Hello miss, how you been" ? Raspberry asked as Isabella answered the phone.

"Hello Mami, I'm fine just getting my outfit ready for tonight. What's up" Isabella replied.

"Chaos got this friend of his name Francisco that I told him I wanted to hook you up with. I told him you was single and you asked if Chaos had any friends. I just need you to play your part as always in the situation and let me handle the rest. I have never met the man to tell you what he's like, we probably will meet him together for the first time. But I will try to get as much as information as I can from Chaos about him and give that to you" Raspberry said explaining the plan.

"Ok Mami, sounds good to me. So when are we to meet this guy ? You know we have to work around our schedules at the club" Isabella replied.

"Yeah I know, let me think about it and I will let you know. We may even be able to meet them at the club. Plus Chaos needs to get familiar with Marks.....yeah that might work" Raspberry said before hanging up the phone.

The night had arrived and Raspberry was merely the emcee this night as Isabella was the headliner, it was a modest crowd on a Thursday. The weekends at Melvins was always the best and it continued even after Melvin was gone. On those weekends most of the time Raspberry and Isabella both were on center stage along with the other beautiful women who worked at the club with them. Those weekends were great times, legendary and epic for both Raspberry and Isabella. It made them who they were at the club. And more importantly it made them a lot of money.

And they still was very much stars at the club, Raspberry decided to do away with her Escort Service and brought those women on at Melvins. Plus she now had her twenty percent stake in the club, so money wasn't an issue with her anymore. She got the approval from Marks, and her girls were on. Everything was going well and working in Raspberry's favor, she couldn't have been any more happier than she was. But Chaos was feeling uneasy about the new management after knowing the place as Melvins and Melvin being an associate of his. Raspberry wanted Chaos to come to the club one night so she could introduce him to Marks and hopefully Blade if he was around. She had promised Chaos that nothing would change when he came to Melvins, he would still get treated the same because he was a personal guest of hers. That was yet to be seen though, he hadn't been to the club since the new ownership had taken over. He didn't know the new management and ownership and didn't know if he really wanted to.

He kept his admiration for Melvin, a man he knew for years. Versus a man he had never met or seen in Marks. Marks had promised Chaos the same treatment because of Raspberry, that was part of the deal. Raspberry wanting Chaos to get the same treatment meant that to her he just wasnt a regular guy. He meant something to her. She wanted to make everyone happy for the time being until her plan could be followed through. The main people she wanted to keep happy were the two dangerous threats to her, Chaos and Blade. Chaos she didn't want to tip off to anything she had planned for him, he never knew her real name. In fear of him connecting the dots to Baltimore and finding out she was Deanna's sister. If he was to ask her real name, she would give him a fake name. He just knew her as Raspberry and he was good with that for now. Blade because after getting rid of Melvin and making him sign over his club, he was a silent partner that had the most stake in the club. Blade had no clue that Raspberry was actually the person that killed Shameek, he was manipulated by her and he didn't even know it. She was able to get herself out of that by convincing Blade Melvin killed Shameek.

In return, Raspberry offered Blade the club for getting rid of Melvin. In which Blade eventually found Marks to be his front man. So in essence it was a win win for Raspberry and everyone was happy for the moment. After talking to Chaos, he was planning on finally coming to the bar for the upcoming weekend. Although he was a little skeptical about the new ownership. Raspberry was hoping Chaos would like it and everything would continue going smooth. A lot was riding on this so she was optimistic about it working, and if it did she would have less to worry about financially. In her mind that was all it was about. She needed Chaos to get along with Marks and Blade for the time being, while she continued with her plan and making her money.

And if it didn't work something had to be done to make it work, she had been used to getting her way and making things happen the way she wanted them to. She figured everyone would be happy in the end if it all worked out. The night came as it was a typical night on the weekend at Melvins, packed from wall to wall with beautiful and sexy women gracing the stage. And it just so happen that everybody was at the club this night, including Blade and Chaos. Blade was already there in V.I.P. after making the trip from

Baltimore. Chaos had just arrived and he was greeted by Raspberry.

"Hey handsome, I want to introduce you to someone" Raspberry said leading Chaos through the crowd to the V.I.P. area over towards Blade. As she got closer she noticed that Blade was no longer in his seat anymore, so she quickly made a split second decision and led Chaos over to the actual front man Marks.

"Marks I want you to meet a friend of mines, Marks this is Chaos and Chaos this is Marks. He is the new owner of the club" Raspberry said introducing them as both men shook hands.

After being introduced both men sat at a table with Raspberry present and talked about a few things.

"So do you like the club and few changes that have been made ? Since you haven't been here since the change in ownership happened....what do you think" ? Marks asked Chaos as he took a sip of his drink.

"I mean it's nice, I just had a good relationship with Melvin. He was an associate of mines. This whole shit about him up and leaving, selling the club doesn't sound like him. Where the fuck is he at anyway" ? Chaos replied.

"I have no clue where he is, the man had a club for sale and I bought it. After I made the purchase that was it. And the end of my business relationship with him. Now if you want to continue to have a good relationship with this club, let's have a good night and enjoy all these beautiful women you see in here. I'm not here to beef with you, or disrespect the relationship you had with Melvin. Or the relationship you have with Raspberry. I'm just a businessman handling my business" Marks said.

"I'm going to have a good time, no matter what. That's exactly what I'm going to do, have a good night" Chaos replied as he got up from the table and went on the other side of V.I.P.

He then sat down and ordered a bottle. Raspberry later followed behind and over to his table.

"What was that about ? I don't understand why you can't just accept that Melvin sold the club. Let's have a good night like you said and enjoy this, you still in V.I.P. You still get everything you want like always" Raspberry said as she sat down next to Chaos.

"Shit is not about that, I know you wanted him gone. After I didn't strong arm him you got somebody else to do it. What yall killed him ? You can tell me" Chaos said. Page 119

After talking to Chaos for a little while longer, Raspberry had to get back on stage and do her job. She was somewhat uneasy about how Chaos was towards Marks but she couldn't worry about that now she had a job to do and she had to do it well. And like always she did just that, took to the stage and was flawless. Sexy as ever while her friend Chaos watched from the V.I.P. section. After blazing the stage she walked off and ran into Blade backstage.

"Hey....where did you disappear to ? I was looking for you to introduce you to my friend Chaos" Raspberry said.

Blade looked at Raspberry and replied. "I'm not trying to meet nobody, and I'm not trying to make any new friends. Unless of course we can be friends, I'm with some shit like that" as he got closer to Raspberry.

"You need to step back and relax because it's not that type of party" Raspberry replied.

"Oh ok, you gonna do me like that. You know you need a real man to handle that, and no I don't want to meet your friend. Only person I'm interested in getting to know better is you. So he's your little boyfriend or something ? No I'm good on meeting anybody that ain't about business....money" Blade said as he walked away.

It was clear from that point on that Blade had no interest at all in meeting Chaos. It was an uncomfortable moment for Raspberry, Blade had never came onto her before so strong and she found the timing strange. After that encounter she went back over to sit with Chaos and enjoyed the rest of the night. She didn't mention anything about Blade and what he did in fear of getting a war started between the two. At this point that was the last thing she needed. She tried to keep the peace but she was beginning to think that Blade was going to be a problem, he was a lose cannon. She had to be very careful in how she dealt with him, after all he was the true owner of the club at this point. And more importantly he had dirt on Raspberry. Not that she thought he would rat her out, but that was an option if he ever got caught up and was going to do a lot of years. With Blade now saying he didn't want to meet

Chaos she had to think of another way for these two men to coexist together or completely scrap the plan all together. In her mind that was not an option, it had to work and she was going to figure out a way that it would.

Meanwhile Isabella was at home and thinking about a lot of different things when she got a call from of all people Blade. "Hey Ma, this is Blade the new owner of the club you work for. I just called you so maybe we can meet up somewhere and talk, get to know one another" Blade said.

"Who the hell is Blade ? I never heard of you, and Marks owns the club I work for" Isabella replied.

Blade laughed a little and responded. "No beautiful, Marks is the face of the club. My front man. I can't be the face of the club because of the life I live and the nature of the business I'm in. I'm your real boss and I can prove it once we meet up" Blade said.

Isabella was somewhat surprised at what she was hearing, Raspberry had told her that Marks was the owner of the club. She was also a little frightened by the call from Blade. Seemed a little creepy to her. Blade had dropped a bombshell on Isabella by telling her he was the actual owner of the club. Isabella was confused and a little concerned and nervous. She wasn't agreeing to meet with anyone name Blade without proof that he was the actual owner. And without talking to Raspberry about it.

"I have to meet with Raspberry about this, I don't know you. So after that maybe we can meet" Isabella replied.

"Oh so you have to talk to Raspberry? Ain't that bout a bitch. Once you do talk to her she will let you know who your real boss is, until then I will be seeing you and I will keep in touch" Blade said before hanging up.

A strange call from a vicious killer, who had a hidden agenda and was instantly attracted to Isabella. Which was the same woman that his homie Shameek was dealing with before he was murdered. The same woman Blade and the rest of his goons was looking for to see if she knew who killed their homie Shameek. But Blade had no clue because he never really saw Isabella before but from a distance. Isabella immediately called Raspberry for some answers.

"Mami I have to talk to you. Some guy name Blade called me saying he wanted to meet with me and he was the real owner of the club, is this true" ? Isabella asked.

"He isn't the owner of the club, Marks is the owner of the club. He's just someone that will be around. And someone that invested in the club. You shouldn't associate yourself with him at all" Raspberry replied.

Raspberry couldn't believe Blade who said he wanted to be in the background and just get his money, had suddenly wanted to play boss and step to the forefront. In a sense it had pissed Raspberry off because she had gave Blade an opportunity to make even more money than he was already making. The club was just another side hustle for Blade who had continued running him and Shameek's drug empire back in Baltimore. And he was supposed to lay low in this business venture and not let anyone know that he was involved with the new ownership. That was what was agreed upon, but Blade had other plans. Raspberry was sure to have a discussion with Blade about him deciding to call Isabella. After talking with Raspberry, Isabella was still somewhat upset and scared. Not knowing if Blade knew where she lived or not. Raspberry reassured her Blade didn't know where she lived. Addresses weren't kept, only phone numbers. But Raspberry did want to get to the bottom of this as soon as possible. The next day Raspberry called Blade and wanted to meet with him. Blade told her to come to the club, and so she did. Her, Marks, and Blade met in Marks office.

"Why did you call Isabella ? You don't call a dancer for anything else but business about the club. And you told us you wanted to be in the background and let Marks run the club, you calling this woman and scaring her" Raspberry said before getting interrupted by Blade.

"So what I called her. It was my muscle that got this club. You needed somebody to strong arm this nigga Melvin, because you couldn't do it. But I did. Marks is just the front man, and he knows that. But don't ever tell me I can't talk to MY dancers. And that includes you, so get back to work and make me some money" Blade said taking a sip of his drink.

Raspberry just looked at Blade and shook her head. Not saying a word, and she got up from the table and left. Marks just sat there in sort of disbelief at what just happened.

"Blade why would you want to piss her off ? We need her. She is our moneymaker" Marks said.

"No YOU need her. Plus that bitch ain't going nowhere. She came and got me, asking for ME to handle Melvin. And the nigga got handled. So now I'm the boss, you know this shit Marks. She just needed to be humbled for a little. That's all" Blade replied kicking his feet up on one of the tables.

Marks knew Blade's reputation in the streets, that alone was enough to assure Marks that Blade was not a person you want to cross. Marks did fear Blade to a certain extent. Among other things he knew about Blade from dealing with Shameek over the years. Blade had changed his tune and decided he wanted a bigger role in running the club. As he would be more of a fixture at the club. Which was something that was not agreed upon at the beginning and wasnt apart of the overall plan. Blade wasn't the public type and if he wanted to be the face of the club it would change some things which would affect the bottom line. Which meant money. Raspberry knew Marks couldn't talk any sense into Blade, nobody could. So it was up to her to handle the situation. Meanwhile Chaos wanted to take Raspberry out and she wanted to bring her friend she had been telling him about. Hoping he would bring Francisco. And much to her delight he did mention it to Francisco. Raspberry had never seen Francisco, she didn't know how she was going to feel when she did. If it would feel similar to the way she felt when she first saw Chaos, or if it would be different. Either way she was eager to finally see who this man was.

So after a few days passed, Chaos came back and told Raspberry that it was a date. Raspberry, Chaos, Isabella, and Francisco were going to go out and enjoy each others company. Raspberry was happy and excited for the night to come, she let Isabella know and the plans were set. Back at the club Marks and Blade were sitting down having a drink discussing the club and their future plans.

"Blade you have to be smart about this, having your face out there wouldn't be smart. That's why I'm here, and you know whatever you ultimately decide I will be behind you one hundred percent. But I'm also here to advise you to do things the right way" Marks said.

"Man I know, but we got this bitch Raspberry thinking she runs shit. You need to be more of a boss.....you hear me" ? Blade replied.

"Yes I hear you Blade, you're right. Just fall back a little, let me handle the public things and you play the background like we orginally planned" Marks said.

After talking to Marks, Blade got up and walked around the club just mingling. He walked past the V.I.P. section and seen a dude that he hadn't seen before. Blade then walked downstairs to the dressing room amid all the women getting dressed and he didn't care. He wanted to see Raspberry right away. After walking through the dressing room he finally found Raspberry and asked to talk to her privately.

"So who's the guy over there sitting in V.I.P. ? And why is he even sitting in V.I.P." ?

"That's Chaos the guy I was going to introduce you to until you disappeared before I got a chance. He spends a lot of money here that's why he's in V.I.P. and he just so happens to be the guy I'm seeing right now. So I gave him full access to V.I.P." Raspberry replied.

Blade just looked at her for a moment and responded. "I guess that's cool for now, but I don't know how long this is going to float. He better continue spending a lot of money in here if he expects the treatment he's getting to continue. And you better make sure he does" Blade said walking away from her.

Raspberry was prepared to deal with Blade and the way he was beginning to be about the club. She had even heard that Blade was thinking of renting an apartment in College Park so he could stay more involved with the club and closer instead of commuting from Baltimore.

Either way it was clear that Blade was going to be more involved. Regardless Raspberry had everything under control and continued being focused on improving the club as best she could. Isabella was running late on this night and happened to walk past Blade on her way into the bar area. Towards the stairs to the dressing room. As she walked past him he winked at her and smiled. Of course she was caught off guard by him and felt uncomfortable around him in general. Especially after the phone conversation. She feared him after speaking with Raspberry about what he was capable of doing. After that awkward moment Isabella went downstairs to the dressing room and got dressed. She was to be the headliner tonight, as it was Raspberry's night to just be the emcee. Chaos sat back on the luxury couch in the V.I.P. area and enjoyed the numerous beautiful women who graced the stage while waiting for Isabella like the rest of the crowd. As he was sitting there, Blade walked past staring at him. Chaos stared back and brushed it off as Blade just walked past and kept moving.

Once he didn't say anything, Chaos dismissed it as nothing. One thing Chaos did was always bring his guns when he traveled anywhere, including coming to College Park to Melvins. So he definitely wasn't worried about having any problems with anybody. Chaos always carried his signature gun of choice, the 45 caliber and his 9mm. They were either on him or in his vehicle at all times. What Chaos didn't know was Blade kept a razor on him inside the club and a glock 40 on his waist inside the club. Something he had never told anyone. He didn't have to go through security check so it was never a problem for him to bring what he wanted in the club. After all he was the boss, and becoming more of a fixture at the club since recently getting his place in College

Blade was beginning to become worst than what Melvin was when he ran the club, Blade was feeling himself and his newfound title. And he loved to throw his weight around letting anyone that would listen know that he was the boss and it was his club. No one could tell him anything, not even Marks who feared him. But Raspberry was growing increasingly annoyed with the way Blade was acting and carrying himself. And more importantly she didn't want him to ruin any of the business at the club. Everybody's job was basically on the line when he was around because of the unprofessional way he went about acting around the customers. Someone had to do something, and they had better do it soon. Chaos was sitting at home waiting for Raspberry to arrive as they were going to go out for dinner at an upscale Downtown D.C. restaurant. After making the drive from College Park and riding with Chaos to the restaurant, Raspberry was tired but Chaos wanted to discuss the new owner Blade.

"So what's with this dude Blade you wanted me to meet so bad ? I saw him the other night at the club. He kind of looked at me funny. Like he had a problem with me or something, I thought maybe I would have to wait for his ass outside. I gave it some thought and then dismissed it. Because it's your place of business. Next time I'm not going to be so nice" Chaos said with a straight face.

"To be honest with you he's starting to become a problem in more ways than one. He technically is the owner. But legally he's not. The club is in Marks name, but Marks works for him and fears him like you wouldn't believe" Raspberry replied.

"He hasn't been a problem to you personally has he"? Chaos asked.

"Of course not, that would never happen. In a business sense for all of us at the club he is a problem, and no one wants to solve it. But sometimes things change, maybe it will handle itself eventually" Raspberry said sounding optimistic.

"You know if you need me to handle this shit it will be handled, I didn't like the way he came up in there. Owner or not. And you know I always keep my heat on me whereever I go, I could've handled him that night. Melvin never did that shit" Chaos said eating his dinner.

"You're partly right, Melvin was never this disrespectful. But that was then and this is now. I can handle myself, just sometimes I worry about the other girls and Isabella. I believe this situation will handle itself. Blade is a street dude and a live wire, most likely has a lot of enemies. It's only a matter of time. Enough about that nonsense, let's enjoy our dinner. This shrimp alfredo is really good too" Raspberry said eating her food.

"Yeah but before we finish the conversation. Just remember I'm a street nigga myself, and like I said if you need me to handle it I will" Chaos said for the second time but more serious.

After his first encounter with Blade, he wouldn't mind at all delivering street justice to him. All she had to do was say the word.

After finishing their dinner and talking for a little while longer they decided to call it a night and go home to Chaos condo. The next morning Chaos was awakened out of his sleep by a phone call from Francisco. Which also woke Raspberry up as she lay in bed listening to Chaos talk. At least for a few minutes until she got up and got in the shower. In the shower she could still hear faintly what Chaos was saying as him and Francisco talked. Before he hung up Raspberry heard Chaos say, "Yeah its time for some action." After getting out of the shower Raspberry walked in the bedroom with nothing on but the towel around her. By then Chaos had gotten off the phone and his attention was solely on Raspberry and that little towel that was around her. Their eyes met and Chaos pulled her close to him as he took her towel completely off while leading her to his king size bed. As he kissed Raspberry from her full lips to her neck and worked his way down finally resting between her thighs as he gave her oral sex. She moaned loudly in approval much to Chaos delight.

He then got undressed and they had some of the most intense passionate sex they had to date. It was just one of those moments driven by passion. Afterwards they both had to go, after of course them both getting a shower and having another session in the shower. Before they both left Chaos condo. It was back to business for Raspberry as she headed back home before heading to the club. Upon arriving at the club Raspberry seen Blade as she walked in.

"Hey Miss, you ready for tonight" ? Blade asked Raspberry looking at her up and down.

"I'm always ready for the night BOSS" Raspberry replied.

Blade just continued having his drink at the bar as she walked past. Raspberry went downstairs to the dressing room where some of the women already were.

"You ladies we have about ten minutes till showtime, let's make them make it rain" Raspberry said hyping the women up for the night.

Raspberry as usual got the crowd ready for the women as the night began and the dollars littered the stage. Marks had mingled through the crowd and made sure that they were happy and had enough drinks. Blade sitting in V.I.P. had a few bottles at his table along with a few of the women dancers who were giving him lap dance after lap dance. For the moment everyone was happy and satisfied. Including Marks, Blade, and Raspberry. But how long could these three coexist running the club together ? Only time would tell as their egos collide. One in particular had outgrown the others. Blade had got out of control of late, and was quickly becoming a serious threat to the club and the people in it.

Page 125

Later that night as the night was ending, Blade came out the club and got in his BMW en route to his apartment. He had just moved in a College Park, Md. apartment a few days prior. He had finally decided to get a place instead of driving back and forth to Baltimore. He had a bottle and a few drinks at the club but appeared fine as he drove home. He finally got home and was walking towards his apartment. But before he could get there he saw someone walking towards him, but it was dark and he couldn't see exactly who it was. As he got closer he saw a hand raise, and before he could get his hand in his waistband to pull out his 9mm Ruger. Three shots were fired at him hitting him with all three, two in the chest and once in the neck. The shots were muffled, probably fired from a gun with a silencer. Blade immediately fell to the ground and was dead at the scene. His neighbors noticed the body laying on the ground as Police were called. And night turned to dawn. They immediately started investigating the scene and looked for potential witnesses. The medics were also called but it was much too late as Blade was already dead. Like other murders in the area, word spread fast about Blade. At the moment Police had no suspects and no leads. Blade most times wore a vest on him, but since he was away from Baltimore he figured he didn't need it. So that particular night he wasn't wearing a vest at all.

There was a gun found on Blade that was near his body, along with a six inch blade that he always kept on him. From the looks of the crime scene, Blade was attempting to pull his weapon, a 9mm Ruger. But failed to do so before he was gunned down. He didn't get a shot off, obviously he was shot before he could. The blade was found in his back pocket. The fatal shot was in his chest, the second shot hit him in his heart. A third shot was fired before he fell to the ground which hit him in the neck. It was a horrific scene at his apartment complex as everyone was outside. A lot of blood was all over the pavement near where the body lay covered with a tarp. Marks was awakened after just getting to sleep at his home early that morning.

He was notified that Blade was murdered at his apartment complex. He quickly drove over there to the crime scene, by then the body had already been taken to the morgue.

Marks was visibly upset learning that his business partner and associate that he knew for the last four years had been murdered. It was a painful pill to swallow and also the fact that Marks had the club now all to himself as it was legally his anyway. The next morning Marks called all the women over to the club saying he had an announcement to make. The women all showed, some knew from watching the news. Others had no clue. He told the women that his business partner and associate Blade had been murdered. Many of the women were in shock, others really didn't care. Blade had made a not so good impression on most of the women at the club anyway with the way he had began carrying himself. And not a lot of women actually knew him. But to them just knowing yet another person that was connected to the club was gunned down, really had them paranoid. It put enough fear in them that some women were questioning if they still wanted to work at Melvins.

Page 126

It was a mix of emotions about Blades murder, Marks wanted to see Raspberry in his office as soon as possible. She knew that he was going to reach out to her, he had no one else. And she also knew that a few of Blades goons would be in College Park shortly looking for revenge. So as she entered Marks office she kind of knew what to expect.

"He's gone and I can't believe it, no one even knew he was here from back in Baltimore" Marks said pacing back and forth in front of his desk.

Raspberry just stared at him and replied. "You know the type of dude Blade was, he was a magnet for trouble. I know because I remember when he first started running with my cousin Shameek."

"I'm just shocked because no one knew he was here. And who even had the balls to kill him ? He was feared any where he was" Marks said sounding confused.

"It's definitely a shock to most of us, but all you have to do is piss off the wrong person" Raspberry replied.

"Even still, how many men were as bad as Blade ? I mean I'm a little worried now, maybe they coming for me next. I gotta get out of here for a few days" Marks said still pacing back and forth in front of his desk.

"Relax Marks, just relax. We can have a Police presence around here if you would like, and we can have the Police escort us out at night. Just try to remain calm and let the Police do their job" Raspberry replied.

Marks was beyond paranoid and swore that whoever killed Blade was after him next because of him and Blade's business relationship. Raspberry tried to calm the waters so to speak, and tried to convince Marks that everything would be OK. For the rest of the women who knew Blade for the short time that they did, were relieved for the most part that he was gone. He was quickly becoming a problem at the club. They figured things would get back to normal when Marks first took over. Sad that his life had to end in such a violent way, but some of the girls were relieved they no longer had to deal with him.

"Maybe you're right, but I am worried that the killer may come for me. We were together a lot" Marks said.

"Just give it some time, in the mean time I will help you with anything you need for the club" Raspberry said reassuring Marks everything would be fine.

Later that day Raspberry met with Isabella for lunch.

"How do you feel about what happened to Blade"? Raspberry asked.

Page 127

Once again Raspberry had got rid of someone who was quickly becoming a thorn in her side. And someone who completely went against their original agreement and didnt care. Raspberry had followed Blade home a few nights before to his apartment, and another night after that to get his routine down. She was basically casing the place to get familiar with his apartment complex. The night of the murder Raspberry had left the club before Blade and sat in the back of his building waiting for him to come home. Once she saw his car pull up she got out of her car and crept through the back to meet him in the front. As he was walking towards the door she came from the back and met him before he got to his front door. Firing three shots in a row, hitting him with all three and killing him instantly. She then quickly went back to her car and drove off. Not many if any people heard the shots because like always Raspberry used a silencer to muffle the sounds. She had grew tired and irritated with the way Blade had become. And she felt that moving forward he would make life difficult for all that worked at the club, so in Raspberry's eyes he had to go.

She didn't tell anyone as she didn't tell anyone about the others she had got rid of. She had tried her best to get someone who would coexist with her and Marks to run the club the right way. Chaos wanted no parts of it because he had felt Melvin was done wrong. So the only other option was Blade who was fine at first. But after running things for a certain amount of time it went to his head and he had to be replaced. It was now up to Marks to take the bar into the future. He was unsure if he could at this point, he was still shook up about Blade's murder. But Raspberry was there to ensure him that he could. By trying her best to cheer him up and make him feel optimistic and more confident about running the club. She also convinced him it was better for him now that Blade was gone. He could now run things the way he wanted to without the interference from Blade. And his not so nice unprofessional ways of doing things.

Blade was a necessary evil to have around in the beginning, Raspberry needed him to force Melvin out. And she honestly thought she could coexist with Blade, him playing the background and being the real money man and enforcer he was. Would've been great for the club. But things had changed, once Blade got his power from owning the club. He took off with it and wasn't being smart. So Raspberry had to stop him before things got even worse. It was yet again another new era at Melvins. It was now solely Marks show. And what he would do with that was yet to be seen. Raspberry was very optimistic that things would work out for the best. And she would try everything in her power to make it that way. There were no more worries anymore, Blade was gone. Isabella happen to be out shopping when she seen a man from a distance that looked like Chaos. As she got closer she noticed it was him.

Page 128

She had only met Chaos once but had seen him numerous times at Melvins.

"Hey what's going on, how are you" ? Chaos asked.

"I'm good and yourself" ? Isabella replied.

"I'm here doing a little shopping, and I suppose you are also. I seen you dance at the club, you look real sexy up there" Chaos said looking directly at Isabella as he scanned her body with his eyes.

"Thanks a lot, that was sweet. But I better get going, nice seeing you. I will tell Raspberry I seen you. Goodbye" Isabella replied walking away quickly.

She was nervous and felt a little uncomfortable about the way Chaos was looking at her. Chaos tried to respond but Isabella quickly walked away from him.

She definitely didn't want to tell Raspberry about that part of their encounter. She didn't want to be in the middle of anything between them. Raspberry had been dating Chaos for some time now. She would only tell her that she saw him. Meanwhile back in Baltimore funeral services were being held for Blade, whose real name was Antonio Bates. A packed funeral home including Marks who had spoke on behalf of his business partner and associate were there. Along with Raspberry who also made the trip from College Park. Blade had left behind three children, a girlfriend, and other family members. His crew was there also, now losing two of their leaders to murder in the last few years.

After the funeral Marks gave Blades mother and girlfriend envelopes of money that was his share of the profits for the family and his children. Driving back to College Park Marks did a lot of thinking about the club and what had happened to Shameek and Blade. Two men that took Marks under their wings and made him a lot of money. And they did so by never letting Marks get involved with the criminal side of the business. They always made sure he kept his nose clean so that he could get legitimate businesses throughout the city of Baltimore. With them supplying the cash. They often used their money to start and finance the businesses, and let him be the front man because he was so beloved in the community. No one ever knew that they were in business together. Shameek and Blade were only known as friends of Marks that grew up around the same neighborhood. Either way Marks was going to miss them both dearly.

He had very little time to dwell on either of their deaths because he had a club to run. And after being closed for a few days in honor of his boy and attending the funeral. He was back and it was business as usual. It was the weekend and it was a packed house as usual. Both Raspberry and Isabella were on tonight. And from the outset it looked as if it was a serious competition between the two like most times. Who could be the most sexy and bring the men their fantasy, without actually having the sexual experience with them. It was always competitive between the two, ever since the beginning and it only got more fierce as the years went by. Some of Shameek and Blades crew remained in the area quietly searching for Blades killer, trying not to tip off the Police of their plans.

But they had to be careful looking for revenge, because Police were everywhere trying to solve the case. The competition between Raspberry and Isabella always made for a great show, which meant more money was being spent. It was another great night. And although it wasn't a consolation for Marks losing his friend. It did cheer him up somewhat as he made a toast to Blade before he let all his workers go for the night. Everyone had left but Raspberry and Marks. Before leaving his office Raspberry wanted to check on Marks to see if he was alright.

"Hey Marks, you ok" ? Raspberry asked peaking her head in his office.

"I'm as good as I can be despite the circumstances yeah. You know Shameek and Blade when I was younger saved my life, there was these kids that always used to jump me......everytime. This one day they was about to do it again until Shameek and Blade came up. Shit Shameek and Blade whooped them kid's ass and sent them home. They never bothered me again. Matter of fact no one ever bothered me again in life once they knew I was cool with them. When I didn't have shit they took care of me, now they're both dead" Marks said shaking his head.

"I understand that it's painful, I've lost people that were close to me also. Just take your time, I'm here to help you with the club if you want to take a day off or anything" Raspberry said.

After talking a little more, the two finally called it a night. Marks felt a little better after talking to Raspberry and being reassured that she was going to be there for him when he needed her. Because at this point she was all he had, and who had his best interest. He needed Raspberry, she had a better relationship with the women who worked there. And they didn't know Marks as well as they knew Raspberry. After working with her for over the last four years. So she was the bridge that led him to some of his best workers at the club so to speak. Isabella was successful in her own right, and was quickly becoming more of a fixture at the club. She was the top dancer besides Raspberry, and incredibly loyal to her. She continued to be loyal to her since the beginning. The next night which was Saturday was here and it would be another great night at the club. Jam packed from wall to wall. Even though Marks was still grieving over Blades death, he couldn't help but to be happy at the profits that were rolling in. And more importantly all the people he was meeting because of owning the club.

Marks found out the business was more lucrative than he first thought, he figured he would dabble with this business until Blade straightened his act out. And cleaned his image and then hand it over to him. As it was originally his to begin with, after he had persuaded Melvin to sign it over to Marks. After Blade's death it was all up to Marks. The direction the club was going in was paying dividends as Marks was making a lot of money. It was moving the right way as everything was going as smooth as it could be. But the question was. With all the violence and mayhem that were around the core people at Melvins, would it continue ? Or would there be nothing but peace from here on out ? Only time would tell. There was uncertainty to a certain extent, but also excitement for what was yet to come.

Page 130

Isabella had been holding in something for some time now, and the only person she could talk to about it was Raspberry. But she was terrified to do so, she wanted to talk to Raspberry about what they did to Shameek. It was something Raspberry told her to never talk about again since that night. But it was really bothering Isabella. Slowly and slowly eating away at her conscience. She was also suspicious about what really happened to Simone and Tricky. Two murders that still remained unsolved. Melvin before he disappeared was suspicious of Raspberry and had Isabella trying to get information about her. She had told Raspberry about it and suddenly Melvin disappears. A lot of thoughts were going on in Isabella's head, and she really didn't know where to turn. She was once again very torn and battling her inner demons so to speak. She felt at some point she had to confront Raspberry about it because she was involved, and she just had to know why Shameek was killed and who he really was to her.

She had no clue and never asked any questions when it came to what Raspberry told her. She was like that because Raspberry always took care of her and made sure she was good. And in a sense, got Melvin off her back. Either way she felt guilty about it all, and hoped Raspberry wasn't apart of any of it besides the Shameek situation. Isabella was frightened when she found out that Blade was Shameek's best friend and he was the actual owner of the club. She thought that he would figure out who she was, although she had never really spent a lot of time around him. Besides their little interaction at the club. It was a very tense time for Isabella, but just like that within a blink of an eye. Melvin and Blade was gone. A few nights had passed and Isabella was still wrestling with her feelings, she would put off making a decision for another day.

Meanwhile Raspberry still didn't know what Chaos was talking about when he said "time for some action". She had assumed that Chaos needed to do a job for Francisco, more than likely a hit. Raspberry knew and Chaos had no idea that she did know some things about him. And the fact he had killed her sister and only sibling. She waited patiently for his call because she knew at some point it was coming. After about an hour the phone rang and it was her mother Denise.

"Hello mom, how have you been" ?

"I'm fine, I was worried about you. Haven't heard from you in a while, have you thought about going back to school" ? Her mother Denise asked.

It was something she hadn't talked to Raspberry about in a while, but Raspberry knew it meant a lot to her mother to get her degree.

"No mother I still have my career going and things are going well. At some point I plan on going back, I will mom I told you that" Raspberry replied.

"Yes you keep telling me, I just don't want you to put it off for too long. And before you know it you will be pregnant and won't ever go back. Or something else could happen" Denise said.

Raspberry laughed a little and replied. "Mother don't worry, that's not happening anytime soon" Raspberry replied.

Raspberry always knew her mother was going to ask her that until she actually went back to school and got her degree. Which in Raspberry's mind wasn't going to happen anytime soon, although she really did want to get her degree and planned to do so. She knew her mother meant well and wanted the best for her, but Raspberry was making a lot of money on her own terms. And that for now was good enough for her. After talking to her mother, Raspberry was just about to go to the gun range when she got a call from Isabella saying that she needed to talk. Raspberry told her that they would meet later, Isabella made it a point that she wanted to meet at Raspberry's apartment. Raspberry agreed. Her annual visits to the gun range made her a marksman. She was a very good shooter and knew how to handle some of the most powerful weapons. She was an accomplished killer who was a person that many would least expect, she was lethal when she killed. And her victims hardly stood a chance against her, because most didn't even see it coming. She would outsmart them and be two steps ahead of them, not leaving a trace for anybody to know. All except Isabella, who knew about and watched Raspberry kill Shameek. Her own cousin, which Isabella had no clue or why she decided to kill him.

Isabella wanting to see Raspberry at her place and specifically saying her place had a lot of thoughts going through Raspberry's mind. Was Isabella wearing a wire and being a snitch ? Was she going to try and kill Raspberry in her own apartment ? Was she trying to set her up ? Some of the many thoughts running through Raspberry's mind. Either way like always she would be prepared for whatever came her way. Later that day Isabella came by her apartment as planned, and from the moment that she stepped in her apartment. Raspberry was all about the subject at hand.

"So what did you want to talk to me about" ?

"I've been holding back talking to you about this for some time now. But why did you have to kill Shameek ? And who was he to you" ? Isabella asked.

"I don't know what you're talking about, and I don't know no Shameek" Raspberry replied.

"I don't have a wire on me Mami, I swear I dont. I wouldn't do that to you" Isabella said taking off her coat then her shirt down to her bra. And was about to pull her bra off until Raspberry stopped her.

"Listen I needed you to do me a favor and you did. Who he was to me doesn't matter. What mattered was he had to go. I told you before that we shouldn't talk about this again, it happened and it's in the past" Raspberry said.

"That's not the only thing. Do you know what happened to Melvin, Simone, and Tricky" ? Isabella asked.

"What are you getting at Isabella ? I know just as much as you know. And I was just as shocked when Melvin left as you were" Raspberry replied.

"I just need to know Mami, it's been eating me up inside. I haven't been able to sleep at night. Especially with what happened to Shameek" Isabella said sounding concerned.

"We been through a lot together Isabella, and we finally good now. We're the major pieces that make the club go. Be happy for what we have now after all the bullshit we been through. When you can do that, the less time you will be spending thinking about what happened to those people. Let the Police do their job, and lets get to this money" Raspberry said taking a sip of her drink.

"You know I guess you're right, I haven't enjoyed myself in some time Mami. I need a vacation, maybe visit my family in Miami" Isabella replied.

"Maybe you do need a vacation, clear your mind. We can hold the club down while you're gone. I can talk to Marks, I'm sure he wouldn't have a problem with it" Raspberry said.

"That would be very nice of you Mami" Isabella said sounding excited.

As always, Raspberry looked out for Isabella. And offered her a getaway. Something Raspberry felt she deserved for being so loyal to her. She also carefully executed a shift in focus within Isabella, quickly taking her mind off Shameek, Simone, Tricky, and Melvin. And more on herself and a much needed getaway. She would talk to Marks about it as soon as possible.

Isabella felt a lot better about everything moving forward, she would do just what Raspberry asked her to do. And let the Police handle what happened to Simone and Tricky. Meanwhile Chaos had still been M.I.A. And Raspberry hadn't heard from him in over a week, she was starting to get worried if she was ever going to hear from him again. She didnt want to completely lose contact with him or his whereabouts. She had worked too hard executing her plan for him. But she continued to wait patiently hoping to hear from him soon. The night was slowly approaching and Raspberry had to get ready to go on and start the night's show. As she took to the stage and started the show. She couldn't help but notice Chaos standing towards the back of the club, she hadn't spoke to him in over a week and out of nowhere he showed up at the club. No emotions could be shown, she had a job to do and she did it. She definitely wasn't too happy with Chaos, but she had to realize that deep down she wasn't in her situation with Chaos for pleasure. It was personal. And it was also business. Taking everything he had was the business part. And getting revenge for her sister's murder was the personal part.

After having a break from the stage Raspberry strolled her way over to Chaos.

"Why hello there, long time no see or hear. It's nice to see you here" Raspberry said sarcastically.

"Listen I'm sorry I didn't contact you, but I had some important shit to handle. And couldn't be hung up on the phone for even a minute. I just decided to come here and see you and then maybe drive back to my place. Maybe a nice breakfast in the morning just me and you" ? Chaos said trying to convince Raspberry to forgive him.

Raspberry stood there for a moment just staring at Chaos and shaking her head. "You lucky I like you, if not I would've told you to go to hell. Let's go" Raspberry replied as Chaos smiled and they got up and left the club en route to Chaos condo in D.C.

Even though Raspberry wasn't too happy with Chaos at the moment, she knew that she would eventually get over it because she needed Chaos. She needed Chaos so she could get revenge for her sister's death. She had slowly brought Chaos along till this point, and she wasn't done trying to get as much information as she could about him and his business practices and finances. And she wasn't stopping at just that, she also wanted Francisco who was the mastermind of the whole thing. And ran the organization that her sister was apart of that got her killed. Isabella as always was riding shotgun to help her with her plan. She often times sat and thought about what Francisco looked like and if his face looked familiar to her from her high school years. That was around the time her sister was hustling for him.

She just had to meet Francisco to keep the ball rolling. She was very confident that if Francisco came into the equation and saw Isabella, they would click and the plan would be in motion. So she kept her composure and waited patiently for the time to come. They had a great time that night and woke up in the morning continuing their episode from last night. One thing about Chaos and Raspberry was their physical chemistry was like magic. They were both hustling in different ways, and hardly ever discussed too much of their personal lives. They were both cold blooded killers on a collision course with one another, but only one knew it. Which was somewhat of an advantage of sorts. Raspberry had her plan in action. After dealing with men who at some point disappointed her. She decided to change her outlook on the way she dealt with each situation pertaining to each man. Her intention was never bad at first, except this situation. After killing Malik and realizing she could do it and get away with it. Set her off on a journey to continue killing when she felt it was necessary. And the more she killed without a trace the more confident she was about what she was doing.

She was beautiful, sexy, smart, ambitious, and a go getter. And she took down some very dangerous men along the way. Along with a very outspoken woman who was the one who gave her a shot as a dancer. In her mind, all for good reason. Most would think for the things her victims did, they could've been handled a lot better without a person losing their life. But that was also a fact about Raspberry. For all the things she had been through in her life, some had affected her in very negative ways. She had a sick mind and was somewhat of a sociopath, but she was also all about her money. A mixed bag of a person but very tempting and irresistible being that she was so beautiful and smart. Most if not all men were instantly attracted to her just as Chaos was. Her body was amazing for a woman who rarely went to the gym, her body was also natural. No surgeries or anything. Her mother Denise was a very attractive woman also when she was younger. So Raspberry got it honest. But Denise's drug addiction had slowly affected her looks over time. Raspberry came from a beautiful woman and maintained her beauty, it was important in her line of work. Plus she took pride in looking good and carrying herself with class.

After getting up in the morning and eating breakfast that Chaos prepared personally for her, she was headed back home to College Park. Upon returning home she checked her messages, and Marks left a message saying to meet him at the club a little later. She didn't really know what Marks wanted, but she was ready for whatever as always. Meanwhile Isabella was home and her phone rang.

"Hey what's going on. I know you might not know who this is, but I'm going to tell you. This is Chaos, and before you say anything. Think before you speak" Chaos said.

"Hello Chaos, what's going on" ? Isabella replied.

"I need to see you, and I need to see you soon" Chaos said sounding like it was urgent.

"Ok we can do that. Is there anything else" ? Isabella asked.

"Just keep your phone near you and wait for me to call back" Chaos replied.

Isabella agreed and hung up the phone. A few hours passed and Chaos called again. "It's me again, so did you decide when we can see each other" ? Chaos asked.

"I guess sometime soon, but I don't want Raspberry to know we know each other" Isabella said sounding concerned.

"So you don't want to let Raspberry know huh ? I guess you don't want to let her know we also used to be involved with one another. Or should I say we used to have a lot of sex" Chaos said laughing.

"This isn't funny, I seriously don't want her to know at all. Let's keep it between us, it was a while ago anyway" Isabella said.

"Don't worry, your secret is safe with me. As long as you do as I ask. If not I will definitely tell her all about us" Chaos replied.

Isabella had never thought about dealing with this issue because up until now Chaos never said anything about it, so she didnt either. But now that he did it had become an issue. If Raspberry found out that all along Isabella and Chaos were lying and did know each other. And not only knew each other but also used to be involved. It wouldn't be a good thing at all. And it could potentially destroy the relationship, bond, and trust that Raspberry had with Isabella. Yet again Isabella was caught in a sticky situation basically because she knew certain people. Isabella had told Raspberry that she knew Tricky when him and Raspberry were dealing with each other. But Chaos she couldn't tell her about just because it was a totally different situation. And she knew Raspberry wanted to go on a double date with Francisco and her.

She met Chaos a few years ago in a local D.C. area club. After meeting each other they exchanged numbers and began seeing each other casually for about three months. They both knew their situation wasn't that serious.

Chapter Seven "Justice Is Served"

Isabella had worked in the D.C. area dancing at a few different clubs throughout the city when she was younger and eventually meeting Malik who introduced her to the call girl game. Which she excelled in and made her and him both a lot of money. Her and Malik's relationship was strictly business, she had worked for him a little over a year when he met and was seeing Raspberry. Once they met, Isabella and Raspberry immediately clicked and developed a good friendship. After Malik was mysteriously murdered her and Raspberry got even closer and she eventually started working for Raspberry after she took over for

Malik. And started her own Escort Service of women. Which included Isabella. Raspberry then started seeing an associate of her brother's and a local gun dealer Tricky. Who dabbled in guns as well as drugs. Her and Tricky had a little fling when she was younger, but nothing real serious. Tricky was also murdered, in which Isabella was suspicious about Raspberry after talking to Melvin. Melvin at the time had her thinking that Raspberry was in some form involved with not only Tricky's death, but also Simone's death.

It was something that was never proven so Isabella left it alone, and after talking to Raspberry she did what she said and let the authorities handle it. But now once again, Raspberry was involved with another man that she had been previously involved with. And by all accounts for the wrong reasons. Isabella had no clue of what Raspberry's plans were regarding Chaos, but she knew what she did to Shameek. So she knew what Raspberry was capable of, and she was once again riding shotgun in another one of her plans. Now what was she to do ? She couldn't tell Raspberry the truth, at least not yet. In fear of her not trusting Isabella again. And what would Raspberry do if she found out about Isabella and Chaos ? That they really knew each other, and had been involved before. She couldn't continue giving Chaos sex when he wanted. Chaos was in a prime position to have his cake and eat it too, and he knew it. He used it to his advantage everytime.

Chaos cared about Raspberry but had women to his disposal. He didn't care at all too much about losing any female because he always knew he could replace them. But for the moment he wanted to keep Raspberry and continue having fun with her. He also wanted to keep in touch with Isabella, even though he wasnt dealing with her at the momemt. Isabella knew that Chaos was a very dangerous man, she knew he had a criminal past. But she didn't know about the plenty of people he murdered in cold blood to get his point across. One thing she didn't do was put anything past him, she had heard some things about his reputation in the streets. So him actually murdering someone wouldn't surprise her. She wasn't taking a chance with him or Raspberry, she didn't want to cross either one of them. But eventually she had to make a decision the longer the situation played out. It was like deja vu all over again, from the Raspberry Tricky situation.

Page 136

Isabella couldn't understand why Chaos wanted to tell Raspberry anything about them when he had already been dating Raspberry for a while now. But much like Raspberry, he loved to use his leverage when he had it. And that's what Isabella believed he was doing to her. Leveraging her so she had to do what he said. Also much like Raspberry, she didn't want to cross him in fear of what he would do. The best thing she could do was focus on what she had to do and let the rest take care of itself. It was all she could do. In the meantime she had to get ready for the night and she wanted to put together her usual great performance. Like the many men that was at

Melvins were used to. On her way in the club she saw Raspberry talking to one of the bartenders but she stopped when she seen Isabella and started talking to her.

"Hey girl, it's been a change of plans tonight. You can headline tonight" Raspberry said.

"Wow, really Mami ? You always love to headline, I do too. But thanks a lot for doing this, I really appreciate it Mami. You sure though" Isabella replied asking Raspberry one last time.

Raspberry just smiled. "Yes I'm sure, you can headline. I got one of the other girls to open up for me."

"Why what's wrong with you ? It's not like you to not dance the night you're supposed to dance" Isabella asked sounding concerned.

"I'm good, just tear the roof off beautiful. Like I know you can" Raspberry replied walking away.

Isabella was somewhat shocked and didn't know what to think, but she couldn't worry about that now. She had a job to do. And just as Raspberry said to tear down the stage, Isabella did just that. She took to the stage like she had something to prove, very confident and commanded the crowd and they loved it. Raspberry stood off to the side of the stage cheering Isabella on and smiling all the while like a proud mother watching her child. She always wanted Isabella to do well, them being competitive brought the best out of each other. Only to make each other better and the club more money. At the end of the day, it would make them both more money.

Isabella lit up the stage in front of Marks, Raspberry, and Chaos who was sitting at his usual table in V.I.P. Of course the stage was littered with ones as they always was when Raspberry and Isabella hit the stage. Isabella came off the stage with her head in the clouds and her confidence level out of this world. She put all her worries to the side and focused on her stage presence. While looking sexy as ever wearing a tiny skirt that was thin enough to see through. It was a great night for Isabella, and a great night for the club. Marks was happy and had recently took a different role as the club's owner by stepping back out of the spotlight. He preferred to play the background. Which was in contrast to the way Blade wanted to be after a while of running the club. Marks was a very smart businessman and he stayed out of the trouble that plagued his hometown of Baltimore. He worked for the city and played a key role in helping out the community. He was generally a good guy, but was surrounded by hustlers and killers.

Page 137

Even though Marks lost two of his good friends and mentors in Shameek and Blade, he felt comfort as time went on. He also eventually found out Raspberry was from Baltimore too. After another great night at the club and Marks was feeling good and he wanted to thank Raspberry personally so he invited her out for lunch to show his appreciation. The next day as they sat in a College Park restaurant and talked about the club and it's direction.

"It was a really great night last night, really has been since I been here" Marks said.

"I got news for you, it's always been great. And it's been even greater since me and Isabella have been here. The crowd knows we're going to give them a great show each time they come out" Raspberry replied.

"And that's what I love about you and her, you both have elevated the rest of the women's stage presence. And for that it's made us a better club and generated more profits. I'm definitely pleased with the way everything is going at the club. Just wanted to let you know and I will do the same for Isabella, that I appreciate you both very much. And for that, I'm going to give you both raises" Marks said.

"That's great and I appreciate you doing that, but I believe I deserve a better raise because of my position and the fact I brought Isabella to this club. I just hope its not a catch to this. And excuse me if I'm assuming, but I'm used to Melvin and Blade. Two men that always had a catch behind their methods" Raspberry replied.

"Of course not, there's no catch. I'm just happy with the way things are going at the club. We have increased profits and you both deserve raises for helping me achieve that. And I agree you definitely deserve a better raise for all that you have done. That is all" Marks said sounding sincere.

Raspberry nodded in approval and was happy there was no catch or clause with her raise. She believed that her and Marks would have a great business relationship moving forward because of that understanding. Leaving the restaurant after their meeting, Raspberry returned home for a little while before she had to get to the club and report to work. Upon doing that she got a phone call from Chaos wanting to see her later that night after work. She told him she had to take a rain check on that because she was already tired, and knew she would be even more tired by the end of the night.

Chaos decided he would stay home if Raspberry wasn't going to come home with him afterwards. So Raspberry would be hitting the stage without Chaos being there. Something that would be different but definitely wasn't something she had never done before. She was focused on getting back on stage after letting Isabella control the stage and taking a break from dancing for a night. She was eager to get on stage and feel the crowd again, something that she always loved about being a dancer. She also felt great and confident after being promised a raise from Marks. Being the center of attention with all eyes on her was addictive, almost as addictive as the money.

Her being back on that stage after a short time away from it brought joy to Raspberry's heart and brought the best out of her. She took to the stage much like her protégé Isabella and raised the roof at the club as the dancers say. Meaning they had a great night as evidenced by the many ones littered across the stage. Like Raspberry did with her, Isabella just watched from backstage still in awe at a woman that she had admired so much as a dancer and leader. Her good friend that always looked out for her, Isabella was her number one fan. After coming off stage Raspberry and Isabella embraced each other with a hug and walked backstage smiling and laughing. They had a chance to talk after Raspberry's performance because Chaos wasn't in attendance.

"Mami you did that. Legendary like always, I don't know how you do it. But nobody, I mean nobody controls this crowd like you do" Isabella said sounding excited.

"Thanks girl, you do your thing too. Proud of you" Raspberry replied as they embraced each other with a hug.

Isabella was trying to put the threat that Chaos imposed on her in the back of her mind. She definitely wasn't going to tell Raspberry now. It would have completely fucked up the mood. She wouldn't dare to put a dim on Raspberry's shine. So she would save it for another time. Chaos for once was at a place for a decent amount of time. He traveled a lot and moved a lot, living anywhere from Washington, D.C. to Tacoma, Washington State. He had put in work all across the country. And was rumored to have been involved with murders in New Jersey, Michigan, Georgia, and Texas. Of course somehow beating each case with high profile lawyers and witness intimidation. Francisco and Chaos had a large amount of soldiers and people who worked for them across the country. They had developed great business relationships with a few heavy hitters in Chicago and L.A. They had a few people they occasionally dealt with from the New York area, but not a whole lot.

Either way Chaos was here now, and he had escaped doing any very lengthy time in prison. Despite being charged with some serious and violent crimes that weren't murder also. All the work he put in was apart of the game, never outside the game. And the only mistake he made to date was accidently killing Deanna, Raspberry's sister. As sad as it was, Chaos had no remorse for killing her. Or having Anita take the charges she took. After he threatened to kill her also if she said anything to anyone about what really happened that night. He hardly knew Deanna or Anita, they were handpicked by Francisco. In Chaos mind he had no ties to Deanna or Anita, he was only doing what he was told. He had no feelings either way about either of the girls. The home invasion wasn't all a mistake or bad, because Chaos still got away with a good amount of cash.

Page 139

It was the same way he felt now about Raspberry and Isabella. Two beautiful women who weren't necessarily in the game and who he was involved with intimately. Chaos also had no clue that he was currently dating the sister of the girl he accidentally killed in Baltimore over four years ago. Meanwhile Raspberry was feeling good about the previous night and the way she tore down the stage. She felt so good that she decided to go shopping for some new clothes and a few pair of shoes. She had not been shopping for quite some time, so she decided to head to Downtown D.C. It was something she did more often than most women do. She owned over sixty pairs of shoes, numerous dresses and outfits. And a bunch of designer bags. A lot of which were gifts from different men that were very fond of her. A few more outfits and a few more pairs of shoes wouldn't hurt. While she was out shopping she saw someone that looked familiar from a distance. It looked like Chaos, no it couldn't be him. She had just talked to Chaos the previous night. But then again his condo wasn't that far away from the area.

And then the unthinkable happened, she saw a female with the man that looked like Chaos. The woman looked like Isabella. She had to completely stop shopping and walked a little closer to see who it was for sure. So she went a little closer but out of plain view sight of either of them. And much to her surprise it was Chaos and Isabella in a shoe store shopping together. She just watched from a far and shaking her head while watching. Someone she had valued as a good friend. Looked after, and was loyal to was obviously doing things behind her back. The same with Chaos. A man that she had been involved with for the last almost nine and a half months. She was shocked that they even knew each other like that. After the initial shock Raspberry got herself together and from that point on she knew what she had to do. She had always trusted Isabella to a certain extent. She had trusted her more than she had trusted anybody since her sister Deanna was alive. She developed a friendship with Isabella similar to her bond with her sister, but of course not as strong because Raspberry and Deanna were actually sisters.

Her and Isabella were not blood related and now their friendship was in serious jeopardy.

Either way it was a crushing blow to Raspberry's plans for Chaos, after finding out what she now knew she had to alter her plans somewhat. And figure out a way to get into Chaos and Francisco's circle without Isabella. Isabella had lied to her and knew Chaos more than she originally led on. Raspberry knew that her and Isabella's friendship would never be the same after that day. But she wasn't going to be obvious with showing her it was anything different at the moment. She would act as normal as she could to not tip her off about what she had recently found out. And what she saw. But now Raspberry had two different plans for Chaos and Isabella, and she was determined to execute each plan to the best of her ability.

Raspberry quickly got out of the area they were in and went directly to her car and drove home. Driving home she was just shaking her head and talking to herself in a somewhat whisper. Yet again another person that was close to her had crossed her, not that she had loved Chaos. Because she didnt. But this was now going to change her plan from what it originally was, it was more the fact Isabella was doing what she was doing. And never told Raspberry that she even knew Chaos. The way they were interacting with one another seemed like they knew each other for quite some time. Raspberry would continue to play clueless, she loved the fact that she knew something that someone was doing to her. And they had no idea she knew about it all along. It was the same way with Simone after she had robbed her apartment and wore her bracelet right in front of her. Simone made a critical and bold mistake by being sloppy. Isabella for all her loyalty she supposedly had for Raspberry, it was all worth nothing at this point. Raspberry had stuck up for Isabella so many times, with Melvin and Blade in particular.

She had gave her lessons as a dancer and took her under her wing since she had met her as a call girl with the Escort Service through Malik. Chaos was the target since Raspberry had got the information from Anita after going to see her. After meeting Isabella and bonding with her, she was supposed to be her right hand person. They were to get to the top together, or so Raspberry thought. But things had changed after Raspberry seen what she seen that day, she continued to act as if everything was normal. But she was not the type to hide her feelings for too long. For now she would keep her composure and keep her eyes on the prize which was Chaos and Francisco. She would also keep a close eye on Isabella from here on out, because the trust was no longer there. But she wanted to see what she would do next thinking that Raspberry didn't have a clue about what was going on. Later that night Raspberry was at the club getting dressed and ready for the night when Isabella walked in the dressing room.

"Hey Isabella, ready for the night" ? Raspberry asked.

"Always mami, I was born ready. You look very sexy and gorgeous as usual" Isabella said looking at Raspberry from head to toe.

"Why thank you, you look very sexy yourself. Well its time for me to go on and get this show started, good luck tonight" Raspberry replied walking out of the dressing room and walking up the steps to the main stage.

That went well Raspberry was thinking as she continued to keep her composure and act as normal as possible. A part of her wanted to spazz out on Isabella, but the other part of her convinced herself to be patient. That time would come and her revenge would be even sweeter, but for now she had bigger fish to fry.

Page 141

Another night on stage and another great night with plenty of money made. By the end of the night Raspberry was ready to go home. Isabella offered to take her out to breakfast but she declined and said she wanted to go home. Once she got home she decided at damn near four in the morning to clean her gun of all things, she was tired but couldn't sleep. So she decided to do just that to keep her occupied. A strange thing to do so early in the morning, but Raspberry was still fuming about the Isabella and Chaos situation. She carefully cleaned the gun, something that she seen Tricky do one time or another when she was at his house, it was how she learned. After doing that it was almost dawn as she lay in her bed looking out the window into the skies. She always figured when she would look up she would see an image of her sister in the skies. Even though it had been well over four years since Deanna's death, Raspberry was still grieving and missing her sister and best friend.

When she prayed she always felt she wasn't just talking to God but she was communicating with her sister. Talking to her sister, asking her questions about what she should do about certain things and promising her she would bring justice to those who took her life. It was something she did of course when she was alone, she let very little people know about her sister and about what had happened to her sister. One person in particular that knew the whole story was her former roommate Candice, who Raspberry still talked to from time to time but wasn't as close with anymore. She still had Candice number even though Candice had been graduated from the University of Maryland, and was working outside her hometown of Washington D.C. Raspberry had heard from some of her fellow classmates about Candice and what she was doing with her life. So Raspberry decided to call her.

"Hey girl, it's been a long time. I hear you got your dream job and working close to home. How's life been treating you" ? Raspberry said.

"Desiree ? Oh shit girl, it's good to hear from you. I didn't know what had happened to you after I graduated. I mean I knew you dropped out and all, but I was wondering where you were" Candice replied.

"I'm still around and still dancing at Melvins, and it's good to hear from you again also. I was thinking one day we can get together for lunch or something and catch up, it's been a while" Raspberry said.

"Sounds good to me, I'm usually off the weekends so I will give you a call to see about your schedule and when you're free" Candice replied.

"Ok sounds like a plan to me, in the meantime take care. I will keep in touch" Raspberry said before hanging up. Raspberry and Candice always had a good relationship, and shared things about their lives with each other. After Raspberry dropped out, they lost touch for a while. She felt it would be good to have lunch with Candice and catch up.

Page 142

Raspberry had a thought for a second. Maybe Candice could ride shotgun on this one and be Raspberry's right hand for her plan of action against Chaos and Francisco. And then she dismissed it for the moment, she had to talk to Candice after not talking to her in quite a while. Before she could even think of asking her to do what she wanted her to do. So at the moment it was wishful thinking, but Raspberry was hoping it could become reality. Later on that day Chaos decided to pay Raspberry a visit and take her to dinner before she had to work later on that night at the club. So as they were sitting there eating, Chaos decided to spark up a conversation.

"So how's everything been at the club since there's no more Blade there to cause havoc" ? Chaos asked.

"As to be expected, it's been real peaceful and things are running a lot more smoother. I'm happy, Isabella is happy as well as the rest of the women. And so is Marks. So yeah everything is good right now" Raspberry replied.

Chaos was happy to hear that, because when Raspberry was happy that translated into her being even happier when she was with him. It was the same for her when she was somewhat angry, there was times she brought her work home with her. Those were the times Chaos would like to forget.

"Anything else interesting happening in your life" ? Chaos asked.

"No not really, still have my friend Isabella that I wanted to introduce to your friend. She's single and been yearning for the attention of a good man in her life" Raspberry said taking a sip from her drink.

"I'm not so sure if my boy is in a position to be worried about a woman right now, he's a very busy man and his mind stays on business. But I will say something to him though" Chaos replied.

"Chaos we both know I'm not talking about my girl Isabella being anyone's lady, we're just trying to have a good time......you know maybe hang out a few times. You know we all would have a great time, so just speak to your boy and tell him there's a bad ass Latina waiting to have a great time with him" Raspberry said getting closer to Chaos and rubbing his leg under the table.

Chaos just smiled and said he could do that. Raspberry always had a way of persuading Chaos to do some things he was at first unsure of and sometimes hesistant about doing. He was always very cautious and careful about letting anyone in his circle. Let alone letting anyone around his close friend and partner. It was just the way they ran things to protect their own privacy and way of business. And that's also what made them so successful for the many years they had been in the game. Raspberry knew deep down that she wasn't really going to introduce Isabella to Francisco, she had already changed her plans after seeing Chaos with Isabella. She was testing Chaos, to see if he would really do it. Page 143

Chaos definitely didn't want Isabella being anywhere near Francisco, let alone hanging out with him. That created a problem for Raspberry, she needed to have someone bring Francisco to the forefront so she could stick to her plan. So she could finally see who this man was. She knew now that Isabella was no longer an option to help her. And Raspberry had no one she could use to take her place at the moment, that was something she had yet to work on. After finding out what she knew about Isabella and Chaos, everything changed. For now she was focused on the night ahead of her. Chaos himself was dealing with some personal issues and had to make a quick trip back to Jersey City, New Jersey where three of his seven children resided with their mother. Their mother called and asked Chaos to come back because there was a situation going on with their children. He agreed and immediately made his way to Jersey City, his hometown. Everytime he went back home he couldn't stay in Jersey City very long, old and some new enemies of his and Francisco were still very much apart of the city. So when he would come back no one would know except his kid's mother. Often times his kids didn't know, he would just show up and surprise them.

This time wasn't about a surprise visit, this was more of a personal visit involving his kid's. While Chaos was handling that situation, Raspberry was all about business herself as she prepared herself for the show tonight. It would be another night that she would hit the stage without Chaos being there, he had called her a little earlier that evening to let her know he had got there safely and wished her good luck. Something she thought was really sweet considering Chaos had never done something like that, or was it the fact he may have had a guilty conscience ? And was trying to make amends for lying and cheating. Either way she knew the truth but continued to play along with what was going on. So she wouldn't ruin anymore of her plan that already had to change. Before Raspberry could go to the club, her old roommate Candice wanted to meet on short notice for a drink. Candice was leaving for a few days herself on vacation and was in the area.

"I just wanted to catch up quick before I go on this vacation. I wanted to see what you been up to. How's Melvins? Didn't get a chance to ask you about the club the last time we spoke" Candice said.

"Well a lot has changed since you first took me there, even though it's still called Melvins. Melvin hasn't been the owner in nearly six months. He just picked up and left, sold the club without telling any of us and we haven't seen him since" Raspberry replied.

"Really ? Wow, I mean I never really knew Melvin that well. But I remember when I used to talk to Simone she said the man absolutely loved that club" Candice said sounding surprise.

"Yeah it was a complete shock to all of us, I still can't believe he did it, but I guess that's what he wanted to do. I wish him well regardless. Hey when you get back from your vacation you should stop by the club sometime" Raspberry replied.

"I might just do that. Like I told you before, I'm working in D.C. now. And I love it, it's great working in my hometown. But I will give you a call when I get back" Candice said.

"I understand, but at least come by for me. It will be like old times, and I got you a spot in V.I.P." Raspberry said trying to convince Candice to come.

Candice just looked at Raspberry for a second and smiled replying, "Ok girl, I guess I will come out. You always did have a way to get people to do shit for you" as they both laughed.

They talked a little while longer before Candice had to go, they embraced each other with a hug and went their seperate ways. It was nice to see Candice after not seeing her for a while. And even better that Raspberry took the first steps in trying to rekindle their friendship after some lost time. Raspberry felt like a night at Melvins would do Candice some good. She could get out for a change and finally step back in that club where her cousin worked. For the first time since she was murdered. Raspberry also was priming Candice to ride shotgun in her plan against Chaos. Candice didn't have the figure that Isabella had but she was still very much a beautiful woman. Meeting with Candice put Raspberry in a somewhat better mood as she was now focused on the night ahead.

The drive to the club from her apartment was a joyous time singing out loud to the latest R&B as it played on her car stereo putting her in an upbeat mood before she even got to the club. Arriving at the club as the guy at the door let her in and she greeted him before walking through and making her way downstairs to the dressing room. Getting dressed Raspberry was looking in the mirror fixing her outfit when she saw Isabella walk behind her and spoke.

"Hey mami, how are you ? Are you ready for tonight" ? Isabella asked.

"Of course I am, like you I was born ready" Raspberry replied smiling and winking her eye at Isabella as she walked past her and went upstairs to the main stage and bar.

Raspberry and Isabella had respect for one another, but that didn't mean that they weren't in almost constant competition with each other when it came to that stage. They both wanted to be the best, and both loved to be in command of the stage. Leaving the crowd in awe was a normal thing to the both of them. In most cases that's who the crowd came to see....them two.

It was the life for them both, fortunately for them they were good friends throughout most of their time as dancers. For Raspberry that all changed as she didn't look at Isabella the same anymore. With Chaos still in Jersey City, Raspberry was going to be on her own once again and it was business as usual. Focused from the very moment she hit the stage. She looked absolutely stunning and wore a sexy piece that had most if not all the men in attendance drooling. It was another night at the office for Raspberry as she did her thing. And walked off the stage with so much sexy swagger, that you had to be there to have seen it .

Page 145

A few days had passed and Raspberry had finally heard from Chaos, as soon as he got back to D.C. he called her.

"Hey baby what's up, just got back into town. How you been" ? Chaos said.

"Well hello stranger, it's good to hear from you. I've been ok" Raspberry replied.

"Come on woman don't act like that, you know I had to go back home and handle some shit with my kids. They good, and now I'm back" Chaos said.

"Glad to hear that they're good. And to be honest with you, I'm also glad you're back. You missed a great show the other night, but I'm sure you will make it up and come through next weekend" Raspberry replied.

"Indeed I will, wouldn't miss seeing your sexy ass glide across that stage for nothing. It's even better knowing that your sexy ass is coming home with me at the end of the night" Chaos said smiling.

Raspberry also smiling on the other end of the phone. "I did want to ask you though about us double dating with your friend, Francisco." ?

And before Raspberry could get another word out, Chaos interrupted by saying, "I don't think that's going to work. Not sure if my homie is down to do that. But if anything changes I will let you know."

"I was going to say that I have another friend that I would like to introduce him to, Isabella seems to be busy at the moment. So I hope he changes his mind and we can all go out and have a good time" Raspberry said hoping by saying she had another friend in mind that Chaos would agree now.

Being that he now knew that other woman wasn't Isabella. It was worth a try although Raspberry had no clue if it would work. Either way she felt she would make it work somehow regardless. Chaos was guarding Francisco and what they did like he was guarding his kids. It was how he always was when it came to his childhood friend. And it was exactly how they were with their business practices. It would be a challenge like no other for Raspberry to break their code and work her way inside their circle. But as long as she was still breathing, she would keep trying until she got what she wanted. Raspberry hadn't spoke to Anita since a little after her sister's murder. So she felt it was necessary to pay her a visit to let her know she hadn't forgot about her. And she also wanted to see if she could get any more information on Franciso.

Anita had been moved to another prison since starting her prison sentence which was a 13 year sentence. She had almost five years in for time served. But she hadn't heard from anyone but her mother since she was sentenced. Pretty sure seeing Desiree after a few years would maybe lift her spirits. Along with the fact that Desiree had finally located Chaos, would make Anita even more happy. So Raspberry made the trip to Jessup to visit her. Page 146

After going through the many security checks, Raspberry made it to the visiting room and took a seat behind the glass and waited for Anita to come out. She sat directly across from her with a huge glass separating the two of them. After waiting for a few minutes, Anita was finally brought into the room. When she first laid eyes on Desiree, they both looked at each other and gave each other a smile as they both put their hands up on the glass.

"Hey Anita, it's good to see you. You look good, seems like they taking good care of you in here. I hope you got that money I sent you" Raspberry said.

"Desiree long time no see, it's also good to see you too. I'm looking as good as I can look considering the circumstances I'm in. And I got the money, thanks. So how's life been treating you" ? Anita asked.

"It's been good, I just been working trying to make it like everybody else you know. But listen, I came here because I wanted to tell you I finally located Chaos. Actually I been seeing him for about almost six months now. And before you trip, I'm just setting him up for the kill. And trying to get my hands on everything he owns. To me, it was the only way I could get inside his circle....inside his world" Raspberry said in a low tone.

After listening to what Raspberry said, Anita replied. "Brilliant idea, me myself I probably would have tried to kill him the old fashioned way. Maybe poison his ass, or leave the gas on. But that probably wouldn't have worked, I trust you know what you're doing. Just be careful, because I do know how him and Francisco are about their business. But I must say that I'm glad you found him. Honestly I didn't think anyone would find him after what he did to Deanna and me that night. Just know I'm with you a hundred and ten percent, all the way. I mean I can't help you in here, but if I hear anything in here I will definitely let you know."

Raspberry knew she would have Anita's support, she was essentially getting revenge for not only Deanna. But Anita also for taking all the charges they could give her without the charge for murder. Anita shot one of the men that they were planning to rob, the shot she fired wasn't fatal. But Chaos finished two of the men off before leaving that house in East Baltimore that fateful night. Chaos also fired the shot that killed Deanna, which was determined by her autopsy.

Chaos was wanted for three murders in one nights work, something that became routine with him being the enforcer of his crew. Regardless of it all, no one wanted him dead more than Raspberry and Anita. Two people who were the closest to Raspberry's sister Deanna. After talking for a few more minutes as visiting hours were coming to a close. Raspberry and Anita put both their hands on the glass that was between them. As they couldn't embrace each other, but showed their love for one another. Raspberry owed Anita a lot for her identifying her sister's killer. Anita felt that was the least she could do knowing she would be incarcerated for thirteen years. And she herself couldn't avenge her best friend's death. The next best thing was to share the information with her best friend's family and let them do what they wanted to do with it. She figured someone in their family was crazy enough to seek revenge, that was why she did it. But she never knew Desiree had murdered several people already. Page 147

On the drive back to College Park, Raspberry felt good about her visit with Anita and the fact Anita knew now that Raspberry had Chaos in her sights. Plus knowing that Anita was doing ok and looking pretty good, made Raspberry feel good. That in itself made the whole visit perfect. Raspberry sent Anita money monthly, she felt like she owed her that. Anita realized now that she should've tried a little harder to talk Deanna out of going through with the robbery they did that night. But she also knew that once Deanna's mind was made up it was hard for anyone to change it. She was healing slowly from it, but being in prison made her think a lot. A lot about what happened and a lot about how she imagined her life would be right now if she was free. She battled many feelings since being in prison for almost five years, only being in contact regularly with her mother who made the drive from Baltimore. Even though it had been a while since she had seen Desiree, she always received her money monthly on time in her account like clockwork.

She appreciated that from Raspberry who she only knew as Desiree, her real name. After getting back from Jessup, Raspberry decided to head to the gun range. A place she enjoyed to frequent. It was also a place she could blow off steam and exude energy, she was a very active person who loved to look good and enjoyed life. She had the finer things in life and dated several men that had long money and were extremely dangerous, just like she was. The Chaos situation was business and personal. Raspberry specialized in getting people to do things that they normally wouldn't do, just by her aura and presence. The attraction would always be there almost instantly, she was drop dead gorgeous and dangerous at the same damn time. But you would never know it unless you brought it out of her. Some of those ways of doing that could vary. Sometimes it's something simple and sometimes it's something complex. She was a wild bag of tricks. But if she loved you, she LOVED YOU.

And there wouldn't be anything she wouldn't do for you. On the surface she was a caring person. That's the Desiree her mother knew. Over the years certain situations changed her, and changed her for the worst. After killing the first time and being as careful as she was, and remains till this day. She felt comfortable to kill again and again. If it made a point if it made sense and life better for her, then she would no doubt kill again. And those around her that meant the most she protected, she protected them with her life. And she would kill for them if she had to. After learning to dance and being the best dancer at the club, Raspberry ran with it and met some of the men that shaped her thoughts moving forward. Those men really never knew how much they were like her. How cold hearted she would be after killing someone just like she was after killing Simone. She loved the fact that no one thought she was capable of what she was doing.....all but Isabella saw it with her own eyes. Isabella had dirt on her, and it was beginning to make Raspberry feel uncomfortable.

Page 148

The night was approaching and Raspberry was about to leave for the club. She had one of the other women be the emcee for the night in place of her, she was to hit the stage tonight. As many times as Raspberry hit that stage and amazed the crowd, her moods shifted from excited to business as usual. Tonight was one of those business as usual nights, but like always she got herself up to perform at her best. This night would be no different, she stepped on stage demanding attention and looking amazing as ever as the crowd that loved her so much watched in awe. Isabella decided to take the night off, so the crowd was enjoying it even more being that at least one of their two favorite dancers were in attendance. After another great performance, Raspberry walked towards the bar and once she got to the bar she seen Candice sitting down having a drink.

"Hey girl, I'm glad you decided to come" Raspberry said sounding excited as she embraced Candice with a hug.

"Hey, yeah I decided to come. It really wasn't easy. First time I've been here since Simone died. But I'm here !!! I see things have definitely changed around here, and you looked great up there. Who's the owner now" ? Candice asked.

"Marks, I thought I told you. Anyway, yeah he's a good dude. He's definitely different than Melvin too. They like night and day" Raspberry replied.

"Girl I seen you up there killing it, you have gotten better and better. And just think, when you first came in here you were shy as ever. I remember Simone saying. "Cousin I don't know if her shy ass is gonna work out or not." Candice said as the both of them laughed.

"Girl I was shy, I had never did no shit like this in my life. But hey it worked out" Raspberry said.

"Yeah you're right, it sure did and I'm happy and proud of your success. You look great out there, remember I told you that you was born for the stage. Just didn't know it was going to be for stripping and dancing on poles" Candice said as they both laughed out loud.

"Girl you're still crazy as ever" Raspberry replied still laughing.

"I could never do that shit, my ass is a little too big to be up there on a pole" Candice said laughing.

"Don't sell yourself short, you're beautiful. Always have been inside and out. That's all that matters, any man would be lucky to have you. Speaking of that, remember that time I had you go to that party looking for Ricky" ? Raspberry asked smiling.

"Yes I remember, had me going to the livest party of the year messing my groove up looking for his ass. I found him though" Candice said laughing.

"Yes you did, and that was the beginning to his end. My first love. I wonder where he is now" Raspberry said. Page 149

"Someone said he was out West somewhere, Cali....Vegas somewhere" Candice said

"Ok good, I won't be running into him anytime soon. You want another drink girl, hey.....hey...can we get another bottle over here please" Raspberry shouted, visibly feeling the effects of the bottle her and Candice had been sipping on and now finished.

It was a fun filled night, the old roommates catching up like old times. After that night and waking up to a hangover, which was unlike Raspberry. She knew she had a little too much fun the previous night. She didn't even know how her or Candice got home last night. After that night, Raspberry knew she didn't want Candice involved in her situation with Chaos and Francisco. She would figure out another way to deal with them. Later on that day Raspberry got a call and looked on her caller I.D. to find it was Isabella. She rolled her eyes in the back of her head and proceeded to answer it.

"Hey mami, how did things go the other night ? I know you tore the roof off" Isabella said.

"It was good, you know business as usual. You have a good time off" ? Raspberry asked.

"Yes, it was very nice. Me and a male friend enjoyed a nice little get away and I needed it Mami. Feel so much better, and can't wait to get back on stage" Isabella replied sounding excited.

Raspberry had a moment of pulling the phone from her ear and looking at it as if to say, why in the hell is she telling me this ?

"Oh really ? Ok girl I hear you, glad you had a good time. I may need one of those soon myself" Raspberry replied.

"Yes you should, every woman deserves that in her life" Isabella said sounding happy.

The women talked and said they would see each other later at the club. Meanwhile Raspberry came up with another way she could get to Chaos and Francisco. And she was starting to put that plan in action. She decided not to go to work that night and claimed she was sick. Instead she drove to Chaos condo in Northwest D.C. She didn't park outside his condo. She parked a ways down from it and watched as Chaos got in his black Cadillac Escalade. And she proceeded to follow him not too far behind. Her purpose was to see his whereabouts and figure out his routine, and more importantly how he could lead her to Francisco and his whereabouts.

As she followed she watched everything and was aware of her surroundings, carefully paying attention to whatever Chaos was doing. She followed him to an abandoned warehouse, she stayed back far enough to where Chaos or anyone else could hardly see her. She watched as Chaos got out of his car and went up to the warehouse, he then was met by two men who greeted him and then they all walked in the warehouse together. Raspberry was unaware of who the other two men were, but she was wondering if one of them was Francisco. She had some binoculars so she could see closer and more clearly. Watching to see if she could see any clues to who these other men were. Page 150

She couldn't see too much as the men went inside the warehouse and disappeared. She crept up slowly and quietly looking through the windows of the warehouse and saw them talking. Chaos and two other men. Were one of these men Francisco ? She thought to herself. There was no way she could hear what they were talking about, she still stayed there outside the window watching. After about fifteen minutes, the three men headed to the door and was about to leave. As Raspberry quickly ran back to her car which was parked around the corner. She wore a wig to hide her identity, she then waited for Chaos to start moving again as she continued to follow him. She followed him for about a half an hour going to various spots in D.C. before she decided to return home. She knew she wouldn't get too much right away. The reason Francisco and Chaos business was so successful was because they both were disciplined. They never let anyone know anything besides the people they were doing business with them.

Raspberry was just as hush about her methods in dealing with her victims, most of them never saw it coming. And she never told a soul or acted any different to incriminate herself. That's what made her so cold blooded, she was calm and focused when she killed. She showed no emotion. This was the challenge of her life, dealing with two men who were responsible for numerous murders in a various number of states. Their methods were also clean and most were not proven to be them, some by witness intimidation. No one wanted to testify even if the prosecution had a strong case, they were that feared. After getting back home from a afternoon of following Chaos, Raspberry was tired and prepared to take a hot bath. Meanwhile across town, Detective Nelson who had been investigating Tricky's murder. He had also helped with Simone's murder after Melvin had told him that he believed both murders were connected.

Detective Nelson wanted to talk to Simone's cousin Candice, someone he had spoke to briefly before. But never told her about the possibility of both murders being connected. So Detective Nelson took a ride to D.C. where Candice and Simone were from. Also where Candice worked and resided these days. He had called her on the phone and asked to see her. Upon arriving at her home he was greeted and went inside to sit in the living room so they could talk.

"You know why I'm here, I know the last time we spoke I just asked you a few questions about the night Simone was murdered. And if you had seen her that night. I spoke to Melvin the club owner and he thought that Simone and Travell "Tricky" Andrews murders were connected" Detective Nelson said.

"I don't know how that could be, I mean Tricky didn't really know my cousin like that. I knew him more than Simone did" Candice replied.

Page 151

"Hmmm....is that so ? Do you know a woman that goes by the name Raspberry" ? Detective Nelson asked.

"Yes, Desiree. She was my roommate when she went to the University of Maryland. I'm the one that introduced her to my cousin Simone and my cousin got her the job at Melvins. She also gave her the name Raspberry" Candice said.

"Well we have reason to believe that Raspberry, or Desiree had something to do with your cousin's murder. And may of had something to do with Tricky's murder also. We have an eye witness that seen a female shoot your cousin at point blank range in the face, and then shoot her twice as she lay on the ground" Detective Nelson said.

Just hearing the details once again after almost five years of her cousin's death still shook Candice to the core. And to make matters worse her former roommate and friend was being accused of her murder. Candice couldn't believe it, she was just with Raspberry and had a great time over the weekend with her reminiscing about old times. When they were roommates. And now a witness had come forward after almost five years.

How could she have killed Simone ? And more importantly....why ? Questions that were floating around in Candice head after Detective Nelson had told her that.

"You sure about this ? I mean is there any more evidence besides someone seeing another female murder my cousin ? I just can't believe this, I can't even fathom this" Candice said feeling confused and shocked.

"Well let me give you some time to think about it. We haven't ID her as a suspect yet, but it is a possibility. I just wanted to let you know, and also to not tip her off to knowing we are onto her. The investigation is ongoing" Detective Nelson said.

Sitting there quiet as ever and just staring into space still in shock, Candice didn't know what to do or what to say. She was pretty much speechless.

"If you do see her or you happen to be around her, don't take the law into your own hands. We are still very much investigating both cases. Here's my card, call me if you have any information you may deem helpful to further the investigation" Detective Nelson said before leaving.

Candice was just sitting in her seat with so many thoughts running through her mind. She was one of the few relatives Simone still had in the area. Her mother moved after she was murdered to Florida. Simone was a only child, it's exactly why her and Candice were more like sisters than cousins. They were first cousins, their mothers were sisters. And the two of them, along with Candice older brother all grew up together and lived only a few blocks from one another in Southeast D.C. What happened in Simone's case was, the eye witness a middle aged white woman was walking her dog late that night when she saw a car pull over alongside the road. After the car pulled over a woman had got out of her car and went toward the passenger side of the car. Once she got on that side she kneeled down to check her tire.

Once the woman leaned over to check her tire, a car pulled over in front of her. A female got out of that car, gun in hand. Walked over to the woman checking her tire and shot the woman at point blank range in the face. As the woman lay there, the killer pumped two more bullets in the woman's body before fleeing in her car. There was no clear description of who that woman was that fired those shots that night that killed Simone. It was too dark out, and after seeing what the woman seen she was too terrified to tell anyone for all these years. But it was slowly eating away at her that she finally came forward and said what she seen that night. Candice was really going through a rollercoaster of emotions after having such a good time with Raspberry. She just knew now that it was best to stay away from her until the Police find out who killed her cousin. It weighed heavily on her mind, and it was hard for her but she had to keep moving. Raspberry and Chaos had met up for dinner, after not seeing one another for a while. It was time for them to catch up.

"I want to start by saying that I'm sorry I been somewhat neglecting you for the last two weeks or so. And I'm going to start spending more time with you. Just been busy with a lot of shit. But no more, taking a break from business and focus on us. And oh yeah, I'm going to introduce you to Francisco" Chaos said smiling.

A little surprised, but happy. Raspberry took a sip of her drink and replied. "Great, sounds good and I can't wait to meet him. I know you guys have been friends for a long time, it's an honor that you introduce me to him because I know how private yall are" Raspberry replied.

"That's right, and that let's you know how real this shit is. And how serious I am about you. I don't introduce everybody to my man's you know what I'm saying" Chaos said.

"Indeed I do, let's eat" Raspberry replied as they both laughed.

They enjoyed their dinner and went back to Chaos condo and enjoyed the rest of the night together. Raspberry was beyond being upset that she was in a situation where she was not the only woman. It was bad enough she had to put on an act to stay close to her sister's killer. Their relationship was business to Raspberry, and personal until she got her revenge. To Chaos it was personal because he was falling deeper and deeper for Raspberry. And began trusting her even more. She never considered feelings in the equation. She had one goal and one goal only, and that was what she was most focused on through it all. Eyes on the prize and anyone in the way would pay, it was her own personal motto.

After waking up the next morning, she had to get home because she had some things to do before she was to hit the stage that night. She and Isabella had talked sparingly but weren't as close as they once were. Raspberry backed off of her because she sensed she no longer had the loyalty she once had for her. She felt like she could no longer trust her, she felt betrayed by a person she had looked after time and time again. But for the moment, Raspberry needed Isabella and she knew it. Isabella was on cloud nine after spending a weekend away with Chaos, she too never cared too much about being the main squeeze. Isabella was an escort for many years, she wasn't the type to get attached to any man.

Just a man showing her that he cared was enough for her, she figured Raspberry wouldn't ever find out about her and Chaos occasional time together. Chaos had took her shopping much like he did with Raspberry, Isabella wasn't used to nice things. She was abused as a child and young teen and really never was showed how to be treated by a man. She had a rough life growing up. Chaos was one of the men that seemed like he cared and she gravitated to him. Even though she had feared Raspberry, Chaos talked her into the idea of Raspberry never finding out and nothing happening to her if she did. He vowed he would protect Isabella at all costs as long as she continued with their relationship. At first she wasn't sure, but Chaos was persistent in his approach and he finally got what he wanted. She enjoyed the time and many gifts he provided for her, but in reality she was walking a very dangerous tightrope and that string was getting weaker by the day. As Raspberry had already found out and knew what was going on.

Later that night at the club, another packed house was awaiting yet another great show. As both Raspberry and Isabella were on tonight. Marks was excited and in a great mood as he was most times on the weekend. It was when the club made its most money. He went around the club to make sure that everyone was taken care of, and everyone had all the drinks they needed. He was a hands on owner when it came to interacting with the crowd, something Melvin did occasionally. Meanwhile Detective Nelson was following up on his investigation after hearing from an eye witness to Simone's murder. And after touching base with Simone's cousin Candice, he was full steam ahead trying to close the case. But there was one problem, he had no proof that the woman that seen the shooter kill Simone was Raspberry. It was too dark outside for the woman to see the model or make of either vehicle. She had a small flashlight as she was walking her dog, something she had done numerous times before. It was like a routine for her every night, but that particular night she seen two cars pulled alongside the road. And after seeing what she seen she quickly turned her flashlight off to avoid drawing attention over towards the woods where she was. She knew the shooter was a female by the way she walked.

It took her this long to come forward because she was scared, but Detective Nelson was glad she did. He had worked long and hard on the case over the course of the last five years. He also worked hard on Tricky's case but had no witnesses or leads. He was determined to solve both cases, and if Melvin was right he was going to do everything in his power to bring Raspberry to justice. That was the other problem, he didn't know where Melvin was. He was told what everyone else knew, that Melvin had sold the club and disappeared to places unknown. So any further information he could have gotten from Melvin being the owner of the club was now lost. All he had was an eye witness, and any information he could get from some of the women at the club.

Page 154

Chaos and Francisco planned a meeting at a Virginia hotel and bar, where they could sit down and talk about some things. Whenever they would meet it would usually be outside the Baltimore/D.C. area. They knew that law enforcement in those areas were aware of them both. As they sat down, they had their usual talk that they had over many years about life and business.

"Is all the orders and shipments been on point on your end" ? Francisco asked sipping on his drink.

"Like clockwork, we may even have to expand a little. I been seeing increased sales on my end, so the more we get in the more we can sale" Chaos replied.

Nodding in approval Francisco replied. "Sounds like a plan, these cats we getting shit from they have it to throw away. We can take it off their hands. In the meantime you keep shit real careful and close up there where you are" Francisco said.

Francisco was the type of man to steady be on the move, never stayed in the same place too long. He was always paranoid about people knowing him, besides the ones he did business with. He never was one to be in the spotlight, him or Chaos. When they noticed Raspberry's younger sister Deanna, they just happened to be passing through the neighborhood and saw her and Anita grinding selling clothes. They saw their drive and wanted them to join their organization, and later sold drugs for them. They then arranged for them to do a robbery accompanied by Chaos, which eventually resulted in Deanna's death and Anita being locked up for many years. After it happened, neither Francisco or Chaos spoke of it again. It was out of sight out of mind, it wasn't the first time either of them had committed murder. For those reasons Francisco stayed on the move, he was currently living in Nashville, Tennessee. Where ever he was, him and Chaos stayed in constant communication. Several times daily. He flew up from Nashville to Virginia to meet with Chaos.

He would be up in the area for a few days before returning to Nashville.

"You still seeing that chick" ? Francisco asked Chaos.

"Chick ? Don't you mean chicks ? I got two beautiful women. One black and one Spanish. They both work together at this club, I deal with the Spanish chick on the low though" Chaos replied.

"Be careful, women are equivalent to poison if not treated right. And I know before you say it, yes I used to be a playboy. But a couple of bad experiences with them makes you smarter on how to deal with others in the future" Francisco said.

"I feel you, and hear you clearly. But you know I was a little late in the game than what you were. You always had a chick, I was in the streets more. But you're right, and actually I believe my chick was going to try and introduce you to my Latin chick" Chaos said laughing.

"Man these women gonna get you killed, see me I will stick with my Porscha. We been rocking for over five years now, and she's still beautiful as ever" Francisco replied.

Porscha was Francisco's girlfriend of five years and the mother of two of his five kids. Although him and Porscha had been through their ups and downs, they managed to stay together despite the way Francisco lived his life and the demands of the line of business he was in. Him and Porscha have lived together for three years now. When he picks up and moves, she is right there with him. Out of all the women he had dealt with, she was his longest relationship. The life that him and Chaos was living, they didn't settle down with too many women. Chaos especially who had seven kids of his own.

"So what did you say once you realized that she wanted to hook your side chick up with me" ? Francisco asked.

"I didn't say shit, I just been putting it off. But I think she got the point, because she stopped saying anything about it" Chaos replied.

"Yeah definitely not something I want to do, I had my days of running around. Shit we both did, you just still out there fucking around. But one day you will find someone who will make you think differently about shit, believe me I never thought I would think like this" Francisco said.

"Yeah maybe some day, but for now I'm doing what ever I want to do with no restrictions. What time Porscha got you going in tonight nigga" ? Chaos asked joking.

"Such a funny guy aren't you. But I tell you what, I got a woman that's home waiting for me when I get home. While you out here chasing these hoes. But anyway, let's stick to business. We got a shipment coming in next week and I will meet you back up here so we can go together and meet them dudes over there that got our product. Until then I will stay in contact and hit you on the hip" Francisco said getting up from the table.

"No doubt, stay up and be safe" Chaos said as he also got up and they shook hands and embraced each other with a hug before going their seperate ways.

As they both came out of the hotel and bar, first Francisco then Chaos. Off in the distance, Raspberry was parked and watching from afar. When she seen the two men, she thought to herself that it had to be Francisco. She just smiled and nodded to herself, she had now put a face to the second man she was looking for. Confident it was Francisco, she was so happy that she didn't even bother to follow Chaos back. She immediately headed back home. Things were going as planned and Raspberry was loving every minute of it, she was excited to know just who Francisco finally was.

Page 156

After getting home, Raspberry would get herself ready for the night. It had got tiring following Chaos throughout the day. Her determination wouldnt let her give up, and it showed and she was excited to finally see who Francisco was. Now it was time for her to do her real job, but tonight thankfully she would just be the emcee. Isabella was to have the stage tonight, and Raspberry was more than welcome to let her have it. After going through a week of following Chaos around. As Raspberry watched some of the women perform, she had noticed someone out in the crowd. It was Candice and she looked rather strange. Candice stood as if looking for someone, so Raspberry decided to go in the crowd and see who Candice was looking for.

"Hey girl, I see you're back" Raspberry said after tapping Candice on the shoulder from behind.

Candice turned around and replied. "Oh hey, yeah I decided to come back and check you out"

"You seemed like you was looking for someone" Raspberry said.

"I was looking for you, glad I found you. I see the Spanish chick you put on is over there. She still dancing here huh" ? Candice said.

"Yes she's still here, and she's actually a money maker" Raspberry replied.

Candice just looked at Raspberry. After talking a little more, it was time for Raspberry to get back to doing her job. She set Candice up in the V.I.P. section and got her a few drinks as she sat and watched the show. It was now time for the headliner Isabella, her confidence level was sky high as she moved across the stage. Men throwing ones and stuffing others inside her breasts and thong. A decent crowd had came out, but nothing like the weekends. Even still the club was always a good place to be to their regular customers. As Isabella continued to amaze the crowd, Candice just watched from her V.I.P. table. After Isabella's set, Raspberry was going to go over and talk a little more with Candice but she was gone. A little strange but Raspberry blew it off and went back to concentrating on her job.

After the night was over Raspberry made her way home and was dead tired, definitely a productive day to say the least. A week went by and it was the day of the meeting that Francisco had told Chaos about. So Chaos once again made his way to Virginia to meet with Francisco. The location was the same as before, but this time Chaos and Francisco weren't alone. There were two other men who came after they had arrived. Those two men also went into the hotel and bar. After being in there for about thirty minutes, all four men got in two seperate cars and started to leave following each other. They drove for another thirty minutes to an abandoned warehouse, somewhere in Virginia. They all got out of their cars and went inside this warehouse.

After being in the warehouse for about twenty minutes, the other two men walked out and got in their car and left. Chaos and Francisco was in the warehouse alone along with about a hundred thousand dollars in cash, they had just made a huge transaction and deal with the two men. Fifteen minutes went by as Francisco and Chaos were talking and preparing to leave with the money when a lone gunman came busting through the door firing shots as soon as they came in the warehouse. Two shots hitting Chaos in the abdomen and shoulder dropping him to the ground, Francisco immediately returning fire and then turned to get out of the warehouse. When he went to turn and run, he was shot in the back of the knee as he fell to the ground. Francisco lay face down on the ground.

"Turn around....turn around" !! The gunman yelled wearing a mask, Francisco turned around on his back.

Chaos laying a few feet away bleeding badly from the abdomen and clinging to life. The gunman then took off their mask, it was Raspberry.

"You know that girl you hired five years ago, Deanna ? That was my sister you sent into that robbery that got killed" Raspberry said.

Francisco interrupting, "I don't know what you talking about, I don't know nobody by that name".

"Yes you do you lying ass bitch, you got my sister killed. And now I'm going to kill you both and take all this fucking money" !!! Raspberry replied as she fired one shot to the face of Francisco, killing him instantly.

Chaos still on the ground crawling trying to get away when Raspberry came behind him and fired two shots to the back of Chaos head killing him. The shots were muffled and fired from a gun that had a silencer. Raspberry then grabbed all of the hundred thousand in cash and immediately ran out of the warehouse.

Chaos and Francisco were dead in a warehouse somewhere in Virginia, they were both found hours later by some kids that were playing nearby. Just like that, two powerful and dangerous men were killed in an instant and robbed of a hundred thousand dollars in cash. Back in College Park Isabella was looking at the gifts she received from Chaos. As recently as three days ago. She never received such expensive gifts from a man before, and everytime her and Chaos were together they had a great time. She decided to call his phone, something she rarely did. He usually was the one to contact her, but she wanted to thank him for the gifts. She called his phone and it just rang and rang with no answer. Maybe he was mad because she called and didn't answer ? Maybe he was busy in a meeting handling business and he couldn't pick up ?

She had no idea, but he didn't pick up. She dismissed it and continued enjoying her gifts and being in the moment. She then got a call from Marks.

Page 158

"Did you hear what happened ? Tney found two bodies in a warehouse in Virginia. And I believe one of the men was Chaos. The guy that comes here and be in V.I.P. the guy that comes here for Raspberry" Marks said.

"Yes I know who you're talking about. He's dead ? No way, I talked to him just yesterday" Isabella replied sounding shocked.

She was really upset and was looking for answers to what happened to Chaos, all she knew was he was found in a warehouse in Virginia with another man and they both were deceased. Chaos had been shot four times, once in the shoulder, once in the abdomen, and twice in the back of the head. It was a pretty gruesome scene at the crime scene, lots of blood. There were no suspects or leads. And no witnesses. The warehouse was abandoned and in the middle of nowhere, not too many people ever even went there. That's why Chaos and Francisco chose that spot. Looking over the crime scene and dusting for prints, the local Virginia authorities were working hard investigating the case. Isabella hadn't talked to Raspberry in a while, but couldn't help but to call her after she heard about what happened to Chaos. Raspberry was sleep when she got the call from Isabella.

"Raspberry, Mami wake up. I got a call that Chaos is dead, did you hear anything" ? Isabella asked.

Just waking up, Raspberry replied. "No, wow. I didn't hear anything. What did they say happened"? Raspberry replied.

"I really don't know, Marks called me and told me he was found with another man in a Virginia abandoned warehouse" Isabella said.

Raspberry was clearly not as upset as Isabella was, which was somewhat strange to Isabella. Raspberry was the woman that was known as Chaos woman. Him and Raspberry would be seen out together most of the time. Isabella on the other hand was considered a side chick, something she was comfortable being because she was well compensated for her services. She knew what her and Chaos had, and Chaos always was sweet to her and always made sure she was good. She just stared at the various gifts he had gotten her while she sobbed heavily, his death had really affected her.

She had asked Marks for a leave of absence from the club, Marks agreed to let her. Although Marks had never known that her and Chaos had any type of intimate relationship. He knew they knew each other but nothing more. It's exactly why he had contacted Raspberry first but got no answer. He was also shocked at Raspberry's cold reaction to Chaos death, she didn't seem like it really affected her being that people knew they were romantically linked. Raspberry had finally got the two men that she had seeked revenge on for the murder of her sister. It wasn't the way it was orginally planned, but she finally executed a plan nonetheless. She had carefully followed Chaos for a series of days, eventually following him to a meeting he attended with Francisco. Where they both were going to make a cool hundred thousand dollars.

And Raspberry was finally able to catch up with Chaos and Francisco, getting them both together at the same place. She couldn't have been more happier. Raspberry would later surface that next day, returning Marks call saying she was sleep and found out about Chaos through Isabella. Who had woke her up. A person who found out about what happened to Chaos also was Detective Nelson. Chaos clearly wasn't killed in Detective Nelson's jurisdiction being it was in Virginia, but he read the papers and found it interesting. He himself had never knew Chaos but had heard of him from investigating murders within the area. And while he was investing Simone's murder. He had remembered that one of the women at the club had mentioned him as being a regular on the V.I.P. list. So it was only natural for Detective Nelson to eventually want to question Marks about just who Chaos was. And who he was affiliated with at the club. Days would go by before that would happen, initially Chaos and Francisco's murder had sent shock waves through the DMV. To any of those people in those areas that knew either one, it was a complete shock. Because they were two men who were feared by a lot of people in that region.

Who had the guts to kill not only one, but the both of them ? And how were they able to do it as private and hush with their business as Francisco and Chaos was ? At the moment no one had a clue. But whoever it was, it was a person that should be feared a whole lot more than Chaos and Francisco. And was a brave and brash soul to kill them the way that person did. Details started to emerge from the crime scene. Francisco was shot in the face, along with being shot in the knee and was basically killed instantly after being shot in the face. Chaos was shot in the shoulder, abdomen, and twice in the back of the head. A total of six shots fired that hit their target. In the end two men were dead and a killer was on the loose. Raspberry had finally gotten up and started moving, taking a shower and getting dressed. She had some running around to do before she was to perform tonight. It was the start of the weekend and the beginning of the best time to make money at the club. Even after killing two men the previous day it was business as usual for this incredibly beautiful and dangerous woman.

Isabella was also slated to perform, but she was still dealing with the news of Chaos murder. Still taking it hard. He was the only guy that seemed like he really cared for her, even though she wasn't his girl. She appreciated everything he had done for her. The gifts, the money, and the wining and dining. Even the times they spent together was constantly running through her mind. It would be a tough night for Isabella, but she knew she had to get through it. It was the weekend and the time the most money was made. And she had to make it. So as the night approached at the club, Raspberry and Isabella found themselves in the dressing room together, just the two of them.

"Well hello Raspberry, it's been a little while since we talked last Mami. I know by now you heard about the details of Chaos murder, being that you two are close I am surprised to see you're here" Isabella said.

"What happened to Chaos was very unfortunate and I am saddened by it. But I also knew the game Chaos was in and knew that something like this could happen at any given time. The life of men in the game, and the game doesn't discriminate against nobody. Black, White, Spanish, Asian. If you in it, there's always a chance that it could happen. But what's your angle ? How are you here tonight after you was his side piece ? What you didnt think I knew that you was with him behind my back ? Its cool though, I got what I wanted from him anyway. Good luck tonight Isabella" Raspberry replied leaving Isabella stunned that she knew about her and Chaos as she walked away and went upstairs to get ready for the show.

Isabella stood froze in the same spot, how did Raspberry know about her and Chaos ? And what was she to say about it now that Raspberry knew ? Her mind was racing and she had little time to think about any of it, because she had to soon go on stage. Raspberry was also hitting the stage on this night, but first Isabella was to go on. Raspberry in her own witty way made it very uncomfortable for Isabella to perform that night. By letting her know that she knew about what she was doing behind her back. She had already feared Raspberry and knew what she was capable of when she witnessed her kill her own cousin

Shameek. Isabella was beyond worried, she was the only person that had real dirt on Raspberry. That alone would make any person that knew her and knew what she was capable of nervous. But Isabella had to focus enough to get through her performance and uphold the standard that she had set for herself at the club. Which was on a level only her and Raspberry remained on.

After introducing Isabella, Raspberry and her walked past each other. Raspberry smiling at her as she walked off stage. It was time to focus for Isabella, no more worrying about anything but commanding the stage. As the music blared from the speakers her body moved to the beats, and for the moment she was flawless as usual. Able to block out whatever she was going through. The more she danced the more dollars flowed to the stage, she felt good and she was proud that under pressure she stood and delivered. The crowd loved it and as she came back off stage, Raspberry smiled and nodded in approval. Raspberry knew that Isabella would be a great dancer, that's why she put her on at the club. She never had jealousy towards Isabella, she had one time valued her as a very close and loyal friend. But things had changed, after she realized that she was no longer loyal to her. More importantly Isabella was the only person to see her kill. That alone made her a potential victim. And Isabella was worried sick about it, she thought about maybe getting a hotel room for a few days and stay away from her residence. Because Raspberry knew where she lived.

After that night it was a whole lot of uncertainty surrounding the club, even though that night went smooth without any problems. It would get a whole lot worse before it got any better. Raspberry and Isabella's relationship was sketchy at best, and Detective Nelson was hot on the trail of taking Raspberry down. After having suspicion that she may have had something to do with Simone's murder. At the moment he still had no proof, but he was slowly but surely building his case. In the meantime, Raspberry decided to head to Jessup to visit Anita and let her know what happened. The drive there Raspberry was in great spirits. She had reached her goal and in the process came across a hundred thousand dollars which she hadn't spent at all yet. She didn't want to draw attention to herself so she was very smart about how she handled it. And even where she kept it. Arriving at the prison and going through the pain in the ass security checks she was face to face with Anita only seperated by a glass once again.

All Raspberry could do was smile, Anita just looking.

"Well I see you smiling but you not saying anything" Anita said.

"Why do you think I'm smiling"? Raspberry replied.

Anita sat there for a few seconds and smiled back. And then replied. "No way, really" ?

"Yes really, I tailed him for about a week. He end up leading me to the boss. Caught the both of them in a warehouse out in Virginia. Couldn't have been more convenient and easy. But now that it's over, to be honest I still got this empty feeling" Raspberry said.

"You always going to have that empty feeling, because we can't bring her back. But it was important for me to give you that information so you could do with it what you eventually did. As long as justice was served either way I'm happy. They got what they deserved the both of them. Now she can truly rest. I really miss my friend and I know you miss your sister" Anita said.

Raspberry nodding in agreement, as tears ran down her face. And realizing now that no matter what happened her and Anita would share a lifetime bond.

"There will be some more money added to your account so look for it" Raspberry said getting up about to leave.

"Thank you Desiree, you send me more money than I can ever spend in here. For that I appreciate it and I appreciate you. So I'm going to ask you to forward that money to my mother please. She needs it more than I do" Anita replied.

"No problem, I will make that happen. Stay strong Anita" Raspberry said before leaving.

Their two fists touched the glass and Raspberry was off back to College Park. As she arrived back home she was surprised to see a car parked outside of her apartment. It was Detective Nelson. He was waiting on her at her apartment. "Raspberry it is right" ? Detective Nelson asked.

" Yes thats me, you're Detective Nelson. What do you need" ? Raspberry asked walking towards her house after getting out of her car.

"I have some more questions about Simone's murder. I had questioned Melvin back when the murder happened. And a year or so afterward, and he was suspicious of you being involved or knowing about Simone's murder. And possibly Tricky's also. Eyewitness said a woman fired the fatal shot that killed Simone" Detective Nelson said.

"What does that have to do with me " ? Raspberry asked.

"I have suspicion that you may have been that female that killed her. And I'm going to do everything in my power to find out if that is true. And if it is true I can assure you that you will go to jail for the rest of your life.

Raspberry just looked at Detective Nelson and laughed. "You said that like you're sure I did this. I think you might want to be careful Detective. I do have rights you know. And I won't hesitate to exercise them. But good luck with your case though" Raspberry said walking into her apartment.

What was missing was of course proof. And as of now Detective Nelson didn't have any. A few days later Raspberry was driving by the club on her way to the gun range when she saw Detective Nelson again. And this time he was with Isabella talking in the parking lot. They didn't see Raspberry because they wasn't paying attention. You can only imagine the thoughts that was going through Raspberry's mind, none of which was beneficial to Isabella.

After talking to Detective Nelson, Isabella went inside the club to Marks office and asked to speak to him. He told her to come in and have a seat.

"I'm really nervous about telling anyone this. And you have to give me your word that you won't tell anyone I told you this. I'm serious you have to promise me this" Isabella said sounding concerned.

"Calm down.....I promise I wont, you can talk to me" Marks replied.

"I seen something that someone did, something real bad. Someone was killed" Isabella said.

Marks put his hand up as if to tell Isabella to wait and don't say anything else. As he walked to the door and opened it to see if someone was listening. Then coming back and replying.

"Do you want to tell me who this person is and who was killed" ? Marks asked.

Isabella took a deep breath and stared off into the distance.

"I saw Raspberry kill a man" Isabella said as she started to cry. Marks looking in disbelief could only stare off into space himself, he was speechless. He was almost afraid to ask who or any other questions in fear of being an accessory to murder.

"Isabella calm down and dont say anything else until i can wrap my head around this one. This is really deep. Go home and relax Isabella, you have my permission" Marks said.

Isabella decided to take Marks advice and do just that, go home and relax. She went home and took a nice hot shower and was planning on relaxing on the couch and watching some T.V. As she got out of the shower and put on her rope, she walked into her bedroom and preceded to get dressed. She had just put her bra and panties on when a single shot hit her in the neck as she fell back into her closet. And then the gunman entered her bedroom and stood over her as she lay on the floor gasping for air. And hit her with another shot to the stomach, which was fatal as she took one big gasp as her heart stopped. She lay in a pool of her own blood dead from two shots. One in her neck and another in her stomach. Once again the sound of the gun firing was muffled by the silencer. And just like that, Isabella was gone. A few hours later, Raspberry was planning on going back home to see her mother for a few days. She decided to call her and let her know she was coming home.

"Hey mom, how are you" ?

"Hey baby, I'm fine. It's been a while since I've heard from you. Is everything ok" ? Denise asked.

"Yeah everything is fine mom, I'm even thinking about going back to school and getting my degree. Planning to enroll the next semester and I have a surprise for you too mom, for one I'm taking you shopping at the finest spots in the city" Raspberry said sounding excited.

"Oh is that right ? Well you know I don't require much but your love and company. Just get here safely to see me, I'll be waiting" Denise replied.

"Ok mom, love you see you soon" Raspberry replied before hanging up the phone.

Raspberry was content, and after all that she had been through and all the terror she had inflicted on the metropolitan and surrounding areas. She was finally ready to be a normal everyday person. Even planning to go back to school and get her degree. She could do it without having her scholarship. She was sitting on a cool hundred grand and still had plenty of money that she had stacked from working at the club. Life was great as she escaped the evil that she had done to many and felt was justified. And without anyone knowing that she did. With the only person that actually saw her commit murder now deceased. And in two days she would head back home and visit her mother with money to burn and a new lease on life.

She was off this particular night so she decided to just spend a quiet evening at home while sipping on a glass of wine. She spent that night alone, and reflected on her life and the direction of her future. She was going back to school and get her degree in business like she had originally planned five years prior. She had already started filling out the paperwork and started the process so she could go back the next semester. But before that, she wanted to go back home and spend about a week with her mother. The next morning she was awakened by her

doorbell ringing, which she thought was strange.
Page 164

Because not too many people knew where she lived. She answered the door and it was Candice.

"Hey girl....what are you doing here this time of morning" ? Raspberry asked.

"I followed you" Candice replied.

"You followed me ? Come on in" Raspberry said turning around and walking inside her apartment.

As she turned around and walked in her apartment, and the door closed. Candice pulled out a forth five caliber handgun and fired a single shot to the back of the head of Raspberry. Raspberry immediately fell to the floor. After shooting Raspberry and killing her instantly, Candice dropped the gun and dropped to the floor crying. After hearing the shot, neighbors immediately called the cops. Detective Nelson was on the scene. And after going in Raspberry's doorway and seeing her laying there lifeless was somewhat frustrating for him as bad as that sounded. Frustrated because he had strongly believed that she was involved with Simone and Tricky's murder. And he was close to solving the case. Now all of that didn't matter, Raspberry was dead and so was Isabella. Two women who gave so much life to Melvin's Bar And Lounge was now gone. Melvin was gone, Simone was gone. The club would never be the same, and Marks was left to pick up the pieces. After hearing the news that both his best dancers were murdered, Marks didn't know what he would do moving forward or if he would even keep the club.

He felt bad about Isabella dying. Did someone see them two talking to get Isabella killed ? Did he have anything to do with her dying ? It was those things that constantly ran through his mind moving forward. There was nothing he could do now about any of it. Raspberry's life had came full circle, with a ending that was very much apart of her life. She had got away with her first kill, and continued to kill again and again. She had finally quenched her thrust for revenge and was on her way to a more stable and financially secure life. Robbing the same people who robbed her younger sister of her life years ago. Not only robbing them of their life, but robbing them of cold hard cash. Only days before going back home, maybe to stay maybe to relocate all together. She felt the sky was the limit for her, she was going to invest the money for her and her mother to live comfortably. She wanted to go home for a week, and come back with a clear head to make better decisions for her life moving forward.

She planned to go back to school with part of the money, and maybe invest the rest. But that was no longer an option now. Denise Knight had now lost her husband and two daughters, she was now alone and back living with her sister Angela. Marks continued to run the club, of course it was nowhere near the place it once was. A whole lot of new dancers and a new direction. Eventually the club closed for good months later. After shooting Raspberry, Candice stayed right there and let the Police take her into custody. Why did she shoot Raspberry? Because after a while she herself had believed Raspberry killed her best friend and cousin Simone. And she was right, and for that she seeked revenge. She felt betrayed by Desiree. Page 165

Candice had a bright future ahead of her and just in an instant she had acted off emotion. Candice wasn't a violent person and it hurt her to find out her former roommate had killed her cousin, and it hurt her even more making the ultimate decision to kill her. Candice very much expressed remorse for killing Raspberry. The whole time she was in Police custody she was crying. Shedding tears for Raspberry and Simone, and wondering where did things go so wrong for them all to get to this point. She didn't do much time thinking when she pulled the trigger and took Raspberry's life. Mostly anger had drove her to take another person's life. Not just any person, but a person she knew well and was pretty close to when they were both in college. They were all such young happy girls when they all met. And in the course of five years all of their lives changed forever. When Desiree first came to college she was a somewhat shy girl straight out of high school from Baltimore's West Side. After going to school a little over a year she had transformed into Raspberry after she started working at Melvins. That alter ego had took on a new meaning once Raspberry became her calling card and Desiree took a back seat. And was only brought out for her mother. Melvin's became one of the hottest spots in the area thanks to Raspberry and later Isabella.

Raspberry was an instant success and she never looked back. The more high demand she was, the more power she held at the club. As her confidence grew she became a person many from Baltimore that knew her, wouldn't recognize. It was no longer

Desiree, it was Raspberry. The first time she killed she always felt after that, she could kill again. And she did, again and again. She not only killed her victims, but often robbed them for everything they had after killing them. She was connected to very dangerous men, men that had killed just as many if not more than she did. They ended up becoming her victims, in the process Raspberry left a trail of blood and a unexpected enemy that was developing right in front of her eyes. And for the first time, like many of her victims. She never seen it coming. The final week and a half of Raspberry's life she had reunited with her former roommate Candice who had been working back in her hometown of Washington, D.C. and was fairly successful. Not only did Raspberry kill Candice cousin Simone, but she also was about to use Candice to set up Francisco and Chaos. Until that fell through and she decided to change her plan.

In the meantime Candice was tipped off by Detective Nelson. Who was hot on Raspberry's trail since suspecting she had something to do with Simone and Tricky's murders. That was ultimately what got Raspberry killed in the end. It was almost like karma had came back full circle for Raspberry at a time in her life when she wanted to make a change and become a better person. But she couldn't escape her past, even though she had finally reached her goal of getting revenge against the two men who murdered her sister. She was planning on going back to school and getting her degree in Business like she had set out to do since coming to College Park. But it was too late, her past had caught up to her future and was the reason for her demise. When Raspberry was found in her apartment laying face down, and her head almost blown off. She was shot at close range with a 45 caliber handgun. She was almost unrecognizable when her mother Denise identified her. Which was the hardest thing Denise had to do in her life, it had trumped everything Denise had ever went through in her quest to become clean.   Page 166

After losing her youngest daughter and her husband, she now lost the one person that she loved so much who had so much promise. The first one to go to college in her family, and the only one she had left that was closest to her. Denise wondered what happened to Desiree, the shy girl from Baltimore's West Side that she gave birth to. Her first born. And why did this woman Candice Joseph want to kill her daughter Desiree ? There was so many things Denise didn't know about her daughter that she was totally lost about the situation. College Park wasn't that far from Baltimore, but Denise didn't have a car to visit her daughter much and her daughter didn't really want her down there. Desiree was a different person in College Park, she had changed a lot from her days as a young girl in Baltimore. She was Desiree to her mother, but Raspberry to the outside world.

Was it her sister's death that made her change ? So many questions and her mother Denise had no answers. She didn't have a whole lot of time to think on it either. Because she had a funeral to plan. But at some point she wanted to talk to Candice, she wanted to face her daughter's killer. A few days later Desiree known to her mother, and Raspberry to the world was laid to rest in a private service just outside her native Baltimore. She was cremated and her ashes were later thrown in the Baltimore Harbor. It was definitely the end of an era. As Marks tried his best to maintain the same level at Melvin's, he eventually found out he couldn't as the bar was not as popular as it once was. Marks was losing money and eventually closed the club. After Raspberry's body was found, the Police searched her apartment and found guns and a hundred grand in cash. The one gun, a nine millimeter was traced to Simone and Tricky's murder.

Further validating Detective Nelson's thoughts. After hearing the news Denise now knew why Candice had killed her daughter. And she was utterly shocked to even find out her daughter had killed several people. It was very hard for her to believe, she just didn't understand what was going on and why all of these things transpired. Her daughter was a cold blooded killer who eventually met the same fate that she bestowed on others. Denise still wanted to talk to Candice, who seemed by all accounts a nice successful woman before all of this happened. So a meeting was set up by the two, Denise would go visit Candice in prison. Something she didn't know was right or wrong at the time, she just knew she had to do it.

Denise Knight made her way to Jessup to visit Candice Joseph, the woman who killed her first born. After sitting down in her seat with glass separating her from Candice who had just walked in.

"Candice, nice to finally meet you. I just want you to know first of all, I forgive you for killing my daughter

Desiree. I know now why you did it. Now I don't condone violence at all but I understood that emotions run high when it comes to a loved one. I know all about that first hand" Denise said.

"Mrs. Knight this isn't me, I graduated from college with a degree in Business and I had a great job inside the same community I grew up in. And just like that I'm here and my life is destroyed. Desiree was my roommate in college until she dropped out, we shared a lot of things about each other to one another. I knew about your other daughter Deanna getting murdered. I believe things changed once she started working at Melvins. And I blame myself, because I'm the one who told my cousin Simone to put her on at Melvins" Candice said feeling remorseful.

"You can't blame yourself Candice, Desiree was old enough to make her own decisions and she knew right from wrong. I'm just glad we are able to finally talk and we both understand each other's views on this. I'm sorry this had to happen to you, and I'm sorry that my daughter made so many bad decisions that led to this" Denise replied.

"Simone was my sister, even though we are cousins. She was the sister I never had. And the void has been missing in my life ever since. My life will never be the same without her, I'm sure you feel the same way about both your daughters. I'm really sorry for what I did, I was acting on emotion and should've let the law handle it. But I wasn't raised to be a snitch" Candice said showing more remorse for her actions.

"I can understand that Candice, I really can. Remember I live in Baltimore and I know how it is on these streets. I'm a recovering addict, I've been clean now for good for the last five and a half years. I started snorting coke and end up smoking crack, there was nights I laid my head on those streets to sleep. That's why this hurts so much, I wanted so much more for both my girls. And now they're both gone" Denise said sobbing quietly.

Candice also began shedding tears, they cried together. A woman and her daughter's killer was not hostile towards each other, but comforting each other and trying to give each other closure. Candice expressed remorse for killing Desiree, her former roommate and a person she shared a lot of memories with. The whole situation was bad, but they tried to make the best of it. And instead of having anger towards one another, they tried to understand each other's point of view. After that day, Denise and Candice would share a bond. And would continue that bond into the future.

After visiting Candice, Denise sort of got closure even though she was still grieving her daughter's death. She felt relieved that she finally knew some of her daughter's secret life. She felt better after her and Candice had talked. Before Denise could head back to her home in Baltimore, she was contacted by Detective Nelson. He had gotten her number from Raspberry's belongings that were found in her apartment after she was killed. Even though Raspberry was dead he still wanted to talk to her mother Denise to get a sense of who Raspberry really was. And what may have made her change into the person she became. So after being contacted by Detective Nelson, Denise made her way to the College

Park Area Police Department. Accompanied by her sister Angela who drove Denise to College Park.

"Hello ladies, have a seat. You want anything to drink ? Water, coffee, soda" ? Detective Nelson asked.

"No we're fine" Denise replied.

"I called you here Mrs. Knight because I was investigating two murders that your daughter may have been involved in. Or should I say we have strong reason to believe she was involved" Detective Nelson said.

"I know about one, Simone. That was also why my daughter was killed, I'm aware of that. But that is the only one I have knowledge of. If you have no proof how do you know my daughter was involved" Denise asked.

"There was the murder of Travell "Tricky" Andrews. Your daughter Raspberry was the last person that was with Tricky the night of his murder" Detective Nelson said.

Interrupting Denise replied. "I do know who you mean when you say Raspberry, I found out that was my daughter's stage name. But I don't refer to my daughter by that name. Her name is Desiree Knight. I am aware that was the name she used to work at that club. That name Raspberry has brought my daughter nothing but bad things and ultimately led to her death. So could you please refer to her by the name I gave her. As I said her birth name is Desiree."

"Yes ma'am I can, like I was saying your daughter Desiree was the last one seen with Tricky that night.

And we believe we found the murder weapon in her apartment. What type of child was your daughter Desiree" ? Detective Nelson asked.

"She was a beautiful and smart child, very ambitious. Wanting to do something with her life, wanting more out of life than the norm. She was born and raised in West Baltimore, Maryland that should tell you how much she wanted more" Denise replied. Page 169

"I'm sorry for everything you have been through Mrs. Knight, I really am. I just wanted to talk to you about your daughter Desiree to see where her life turned. That's why I asked what type of child she was. But it seems like it's been enough for you today. If you still want to talk sometime, not just about what happened but just in general. Here's my card I know it has to be hard losing your daughter regardless of what she did" Detective Nelson said.

"Thanks. And if I need anything I will let you know. Both my girl's were very ambitious. The lives they lived and the way they both died wasnt them at all. I almost feel like I had a hand in this. But I can't take back all the things I put them and my husband through. They were the reasons i tried my hardest to stay clean. And I did it, with some help from my sister Angela also. She's been my rock through all of this. I'm the only one left in my family. And now when I go to the cemetary to visit Deanna and her father. I can now also go see my Desiree. I really miss them, but my faith will get me through. And I got closure today, after talking to Candice.Take care Detective Nelson" Denise said as she got up and Detective Nelson gave her a hug. And her sister Angela grabbed her arm and led her out of the Police Station.

The ride home the two sisters had a heart to heart talk about the whole situation.

"Denise you can't no longer blame yourself for the way your girls lives went. I understand you feel bad about the fact you wasn't there for periods of their lives, but those girls knew you loved them. When Robert was alive he reassured them plenty of times. And so did I while you were gone. They chose those lives, you had no idea that Desiree was actually this other person Raspberry" Angela said.

"As sad as it sounds, no I didn't have a clue. Whenever I talked to her she would tell me she had a new job. As much as I tried to find out she wouldn't tell me. I guess she was ashamed because I would always ask her if she was ever going back to school after she dropped out and pursued her career. And when she finally said she was going back to college, the next morning she was killed. She was supposed to come home and stay with me for a week, that was the day she was killed. It's still so shocking both my girls are gone" Denise said looking out the window as they were heading back to Baltimore.

"Sis you will get through this, we will get through this. I miss my nieces so much, but now it's just us. You're my sister and just know I will always have your back no matter what. Now let's get home" Angela said as they hit the highway.

The End.

Made in the USA
Middletown, DE
05 September 2019